秒懂！
關鍵英文
文法輕鬆學

Fast & Easy! Basic English Grammar

國家圖書館出版品預行編目資料

秒懂！關鍵英文文法輕鬆學／張文娟著.
--初版.--新北市：雅典文化,民110.01
面；公分.--（生活英語系列：19）
ISBN：978-986-99431-2-3 (平裝)
1. 英語　　2. 語法
805.16　　　　　　　　　　109017911

秒懂！
關鍵英文
文法輕鬆學

生活英語系列：19

著 ◎ 張文娟
出 版 者 ◎ 雅典文化事業有限公司
登 記 證 ◎ 局版北市業字第五七〇號
執行編輯 ◎ 張文娟
封面設計 ◎ 林鈺恆
內文排版 ◎ 鄭孝儀
編 輯 部 ◎ 22103 新北市汐止區大同路三段 194 號 9 樓-1
電 　 話 ◎ 02-86473663
傳 　 真 ◎ 02-86473660
法律顧問 ◎ 方圓法律事務所　涂成樞律師
總 經 銷 ◎ 永續圖書有限公司
　　　　　 22103 新北市汐止區大同路三段 194 號 9 樓-1
　　　　　 E-mail: yungjiuh@ms45.hinet.net
　　　　　 網站◎ www.foreverbooks.com.tw
　　　　　 電話◎ 02-86473663
　　　　　 傳真◎ 02-86473660

出版日 2021 年 01 月
Printed in Taiwan, 2021 All Rights Reserved

前 言

　　或許有人會問，一定要學習文法才能學好英文嗎？憑藉著語感難道不能駕馭英語的應用嗎？由實務經驗上看來，除非是在英語系國家住過多年，或是已經達到英語母語水準的人，文法架構以及文法解析能力都是必備條件，這一點在閱讀或寫作上更為明顯。

　　本書看似厚重，實際上除了可以按照順序來循序漸進研讀，也可以用來查詢文法問題，解決文法的疑難雜症之餘，可以視需要研讀文法需要補強的章節。各章關於文法的結論力求清楚明白，以簡御繁，佐以生活化的例句，於學習文法概念的同時也讓英文更上一層樓。各章後的練習題皆附解答，可以於讀完各章內容後做練習，也可先來個文法小體檢，先做測驗之後再來決定是否讀該章內容，或讀該章的哪一個部分。

　　總之，無論是想要提升一般文法能力，或是要參加英文各類的檢定考試，本書都是最佳利器。

秒懂！關鍵**英文**文法**輕鬆學** Fast! Easy English Grammar

前言

Chapter
① 句子（Sentences）

Chapter
② 名詞（Nouns）

Chapter
③ 冠詞（Articles）

Chapter
④ 代名詞（Pronouns）

Chapter
⑤ 動詞（Verbs）

Chapter
⑥ 形容詞（Adjectives）

Chapter
7 副詞（Adverbs）

Chapter
8 介系詞（Prepositions）

Chapter
9 連接詞（Conjunctions）

Chapter
⑩ 感歎句（Exclamations）

Chapter
⑪ 句子的5種型式
（5 structures of sentences）

Chapter
⑫ 特殊句型
（special structures of sentences）

Chapter
⓭ 時態（Tenses）

Chapter
⑭ 疑問詞（Interrogative Words）

Chapter
⑮ 附加問句（Tag Questions）

Chapter
⑯ 祈使句（The Imperative Sentences）

Chapter
⑰ 假設法（The Subjunctive Mood）

Chapter
㉔ 標點符號（Punctuation Marks）

附錄

ABCDEFGH
IJKLMN
OPQRSTUV
YZ!?.,

1

句子（Sentences）

Unit
1

句子的定義

什麼是句子

　　一個句子由一組詞構成，並表達一個完整的意思，句首第一個字母要大寫。一個完整的句子至少包含兩個重要的部分：主詞部分（subject）和述語部分（predicate）。

 例句：

例　The student / laughed.
　　　主詞　　　述語
　　這個學生笑了。

例　The student who laughed / is my son.
　　　　　主詞　　　　　　　述語
　　在笑的學生是我兒子。

> 主詞和述語這兩個部分就是句子的基本結構。

　　句子＝主詞部分＋述語部分

主詞（subject）

句子中的主詞主要由名詞、代名詞或帶有修飾語的名詞詞組組成，而修飾名詞的修飾語通常為形容詞、分詞、形容詞子句，具有形容詞的特質。總而言之，必須具有名詞性質的結構才能成為句子的主詞。

 例句：

例 Spring is coming.（名詞）
春天來了。

例 Claire and Clara are twins.（名詞）
克萊兒和克萊拉是一對雙胞胎。

例 She does not talk much.（代名詞）
她的話不多。

例 They support each other.（代名詞）
他們互相扶持。

例 The girl playing basketball is Cathy.（名詞詞組）
在打籃球的女孩是凱絲。

例 The tall guy with many shopping bags was her assistant.
（名詞詞組）
提著很多購物袋的是她的助理。

述語（predicate）

述語是用來說明或描述主語，主要成分是動詞，為了使句意完整，除了動詞之外還可以有修飾動詞的副詞以及受詞與補語。

 例句：

例 That boy screamed.（動詞）
那男孩在叫喊著。

例 That book sells well.（動詞 + 副詞）
那本書賣得很好。

例 The girl watered the plants.（動詞 + 受詞）
那女孩在澆花。

例 They elected him the president.
（動詞 + 受詞 + 受詞補語）
他們選他作為總統。

例 Calvin reviewed his lessons every day.（動詞 + 受詞 + 時間副詞）
卡文每天都複習功課。

省略句除外

 例句一：

例 A：Who is talking so loud outside?
　　誰在外面那麼大聲講話？

例 B：John.
　　約翰。

 例句二：

例 A：What else have you brought with you?
　　除此之外你身上還帶了什麼？

例 B：Water.
　　水。

句子的種類

1. 敘述句：敘述句用來陳述事實，表明說話者的看法包含肯定句與否定句。

肯定句：用來陳述事實或觀點，並對所陳述的內容加以肯定，以句號結尾，肯定句中不含否定詞。

 例句：

例 I like to learn English.
我喜歡學習英語。

例 English is an international language.
英語是個國際語言。

例 So far I have won many prizes for my photography.
到目前為止我已贏得很多攝影獎項。

例 This writer wrote stories of all sorts of topics.
這個作家寫了各種題材的故事。

否定句：動詞前加上否定詞，例如：not, no 不, never 不曾, seldom 非常少, hardly 幾乎不，就形成否定句，否定句也以句號結尾。

例句：

(例) I do not like to learn English.
我不喜歡學習英語。

(例) We have never received any greeting cards from him.
我們不曾收到任何他寄的任何賀卡。

(例) Kay seldom attends class in the morning.
凱非常少上早上的課。

(例) The secretary hardly loses her temper.
這位秘書幾乎不會情緒失控。

(例) We have never seen such an effective way to boost sales in this company.
這樣有效的促進銷售方式在這家公司還是前所未見。

2. 疑問句：疑問句用來提出問題，以問號結尾。

例句：

(例) Do you like to learn English?
你喜歡學習英語嗎？

例 Do you want to have some sweets?
你想要吃些點心嗎？

例 Did he really say that to her?
他真的這樣跟她說？

例 Has Mr. Wang been to a baseball game in person before?
王先生曾經親自去看過棒球比賽嗎？

例 Will you take part in the English speech contest next month?
你會參加下個月的英語演講比賽嗎？

例 Are you going to move to a bigger house in the near future?
你會在不久的未來搬到一間更大的房子嗎？

例 Had you finished all your homework by the time your favorite show was on TV?
你是否在你最喜歡的節目在電視上演前做完了所有功課？

3. 祈使句：祈使句用來表示命令、請求、號召等，通常以句號結尾，但如果是一個強烈命令則以驚歎號結尾。

 例句：

例 Be quiet!
安靜！

例 Be your best friend!
當自己最好的朋友！

例 Listen to the questions carefully and write down the answers.
仔細聽問題然後寫下答案。

例 Let's learn English together!
讓我們一起學英語！

例 Let's cherish what we have.
讓我們珍惜我們所擁有的。

◎詳細解釋請參見Chapter 16 祈使句

4. 感歎句：感歎句用來表示說話時的某種強烈感情，如驚訝、懷疑、氣憤、讚歎，以驚歎號結尾。

 例句：

例 How tasty!
真好吃！

例 How nice of you!
你人真好！

例 What a lovely day it is!
今天天氣真好！

例 What a journey!
真是趟不凡的旅程！

例 What an excellent job you did!
你做得真好！

◎詳細解釋請參見Chapter 10 感歎詞

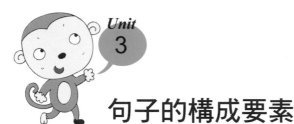

句子的構成要素

英文句子是由不同詞性的詞類所組成，主要分為以下的八大詞類（the parts of speech）：

1. 名詞 (nouns)

名詞用來表達人、事、物、地等。英文句子的構成要件就是主詞與動詞。名詞用來當主詞、受詞與補語，名詞當主詞時放在句首，當受詞與補語時放在動詞後面。主詞一定要是名詞，只有形容詞才可以用來修飾名詞。例如：city 城市，a beautiful city 一個美麗的城市；doctor 醫師，a tall doctor 一位長得很高的醫師……等。

2. 代名詞 (pronouns)

是用來取代名詞的字，前面已經提過的名詞或是彼此都知道的名詞都可用代名詞代替，主要是避免重複，用法與主詞雷同。例如：he 他，she 她，himself 他自己，herself 她自己，this 這個，that 那個，it 它……等。

3. 動詞 (verbs)

動詞用來描述主詞的行為或狀態，通常置於主詞之後。例如：walk 走路，talk 談話，sing 唱歌……等。

 例如：

例 He talks too fast.
他說話太快。

例 She takes care of the baby.
她照顧這個小嬰兒。

例 Teresa sings like a star.
德瑞莎唱起歌來像個明星。

4. 形容詞 (adjectives)

用來修飾一個名詞或代名詞，形容詞多放在修飾的名詞前或放在連綴動詞後，例如：gentle 溫柔的，rude 無禮的，hot 熱的，cold 冷的⋯⋯等。另外，形容詞還有比較級與最高級。

 例如：

例 a gentle nurse
一位溫柔的護理師

例 a kind consultant
一位仁慈的諮商師

5. 副詞 (adverbs)

副詞用來修飾動詞、形容詞、副詞、整個句子，以表達程度、次數、頻率等等。副詞不可以修飾名詞。副詞的移動性很高，常放在動詞後，形容詞前，也可放於句首或句尾。不同的副詞按照強調的部分不同，可放於不同地方，意義也會有所不同，例如：very 很，certainly 確實地。頻率副詞多放於be動詞後，一般動詞前，例如：always 總是，usually 通常，sometimes 有時候，never 從不……等。

例句：

例 Bob usually studies English vocabulary in the early morning.
鮑伯通常一大早研讀英文字彙。

例 Cherry blossoms are very beautiful but last only for a short time.
櫻花非常美，但是很短暫。

例 Rarely did he dine in a restaurant while he was a student.
他在求學時很少在餐廳吃飯。

6. 介系詞 (prepositions)

用來表達兩件事物的關係，如位置、方向、空間、時間、因果等，後面一定要加名詞、代名詞、動名詞結合成介系詞片語，例如：about 關於，around 在附近，in 在，of 的，under 之下，between 之間……等。

 例句：

例 Please don't talk about this issue in public.
請不要在公開場所談論這件事。

例 This is a matter between you and your parents.
這是你跟你父母之間的事。

例 This is a matter of life and death.
這是件生死交關的事。

7. 連接詞 (conjunctions)

用來連接單字 (words)、片語 (phrases)、子句 (clauses)。
注意連接詞所連接的詞性必須一致。連接詞分為：

(1) 對等連接詞 (coordinating conjunctions)：
and, but ,for ,or ,yet ,so...

 例句：

例 Scott passed the test, and his little sister did so, too.
史考特通過了這個測驗，他妹妹也一樣。

例 Scott passed the test, but his little sister failed.
史考特通過了這個測驗，但是他妹妹沒通過。

例 Scott finished all the homework, so he could go swimming.
史考特做完了所有功課，因此他可以去游泳。

例 Sharon finished all the homework for today, yet she wanted to do homework for tomorrow as well.
雪潤做完了今天的所有功課，不過她還想要做明天的功課。

(2) 附屬連接詞 (subordinating conjunctions):
if, because, when...

例句：

例 Jessica can stay here if she wants to.
如果傑西卡想要的話，她可以待在這兒。

例 You should be proud of yourself because you did your best.
你應該以自己為榮，因為你盡了力。

例 You should reward yourself when you achieve a goal.
當你達到目標時，你應該獎勵自己。

(3) 關係連接詞 (correlative conjunctions):
either…or..., neither…nor..., both…and..., whether…or..., not only…but also...

例句：

例 Students can choose either Japanese or French as the second foreign language.
學生可以選擇日語或法語作為第二外國語言。

例 Samantha likes neither cooking nor baking.
莎曼沙既不喜歡烹飪也不喜歡烘焙。

例 This summer we will go to both Milan and Paris for excursion.
今年夏天我們會到米蘭和巴黎校外教學。

例 Whether you believe it or not, Ada is getting married soon.
不論你相信不相信，艾達快結婚了。

例 Not only you but also your family are invited to the fashion show to see my collection of the year.
不只是你還有你全家人都受邀參加時尚秀來看我今年度的作品展。

◎詳細解釋請見Chapter 9

8. 感歎詞 (interjections)

用來表達強烈的情緒或驚訝。例如：oh, wow, yeah, ouch...等。

 例句：

例 Wow, you made it just at the last minute.
哇，你剛好在最後一分鐘趕到。

例 Oh! Your outfit is gorgeous.
喔！你穿得真好看。

例 Yeah, we are going to see each other soon.
嘩，我們將要再見面了。

例 Ouch! you just stepped on my toes.
哎呦！你剛踩到我的腳趾了。

◎詳細解釋請見Chapter 10

Unit
4

句子的結構

句子有以下四種結構：

1. 簡單句：只有一個子句（它一定是獨立子句）的句子。

例句：

例 David had no time for breakfast.
大衛沒時間吃早餐。

2. 對等句：由兩個或兩個以上的獨立子句構成，以對等連接詞連結。

例句：

例 David got up late, and he had no time for breakfast.
大衛太晚起床，沒時間吃早餐。

3. 複合句：由一個獨立子句和一個或一個以上的從屬子句所構成的句子。

例 David had no time for breakfast because he got up late.
大衛沒時間吃早餐，因為他太晚起床。

4. 混合句：由兩個獨立子句和一個或一個以上的從屬子句所構成的句子。

例 Because David got up late, he had no time for breakfast, and he was late for school.
因為大衛太晚起床，他沒時間吃早餐，而且上學遲到了。

這裡的非獨立子句副詞子句 because he got up late 加上獨立子句 he had no time for breakfast就可以是一個完整的句子，但是可以再用對等連接 and 把獨立子句 he was late for school 結合在一起，就成了一個完整的混合句。

Exercises 練習題

一、請標示出哪些部分是主詞，哪些部分是述語？

1. They never called back.

2. The little girl did not know when her parents will be back.

3. The main reason I left the company was that I could not have my voice heard.

4. The girl with many questions probably thinks too much.

5. Our perspective on life changes as we get older.

二、請寫出各句子所屬的句子種類。

1. Do you know when she will come back to the office?

2. What a lovely day it is!

3. I think he is telling a lie.

4. What a liar he is!

5. There is no use crying over spilt milk.

6. Why do you always make the same mistakes?

7. What is truth cannot be denied.

8. Focus on your work at hand.

秒懂！
關鍵 英文
文法 輕鬆學　Fast! Easy English Grammar

9. I heard you bought a new apartment with a parking space.

10. Save your smiles for those who deserve them.

● 找題目

三、請寫出劃線部分所屬的詞類。

1. If I finish the work by April 22, I will attend your birthday party.

2. What a load of lies!

3. Please think about your performance in the company in the previous year.

4. Why do you focus so much on the negative side?

5. Everything happens for a reason.

6. If you can stay calm, problems can be solved more easily.

7. When are you going to face the reality?

8. Like most companies, we face financial difficulties for quite some time.

9. Once you start to work on it, you will find it not as hard as you thought.

10. Julia is an ambitious girl who embraces challenges.

Key to Exercises 解答

一、

1. 主詞：They

   述語：never called back

2. 主詞：The little girl

   述語：did not know when her parents will be back

3. 主詞： The main reason I left the company

   述語： was that I could not have my voice heard

4. 主詞：The girl with many questions

   述語： probably thinks too much

5. 主詞：Our perspective on life

   述語：changes as we get older

二、

1. 疑問句

2. 感歎句

3. 敘述句

4. 感歎句

5. 敘述句

6. 疑問句

7. 敘述句

8. 祈使句

9. 敘述句

10. 祈使句

三、

1. 動詞

2. 名詞

3. 介系詞

4. 形容詞

5. 名詞

6. 形容詞

7. 動詞

8. 副詞

9. 形容詞

10. 動詞

TOEIC Exercises
多益題演練

1. The majority of the employees _____ the strike essential.

    (A) considers

    (B) consider

    (C) has considered

    (D) is considering

2. Do you think the applicant has professional _____ that meet the requirements for the position?

    (A) to qualify

    (B) qualify

    (C) qualified

    (D) qualifications

3. Have you _____ a welcome dinner for the new manager?

    (A) to arrange

    (B) arranging

    (C) arranged

    (D) arrangement

Questions 4 - 6 refer to the following e-mail.

To: Kate Kao

From: Ted Cheung

Subject: AI 2.0 Conference

Date: July 1, 2019 14:12

Dear Kate,

This is to confirm that I will represent our company to attend the AI 2.0 Conference in Kaohsiung on Nov 12, 2019. The _____

4. (A) objective

(B) objectionable

(C) objection

(D) objected

would be to strengthen the collaboration in the field Artificial Intelligence between Hong Kong and Taiwan.

As you probably already know, our company made a major breakthrough in developing Apps for language learners. In the conference, I would like to _____ the use and

5. (A) demonstrated

   (B) demonstrate

   (C) demonstration

   (D) demonstrative

function of the mobile devices for learning.

Attached is the related information. Please let me know if you have any _____ concerning this presentation.

6. (A) suggest

   (B) suggesting

   (C) suggestive

   (D) suggestions

Ted Cheung

CEO, Speedy Learning

e-mail: tedcheung@ml.com.hk

http://www.speedylearning.com.hk/

Address: 20/F., One Kowloon, 1 Wang Yuen Street, Kowloon Bay, Hong Kong

Key to TOEIC Exercises
多益題解答

1. B
2. D
3. C
4. A
5. B
6. D

有些字可以當動詞也可以當名詞，例如face作名詞意思是「臉」，但是作動詞意思是「面對」；有些字可以當形容詞也可以當副詞，例如 "hard" 可以形容事情很難，但是如果是在 "study hard" 中當作副詞則表示勤奮努力，當形容詞與副詞意思稍有不同。因此要特別看清楚字詞於文中的詞性與用法，才能判別其所代表的字義。

名詞（Nouns）

Unit 1

名詞的定義

表示人、事、物、地點、抽象概念等名稱的詞，稱為名詞。

Unit 2

名詞的種類

名詞可以分為專有名詞和普通名詞：

名詞主要分為兩大類：專有名詞和普通名詞。專有名詞是指「特定」的名稱，第一個字母通常必須大寫；普通名詞則是指「一般」的名稱，第一個字母通常不須大寫，除非是在句子的開頭或是作為標題時。

1. 專有名詞 (Proper Nouns)

代表獨一無二的名稱，第一個字母要大寫，例如：Jessica 潔西卡（女性名字），Friday 星期五，Thanksgiving 感恩節，Christmas 聖誕節，Taipei 台北，Tokyo 東京……

2. 普通名詞 (Common Nouns)

(1) 具體名詞 (Concrete Nouns)
代表某類具體人、事、物中的個體，例如：pencil 鉛筆，girl 女孩， school 學校，hospital 醫院……

(2) 集合名詞 (Collective Nouns)
代表許多個體組合成的集合體，
class 班級，staff 全體員工，
committee 委員會……

(3) 抽象名詞 (Abstract Nouns)
代表之物無具體形狀，常為一抽象概念，例如：love 愛，hate 恨，peace 和平……

(4) 物質名詞 (Material Nouns)
代表由某材料所組成，無法用單位數量詞計數的物質，例如：water 水，milk 牛奶，coffee 咖啡，gold 金，silver 銀……

專有名詞和普通名詞對照表

普通名詞	專有名詞
city（城市）	Taipei（台北）
car（車子）	Ford（福特）
company（公司）	Facebook（臉書）

weekday（工作日）	Tuesday（星期二）
uncle（舅舅、叔叔）	Uncle Tom（湯姆叔叔）
river（河流）	Tamsui River（淡水河）
temple（寺廟）	Longshan Temple（龍山寺）
tablet（平板電腦）	iPad（蘋果公司產品 ）

Unit
3

可數名詞與不可數名詞

- -

1.　可數名詞 (Countable Nouns)

大部分名詞都是可數名詞，意即這些名詞所代表之人、
事、物可以計數。單數名詞之前要加冠詞：a（名詞字
首為子音），an（名詞字首為母音）；複數名詞之後要
變為複數形式。

2.　不可數名詞 (Uncountable Nouns)

無法計數，單數名詞之前不可加冠詞（a, an）；複數名
詞之後不可變為複數形式。抽象與物質名詞皆屬於不可
數名詞。

3.　可作可數也可作不可數名詞

(1)　有些名詞可作可數也可作不可數名詞，但意思不同。

例如：coffee 咖啡

I like to drink coffee in the morning.
（表示一般的咖啡，不可數）
I'd like to have 2 coffees.（表示兩杯咖啡）

(2) 有些名詞表示整體物質時，是不可數名詞；表示某物質的一例時是可數名詞。

例如：hair 頭髮

He has black hair.（指的是整頭黑色的頭髮）
He found a hair in the hamburger.（指的是單根的頭髮）
He has quite a few white hairs.（指的是一根根的頭髮）

名詞的單複數形式

1. 通常於名詞字尾加 s，例如：pen, pens 筆；student, students 學生；town, towns 鎮……

2. 名詞若以 s, sh〔ʃ〕, ch〔tʃ〕, x, z 結尾，則於名詞字尾加 es。例如：dish, dishes 餐點；church, churches 教堂；box, boxes 盒子……

★ 但是如果字尾 **ch** 發音為〔k〕，則於名詞字尾加 **s**。例如：**stomach, stomachs** 胃; **monarch, monarchs** 君主……

3. 名詞若以子音加上 o 結尾，則於名詞字尾加 es。例如：tomato, tomatoes 番茄；potato, potatoes 馬鈴薯；hero, heroes 英雄……

★ 但是如果字尾為母音加上 **o** 結尾，則於名詞字尾加 **s**。
例如：**radio, radios** 收音機；**studio, studios** 工作室；
zoo, zoos 動物園……

4. 名詞若以子音加上 y 結尾，則將 y 改為 i，再加
es。例如：story, stories 故事； dragonfly,
dragonflies 蜻蜓； family, families 家庭……

★ 但是名詞若以母音加上 **y** 結尾，只加 s。例如：**boy,**
boys 男孩；**day, days** 日子；**ray, rays** 光線……

5. 名詞若以 f, fe 結尾，則將 f, fe 改為 v，再加 es。
例如：half, halves 半個；knife, knives 刀；life, lives
生命……

6. 通常以複數形式出現的名詞，例如：pants 褲子；
glasses 眼鏡；scissors 剪刀……

7. 有些名詞以 -ics 結尾，但是卻並非複數，例如：
athletics, economics, electronics, gymnastics,
mathematics, physics, politics。

8. 有些名詞以 -s 結尾，但是可以視情形與單數或複數動詞連用，例如：means, series, species。

9. 有些單數名詞經常會接複數動詞，例如：audience, committee, company, family, firm, government, staff, team。

10. 單複數形式相同的名詞

例如：

- one sheep - two sheep   綿羊
- one deer - two deer   鹿
- one fish - two fish   魚

one sheep

- one cattle - two cattle   牛
- one trout - two trout   鱒魚
- one moose - two moose   麋
- one Chinese - two Chinese   中國人
- one corps - two corps   軍團

two sheep

- one means - two means   手段
- one species - two species   物種
- one offspring - two offspring   後代

11. 複數變化不規則名詞

(1) 改變母音

- man - men 男人；woman - women 女人；
- goose - geese 鵝；foot - feet 腳；
- mouse - mice 老鼠；louse - lice 蝨子……
-

one foot

two feet

(2) 改變字尾

★ 字尾加 -en 或 -ren

- ox - oxen 牛；　　　　　child - children 小孩

★ 字尾為 -sis 改為 -ses

- crisis - crises 危機；oasis - oases 綠洲；
- analysis - analyses 分析；thesis - theses 論文；
- basis - bases 基礎；hypothesis - hypotheses 假設；
- parenthesis - parentheses 括號

★ 字尾為 -us 改為 -i

- alumnus - alumni 校友；syllabus - syllabi 課程表；
- stimulus - stimuli 刺激；radius - radii 半徑；
- fungus - fungi 真菌

★ 字尾為 -um 改為 -a

- datum - data 數據；medium - media 媒體；
- curriculum - curricula 課程；bacteria - bacterium 細菌；
- memorandum - memoranda 備忘錄

★ 字尾為 -on 改為 -a

- phenomenon - phenomena 現象；criterion - criteria 標準

★ 字尾為 -a 改為 -ae

- alumna - alumnae 女校友；
- formula - formulae 公式

★ 字尾為 -e 改為 -ce

- die - dice 骰子

★ 字尾為 -x 改為 -ces

- appendix - appendices/appendixes 附錄；
- index - indices/indexes 索引

Exercises 練習題

一、請將下列的單字填入空格中，並於前面加上 a 或 an，
　　還有名詞適當的單複數變化。

pant, staff, air, mathematics, glass, basketball, advice, sugar, question, water, mouse, committee

1. Jenny does not like to wear a skirt. She always wear
　　_____ .

2. Open the window to let some _____ in.

3. Johnny has to wear _____ to read the words on the blackboard.

4. I really don't know which dress I should buy. Could you give me some good _____?

5. The secret of this dish is to put _____ in.

6. Most athletes cannot make a living by just playing __
　　____.

7. Last night I found two _____ in the kitchen.

8. The _____ of this company are planning a strike for tomorrow.

9. _____ was never easy for me in school.

10. The _____ are investigating this case right now.

11. _____ is indispensable in maintaining a life in a desert.

12. We welcome all _____.

二、請將下列空格中兩個項目當中錯誤的劃掉，保留正確的。

1. Gymnastics is / are my favorite sport.

2. My eyesight is getting worse, and I need new glass / glasses.

3. The police is / are trying to find the stolen car.

4. Three years isn't / aren't enough to learn a language well.

5. The news is / are spread out in the whole town.

6. Physics is / are my favorite subject in high school.

7. The people of this small town is / are very used to tourists.

8. The New York Times is / are what most local people read every morning.

9. My scissors is / are too rusty. Please lend me yours.

10. Two hundred dollars was / were missing in my wallet.

三、請將下列句子改正，如果不用修改則請填上 OK。

1. The policeman was ringing the bell of the apartment.

   _____

2. The police was trying to find the gun. _____

   _____

3. I appreciate your good advice.

   _____

4. Jenny wears a blue jeans. _____

   _____

5. Ten hundred dollars are not enough for me.

   _____

6. The news are overwhelming for his parents back home.

   _____

7. That pair of new pants look good on you.

   _____

8. The new pants looks good on you.

   _____

9. The Vietnamese celebrates the Lunar New Year.

   _____

10. The Johnsons is going to Spain during Christmas holiday.

    _____

Key to Exercises
解答

一、

1. pants	2. air	3. glasses
4. advice	5. sugar	6. basketball
7. mice	8. staff	9. Mathematics
10. committee	11. Water	12. questions

二、

1. is / ~~are~~   2. ~~glass~~ / glasses   3. ~~is~~ / are

4. isn't / ~~aren't~~   5. is / ~~are~~   6. is / ~~are~~

7. ~~is~~ / are   8. is / ~~are~~   9. ~~is~~ / are

10. was / ~~were~~ .

三、

1. OK

2. The police were trying to find the gun.

3. OK

4. Jenny wears blue jeans.

5. Ten hundred dollars is not enough for me.

6. The news is overwhelming for his parents back home.

7. That pair of new pants looks good on you.

8. The new pants look good on you.

9. The Vietnamese celebrate the Lunar New Year.

10. The Johnsons are going to Spain during Christmas holiday.

TOEIC Exercises
多益題演練

1. The secretary is organizing her supervisor's _____
___.

   (A) appointed

   (B) appointing

   (C) appointments

   (D) appoint

2. You should listen to your parents' _____.

   (A) advise

   (B) advice

   (C) advisor

   (D) advisee

3. In the end of the year, all employees are asked to write
their own performance _____.

   (A) evaluating

   (B) evaluated

   (C) evaluations

   (D) evaluators

Questions 4 - 6 refer to the following e-mail.

To: Daniel Brown

From: Michael Chen

Subject: A Training Session of Public Speaking

Date: February 1, 2019 10:22

Dear Mr. Brown,

I am writing to let you know that you are invited as the special guest speaker to give a training session of Public Speaking to our interested employees. Please pick a Saturday afternoon suitable to you between February 16 and the April 27, 2019 and inform us of your _____.

4. (A) decide

   (B) deciding

   (C) decision

   (D) decide

We'd like to have your profile with your _____ to

5. (A) published

(B) publications

(C) public

(D) publicity

present you to those who do not know you yet. If there is anything special you would like to request for your training session, please advise us so that we can prepare it for you in advance. In addition, you are also entitled to apply for transportation _____.

6. (A) subsidies

(B) supplements

(C) subordinates

(D) subjects

Michael Chen

Human Resource Manager

Chen Porcelain International Company

E-mail: mchen@jjlanguage.com

Address: 101 Fuhua San Road, Futian District

Shenzhen, 518048 China

Tel: +86-755-88888888

Key to TOEIC Exercises
多益題解答

Part **2**

1. C

2. B

3. C

4. C

5. B

6. A

結論

英文名詞的單複數概念是不是與中文有很大的不同呢？剛
開始學習的時候，搞不清楚何為可數、何為不可數名詞是
在所難免的，還有複數名詞字尾的不規則變化，如果不甚
確定的話，強烈建議還是上網查一下英文字典，順便看一
下該名詞的例句，才不會貽笑大方。

3

冠詞（Articles）

英語的冠詞通常置於名詞前面，用來表示
名詞所指的人事物為特指或泛指，冠詞分為
三種：
1. 定冠詞 (definite articles)
2. 不定冠詞 (indefinite articles)
3. 零冠詞 (zero articles)

Unit
1

定冠詞

定冠詞 (definite articles)"the"用於名詞前面，以表示名詞所代表的人事物為特定的或已提及過的。使用"the"的情形如下：

1. 用於指前面提及過的人事物

例 This is the restaurant I mentioned to you before.
這就是我曾對你提及的餐廳。

例 Have you tried the banana cake she recommended?
你嚐過她推薦的香蕉蛋糕嗎？

例 Have you received the greeting card from her?
你收到了她的賀卡嗎？

例 Could you please pass the salad?
你可以將那盤沙拉遞過來嗎？

2. 用於指已知的人事物

(例) Do you know the result of the exam?
你知道了考試的結果了嗎？

(例) We haven't heard of the latest development.
我們還沒聽說最新發展情形。

(例) Have you seen the new teacher, who is going to teach us from tomorrow on?
你看過這位從明天起要教我們的新老師嗎？

(例) Are you aware of the fact that you have been absent too many times in this semester?
你知道你這學期已經太多次缺席這個事實嗎？

3. 用於指宇宙獨一無二的人事物

(例) The moon is a frequently mentioned subject in the Chinese poems.
月亮是中國詩句中很常提及的主題。

(例) The sun gives us sunshine and warmth.
太陽給我們帶來陽光和溫暖。

(例) I wish I could see the earth from space.
但願我能夠從太空中看見地球。

4. 與最高級、only, very 等修飾語連用

例 She is probably the most popular Taiwanese teenage pop star in South Korea.
她大概是台灣於南韓的青少年流行藝人中最受歡迎的一位了。

例 The best food is often prepared with love.
最好的食物通常是用愛準備的。

例 This is the only English grammar book I could find in the library.
這是我在圖書館僅能找到的英文文法書。

例 That is the very English grammar book you need at this stage.
那本英文文法書正是你現階段所需要的。

5. 與序數詞連用

例 Margret is the first child in her family.
瑪格列特是她家中第一個出生的孩子。

例 The last semester was very intensive, and now I need a break.
上學期真是密集，我現在需要休息一下。

6. 與彈奏樂器名稱連用

例 She enjoys playing the piano before going to bed.
她喜歡於睡前彈鋼琴。

例 Daniel plays the flute in the army band.
丹尼爾在軍樂團裡吹長笛。

例 Unlike most of her friends, Sarah can play the cello very well.
莎拉能將大提琴拉得很好，不像她大部分的朋友。

例 Not many children can play the violin very well from the beginning.
並沒有很多小孩能一開始就將小提琴拉得很好。

7. 地理名稱

(1) 河流
- the Tamsui River   淡水河
- the Yangtzi River   長江
- the Yellow River   黃河
- the Ganges River   恆河
- the Mississippi River   密西西比河

(2) 海洋
- the Pacific Ocean   太平洋
- the Atlantic Ocean   大西洋
- the Indian Ocean   印度洋

(3) 山脈

- the Himalayas 喜馬拉雅山
- the Alps　　　　　　　　　阿爾卑斯山脈
- the Rocky Mountains　　　　落磯山脈

(4) 群島

- the Pescadores.　　　　　澎湖群島
- the Marshall Islands　　　馬紹爾群島
- the Hawaiian Islands　　　夏威夷群島
- the Solomon Islands　　　索羅門群島

(5) 沙漠

- the Gobi Desert　　　　　戈壁大沙漠
- the Sahara Desert　　　　撒哈拉沙漠
- the Thar Desert (the Great Indian Desert)
  塔爾沙漠（印度大沙漠）

(6) 湖泊

- the Sun Moon Lake　　　日月潭
- the Great Lake　　　　　五大湖

(7) 運河

- the Suez Canal　　　　　蘇伊士運河
- the Panama Canal　　　　巴拿馬運河

(8) 海灣

- the Persian Gulf　　　　波斯灣
- the Gulf of Mexico　　　墨西哥灣

(9) 海峽

- the English Channel 　　　　英吉利海峽
- the Taiwan Straits 　　　　　台灣海峽
- the Straits of Gibraltar 　　直布羅陀海峽

8. 與組織、國家等名詞連用

- the United States (of America) 美國
- the United Nations 聯合國
- the Netherlands 荷蘭
- the European Union 歐盟
- the Philippines 菲律賓
- the Bahamas 巴哈馬

當機關組織縮寫唸起來是一個字，而非個別字母則不需要加冠詞，例如：ASEAN, The Association of Southeast Asian Nations 東南亞國家協會；但是如果是依個別字母來唸，則需要加定冠詞the，例如：the FBI, The Federal Bureau of Investigation 聯邦調查局。

9. 姓氏

- the Simpsons 辛普森家
- the Richardson 李察森家
- the Wangs 王家

10. 約定成俗的用法

- the Big Data　大數據
- the cause and effect　因果關係
- the demand and supply　供給和需求
- the food chain　食物鏈

Unit
2

不定冠詞

不定冠詞 (indefinite articles) "a/an" 用於名詞前面，相對於定冠詞，不定冠詞不作特別指定，而是泛指一般的人事物。以下為其特質：

1. 不定冠詞只能與單數可數名詞連用

(1) 名詞以子音起始則冠詞用 "a"，例如：a friend 一個朋友, a book 一本書, a house 一間房子。

(2) 名詞以母音起始則冠詞用 "an"，例如：an incident 一個事件, an inch 一英吋, an apple 一個蘋果。

2. 首次提到的人事物

例 Have you experienced an earthquake in your life?
你生平是否曾經體驗過地震？

例 A typhoon can cause great damage to the farms.
颱風會對農地造成很大的損害。

3. 泛指一類人事物中的一例

例 A good book can change a person's life forever.
一本好書可以永久改變一個人的一生。

例 An error can cause the entire operation to shut down.
一個錯誤可以造成整個運作停止。

4. 用於動物或植物名稱，表示同類的總稱

例 A dog is a person's best friend.
狗是人最好的朋友。

例 An ant can find sugar easily.
螞蟻可以輕易找到糖。

5. 等於 each, every, per

例 We have brought with us a book for a student.
我們為每個學生都帶來了一本書。

例 Write an English composition a day.
每天寫一篇英文作文。

6. 與專有名詞連用，可代表具有與某人相同特質的人事物

例 A Renaissance man is a person who has wide interests and is expert in several areas.
文藝復興時期的人指的是興趣廣泛，精通許多領域的人。

7. 表示單位的數量詞

- 20 dollars a pound   一磅 20 元
- 2 USD an inch   一吋兩美元

Unit
3

零冠詞

零冠詞 (zero articles) 表示某些名詞或名詞片語前面不要使用冠詞。下列情形的名詞前面要用零冠詞：

1. 複數名詞表示同類的總稱時，前面不要用冠詞。

例 Dogs are people's most loyal friends.
狗是人類最忠實的朋友。

例 Cats are usually very domestic animals.
貓通常是居家型動物。

例 Monkeys resemble human beings very much.
猴子與人類非常相似。

例 Tigers face the danger of extinction.
老虎面臨絕種的危機。

2. 抽象名詞前面不要用冠詞。

例 Honesty is one of his best characteristics.
誠實是他最佳人格特質之一。

例 Sue is known for her gentleness and kindness.
蘇以溫柔又仁慈而出名。

例 In my opinion, Ann has to work on generosity.
依我看來，安必須要多慷慨一點。

3. 專有名詞前面不要用冠詞。

"Fusion" means combining two cooking styles.
「融合」意指兩種烹飪風格的合併。

4. 同位語或補語的職位名稱前面不要用冠詞。

例 Mr. Richardson, president of our company, is going to attend this meeting today.
我們公司總裁李查森先生會出席今天的會議。

例 May I introduce Mr. Huang, CEO of "Greenlife", the company we have been dealing with for a couple of months?
容我介紹黃先生，他是綠生活的執行長，我們已跟他的公司來往兩三個月了。

5. 表行為能力的機構名詞前面不要用冠詞。

例 He is going to hospital.
他要去醫院。

例 At what age do the children here start to go to school?
這裡的小孩幾歲開始上學？

---

6. 泛指三餐、四季的名詞前面不要用冠詞。

例 Let's meet for lunch tomorrow.
明天我們一起吃午餐吧。

例 Autumn is my favorite season.
秋天是我最喜愛的季節。

---

7. 疾病名稱前面不要用冠詞。

- Parkinson's disease 　　　　帕金森氏病
- diabetes 　　　　糖尿病
- Alzheimer's disease 　　　　阿茲海默症
- ADHD (attention deficit hyperactivity disorder)
　　　　　　　　　　　注意力不足過動症

---

8. 與介系詞 after, at, before, by 連用，表一天時光的時間名詞前面不要用冠詞。

- before sunset 　　　　日落之前
- after sunrise 　　　　日落之後
- at noon 　　　　中午
- by midnight 　　　　凌晨前

---

9. 與介系詞 by 連用，表示交通的交通工具名稱前面不要用冠詞。

- by bus   搭巴士
- by car   搭車子
- by foot   走路

10. 運動名稱前面不要用冠詞。

- play basketball   打籃球
- play tennis   打網球
- play badminton   打羽球
- play table tennis (ping pong)   打桌球

11. 習慣片語前面不要用冠詞。

- day and night   日夜
- day in and day out   一天又一天
- bread and butter   主要收入的來源
- life and death   生與死

Exercises 練習題

★ 請於空格填入 **a / an** 或 **the**。

1.1 The building is quite special. Has it got ____ good view?

1.2 ____ view of this room is awesome.

2.1 We have been waiting for ____ hour for the speaker to arrive.

2.2 Nobody likes ____ working hours of this job.

3.1 Have you been to New York? ____ city is also called the Big Apple.

3.2 My parents do not like living in ____ big city.

4.1 Could you recommend ____ useful Grammar book?

4.2 I find ____ Grammar book very useful.

4.3 This is ____ best Grammar book in my opinion.

5.1 He currently works 40 hours ____ week.

5.2 ____ week that he went to Japan for business was extremely busy.

5.3 Yvonne applied to take ____ week off next month.

★ 請視需要於下列句子的空格中填入 **the**；如果不需要
用到 **the** 則空白，不需填入任何字。

1.1 Susan's family go to ____ church every Sunday.

1.2 ____ church has a long history in this country.

2.1 Does your son like ____ school he goes to right now?

2.2 At what age do children start to go to ____ school in your country?

2.3 Today is Children's Day, and all school children are not at ____ school.

3. 1 Could you call someone to fix ____ television? It is broken again.

3.2 I tend to watch ____ television too long.

4.1 Have you cooked ____ dinner?

4.2 ____ dinner at the Grand Hotel is unforgettable.

5.1 I like to have breakfast in ____ bed when I am in a hotel.

5.2 I'd like to buy ____ new bed I just saw the other day in the furniture store.

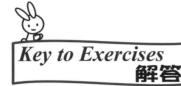

Part 3

Key to Exercises 解答

一、

1.1 a	1.2 The	2.1 an
2.2 the	3.1 The	3.2 a
4.1 a	4.2 the	4.3 the
5.1 a	5.2 The	5.3 a

二、

1.1 ___	1.2 The	2.1 the
2.2 ___	2.3 ___	3.1 the
3.2 ___	4.1 ___	4.2 The
5.1 ___	5.2 the	

TOEIC Exercises
多益題演練

1. Those who did not attend ＿＿ meeting last week have to write a short report.

   (A) an

   (B) a

   (C) the

   (D) ＿＿

2. We should visit ＿＿ Browns during the holidays.

   (A) those

   (B) the

   (C) these

   (D) that

3. Mr. Chen is excited about hosting the dinner in English for ＿＿ guests from abroad.

   (A) the

   (B) a

   (C) an

   (D) this

Questions 4 - 6 refer to the following announcement.

To: All employees

From: James Wang

Date: March 20, 2019

Dear All,

　　We are glad to announce that the new service of child care provided by our company will start on April 10, 2019. It is going to be on the second floor of the same building, where our office is located. The eligible age range of the children is 3 to 6 years old. Please check it out because ___ _____ openings are limited.

4. (A) an

　 (B) the

　 (C) a

　 (D) that

　　　　　　_____ special tour of the child care facility can

5. (A) A

   (B) An

   (C) This

   (D) That

be arranged at your convenience. English courses in _____

___

6. (A) a

   (B) an

   (C) the

   (D) that

afternoon will be taught by qualified teachers with extensive years of child care.

James Wang

Manager

Key to TOEIC Exercises
多益題解答

1. C

2. B

3. A

4. B

5. A

6. C

英文中冠詞的概念與中文非常類似，但仔細比較起來，英文中使用冠詞（無論是不定冠詞或定冠詞）的頻率還是較中文高許多，例如我們稱「撒哈拉沙漠」，而英文則要加上定冠詞："the Sahara Desert"，因此本章的整理可以對學習英文冠詞有很大的幫助，平時閱讀英文文章時多留意些冠詞的使用，也會很有助益。

4

代名詞（Pronouns）

Unit
1

代名詞的分類如下：

1. 人稱代名詞　　　2. 所有格代名詞
3. 指示代名詞　　　4. 不定代名詞
5. 相互代名詞　　　6. 反身代名詞
7. 疑問代名詞　　　8. 關係代名詞

人稱代名詞變化詳細表格如下：

人稱 性、數、格	主格	所有格	受格	所有 代名詞	反身格	中文
第一(單)	I	my	me	mine	myself	我
第一(複)	we	our	us	ours	ourselves	我們
第二(單)	you	your	you	yours	yourself	你
第二(複)	you	your	you	yours	yourselves	你們
第三(男單)	he	his	him	his	himself	他
第三(女單)	she	her	her	hers	herself	她
第三(中單)	one	one's	one	...	oneself	一個人； 任何人
第三(男/女單)	he she	his her	him her	his hers	himself herself	他或她
第三(中單)	it	its	it	its	itself	它；牠
第三(複)	they	their	them	theirs	themselves	他們

附註：出自《簡明當代英文法》232 頁，作者：蔣炳榮，2013 年

以下就此 8 類代名詞一一解說：

1. 人稱代名詞

人稱代名詞顧名思義是主要用來代替人稱的代替名詞，也可以用來代替物：

I, me

you, you

he, him,

she, her

It

we, us

they them

 例句：

(例) Gray had a serious cold, and Gray had to take a day off.
蓋瑞重感冒，蓋瑞必須請假一天。

替代後-->

Gray had a serious cold, and he had to take a day off.
蓋瑞重感冒，他必須請假一天。

(例) Rachel's father asked Rachel to study medicine.
瑞秋的父親要瑞秋習醫。

替代後-->

Rachel's father asked her to study medicine.
瑞秋的父親要她習醫。

◎人稱代名詞可以用來代替物或動物，例如 she, her, he, him, it, they, them。

(例) She is a fancy yacht, isn't it?
她是艘豪華的遊艇，對吧？

(例) They are the missing children.
他們就是失蹤的孩子。

此外 one, ones 可以作代名詞，代替上下文中的名詞，還可作不定代名詞表示任何人。

(例) There came several students. Do you know the one with a basketball hat?
那邊有幾個學生走過來，你認識那個戴著棒球帽的那個學生嗎？

(例) One should never underestimate the importance of health.
我們不該輕估健康的重要性。

2. 所有格代名詞

mine = my + 名詞
yours = your + 名詞
his = his + 名詞
hers = her + 名詞
his or hers = his or her + 名詞
its = its + 名詞
ours = our + 名詞
theirs = their + 名詞

 例句：

例 This cup is hers. Yours is on that table.
= This is her cup. Your cup is on that table.
這杯子是她的；你的在那張桌子上。

例 Those books are theirs. Ours are over there.
= Those are their books. Our books are over there.
那些書是他們的；我們的在那邊。

3. 指示代名詞

◎指示代名詞 this、that、these、those
這些字用來當作指示代名詞時，this、that用來當作單數指示代名詞，而these、those用來當作複數指示代名詞。其中this、these代表靠近我們這裡的人或東西，that、those代表離我們較遠的人或東西。

	單數	複數
here (這裡)	this	these
there (那裡)	that	those

近　　this（這個）= this ＋ 名詞
遠　　that（那個）= that ＋ 名詞
近　　these（這些）= these ＋ 名詞
遠　　those（那些）= those ＋ 名詞

其中 this、that 也可以代表以上所述的陳述，例如：
Recently AI has been applied in many fields, and this is especially obvious in household supplies.

He got a serious cold, and because of that, he could not attend this meeting.

 例句：

(例) This is my bag. That is yours.
　　= This bag is mine. That bag is yours.
　　這是我的袋子；那個是你的。

(例) These are my books. Those are hers.
　　= These books are mine. Those books are hers.
　　這些是我的書；那些是她的。

4. 不定代名詞

all, another, any, both, each, either, enough, (a) few, (a) little, many, much, neither, one, ones, others, several, some, the other, the others, one, two,(數詞)...

 例句：

例 On that day all of the students can take part in picnic.
當天所有學生都可以參加野餐。

例 Both of us have much work to catch up.
我們兩個都有很多工作要趕上進度。

例 The two books are both very interesting, but I prefer this one to the other.
這兩本書都很有意思，但是相較而言我偏愛其中這本書。

例 Among all books I like this most; the others are not that interesting to me.
在所有書當中我最喜歡這本；我覺得其它的書沒有那麼有意思。

例 There came many students, and I know several of them.
那兒有許多學生走過來，我認識當中幾個。

例 Three of your friends you invited did not show up at the dinner party.
你所邀請的朋友中有三位沒有出席晚宴。

5. 相互代名詞

each other（所有格 each other's）
one another（所有格 one another's）

 例句：

例 They love each other very much.
他們深愛著彼此。

例 They are each other's best friend.
他們是彼此最好的朋友。

例 You should help one another.
你們應該互相幫忙。

例 You should be one another's friend.
你們應該作彼此的朋友。

6. 反身代名詞

反身代名詞有以下幾種：

單數	複數
myself	ourselves
yourself	yourselves
herself, himself, itself, oneself	themselves

 例句：

例 I cut myself in the kitchen.
我在廚房割到手。

例 You don't have to do everything yourself.
你不需要每件事都親自做。

例 The work itself is not hard, but it is hard for the team members to do it together.
這工作本身不難，但是要叫團隊成員合作卻很難。

7. 疑問代名詞

疑問代名詞共有以下幾個：

who, which, what, whose, whom

用法請見以下的表格：

	中文	主格	所有格	受格
人稱	人	who	whose	whom
人稱	哪一位	which	---	which
非人稱	何事／物	what	---	what
非人稱	哪一個	which	---	which

附註：出自《簡明當代英文法》247 頁，作者：蔣炳榮，2013 年
（請參考第 14 章）

例句：

例) Who is that girl?
那個女孩是誰？

例) The girl whose name I cannot remember is his daughter.
那個我忘了名字的女孩是他女兒。

例) Do you know whom they are talking about?
你知道他們在談論的是誰？

例) Now your books are mixed up with my books. It is hard to tell which is which.
現在你的書和我的書混在一起了，很難分辨出哪些是你的，哪些是我的。

例) What I know is that I should do more and talk less.
我所知道的是：我該多做事少說話。

8. 疑問代名詞

（請見第21章）

Exercises 練習題

一、請用 some 或 any 填入空格。

1. I can lend you ＿＿＿ books on the subject if you want need.

2. Is there ＿＿＿ more item you would like to purchase?

3. At the moment, he would be glad if he could find ＿＿＿ job.

4. There are ＿＿＿ problems with your project, but they are not serious.

5. Is there ＿＿＿ new issue you would like to raise in this meeting?

6. Some of the tasks are well done, but ＿＿＿ are not.

7. Are there ＿＿＿ new students in this classroom?

8. Of all the assignments, some are interesting, and ＿＿＿ are not.

9. I cannot think of ＿＿＿ teachers that does not like me.

10. Is there ＿＿＿ neighbor that you don't know?

二、 請用 myself/yourself/ourselves etc 來完成句子。

1. Tom blames _____ for not taking good care of his little brother.

2. Kelly had a good time at the party. She enjoyed _____.

3. I cut _____ in the kitchen today.

4. If I get this work done in time, I'm going to reward _____ with a trip to the mountain.

5. Don't burn _____ when you set up the fire.

6. He was ashamed of _____ for what he had done.

7. When you are overseas, you have to look after _____.

8. We should not blame _____. It was not our fault.

9. They were so careless that they hurt _____.

10. Allen, please help _____ with the desserts.

三、 請用 no- 或 any- 加上 -body/-thing/-where 來完成以下句子。

1. I have _____ to say. You can think whatever you want to think.

2. We welcome _____ that would like to join us.

3. Is there _____ you left in the room?

4. There is _____ like home.

5. _____ you go, I go with you.

6. _____ likes to be around with a sad person.

7. _____ has changed in the school. It is almost the same as it was thirty years ago.

8. When Dave's mother is around, he usually stays quiet and does not say _____.

Key to Exercises 解答

 一、

1. some	2. any	3. any
4. some	5. any	6. some
7. any	8. some	9. any
10. any		

 二、

1. himself	2. herself	3. myself
4. myself	5. yourself	6. himself
7. yourself	8. ourselves	9. themselves
10. yourself		

 三、

1. nothing	2. anybody	3. anything
4. nowhere	5. Anywhere	6. Nobody
7. Nothing	8. anything	

TOEIC Exercises
多益題演練

1. Please familiarize _____ with the new software of the company in a week.

   (A) ourselves

   (B) yourself

   (C) themselves

   (D) himself

2. Because her husband was ill, she had to do all the driving by _____.

   (A) himself

   (B) him

   (C) her

   (D) herself

3. _____ who are interested in applying for the position, please do so by the end of this month.

   (A) Those

   (B) These

   (C) They

   (D) Anyone

Questions 4 - 6 refer to the following e-mail.

To: Jane Wang

From: Tom Lin

Subject: Trade Fair in Seoul

Date: July 28, 2019 8:16

Dear Jane,

　　We are glad to know that you are going to represent our company to attend the trade fair in Seoul. For _____

4.　(A) whoever

　　(B) this

　　(C) those

　　(D) someone

who has not done this job before like you and four other employees, we strongly suggest a workshop of preparation. Our Korean language specialist will not be going on the business trip with you this time. All of you are therefore expected to do all the presenting our products by _____.

5. (A) yourself

(B) yourselves

(C) them

(D) themselves

In the workshop, you will learn practices and customs of Korean culture as well as some case studies of success and mistakes in communicating with Korean business partners. In the end, only you _____ can decide your own style of communication in Korea.

6. (A) your

(B) yourselves

(C) yours

(D) yourself

Tom Lin

Sales Manager

Golden Star Trading Company

No.62, Hengyang Rd., Zhongzheng Dist., Taipei 100, Taiwan

E-Mail: tomlin@goldenstar.com.tw

Website: http://www.goldenstar.com.tw

Key to TOEIC Exercises
多益題解答

1. B

2. D

3. A

4. D

5. B

6. D

 結論

英文中使用代名詞的頻率遠大於中文，因為中文無論已經
提及此名詞多少次，還是經常重覆已提過的名詞，而且如
果不是特別需要，並不會常常用到「它」、「它們」。想
要培養出英文的語感，需要平時仔細聆聽，詳細閱讀，這
樣於口說及寫作時才能輕鬆使用代名詞。

5

動詞（Verbs）

動詞的定義

動詞是用來表示各種的動作過程，依文法上的不同形式，動詞有以下不同的分類：

動詞的分類

1. 及物動詞 vs. 不及物動詞

及物動詞又分為：單及物動詞 ＆ 雙及物動詞

(1) 單及物動詞：只有一個受詞的動詞
主詞 - 及物動詞 - 直接受詞

 例句：

⑦ I love English.
我喜愛英語。

⑦ She hates him.
她痛恨他。

⑦ At the party last night Michael was playing the piano while his mother was singing.
在昨天晚會上麥可彈鋼琴時，他的母親在唱歌。

⑦ Many art lovers often visit museums and galleries.
很多藝術愛好者經常參觀博物館與畫廊。

⑦ Nowadays many people read ebooks online.
現在很多人閱讀線上電子書。

⑦ Quite a lot of young people must have the latest smartphones.
相當多的年輕人一定要擁有最新的智慧型手機。

(2) 雙及物動詞：有兩個受詞的動詞

主詞 - 及物動詞 - 間接受詞 - 直接受詞
= 主詞 - 及物動詞 - 直接受詞 - 介系詞 - 間接受詞

★ 請注意介系詞

 例句：

例 Her mother gave her an English book.

= Her mother gave an English book to her.

她的母親給了她一本英文書。

例 My friend brought me a sandwich and a drink.

= My friend brought a sandwich and a drink for me.

我的朋友帶了一個三明治和一瓶飲料給我。

例 The teacher showed the students what they should practice.

= The teacher showed what they should practice to the students.

這位老師示範學生該做的練習給他們看。

例 Howard told his parents many lies.

= Howard told many lies to his parents.

霍華德對他父母撒了很多謊。

例 I wish you great health and happiness.

= I wish great health and happiness for you.

我祝您健康幸福。

◎附註：「受詞」即「賓語」。

2. 完全動詞 vs. 不完全動詞

(1) 完全動詞

a. (完全)及物動詞

例 I love you.
我愛你。

例 William plays the drum in the band.
威廉在樂團是打鼓的。

例 Johnson fixed the guitar by himself.
強森是靠自己把吉他修好的。

例 Please wash the cups.
請洗杯子。

例 Don't waste money to buy useless things.
不要將錢浪費在買沒用的東西上面。

b. (完全)不及物動詞

例 I walk to school.
我走路上學。

例 Birds fly in the sky.
鳥在天上飛。

例 Fish swim in the pond.
魚在池子裡游。

例 Henry seldom cooks because his mother cooks well.
亨利很少下廚因為他母親很會燒菜。

例 The monks meditate in the temple.
和尚在寺院裡禪修。

(2) 不完全動詞

a. 不完全及物動詞

這類動詞有：

elect, keep, find, call, consider, believe, appoint, regard, name, deem, force, leave, suppose, prefer

例 I consider her an angel.
我視她為天使。

例 I regarded him as my mentor.
我視他為我的導師。

例 He named his dog Flash.
他將他的狗命名為閃光。

例 Some people might find her very strict.
有些人可能會覺得她很嚴苛。

例 The teacher appointed her the leader of the class.
老師指定她作班長。

b. 不完全不及物動詞

不完全不及物動詞主要為連綴動詞

★ 連綴動詞

- be 動詞：am, is, are, was, were, be, being, been
- 帶有助動詞的 be 動詞：shall be, should be, can be, could be, will be, would be, may be, might be
- ......起來：look 看起來, smell 聞起來, sound 聽起來, taste 嚐起來, feel 覺得
- 似乎：seem 看似, appear 顯現
- 仍然：remain 仍然, stay 保持, keep 保持
- 變得：become 變成, grow 成為, turn 變成, go 變成, get 成為

 例句：

⑩ Brian was very sad.
布萊恩很難過。

⑩ Andy was shocked and speechless.
安迪震驚到說不出話。

⑩ They remained silent.
他們保持沉默。

⑩ She looks fine.
她看起來很好。

⑩ The pork tastes sweet and sour.
這豬肉嚐起來酸酸甜甜的。

例 The tea tastes a bit bitter.
這茶嚐起來有點苦。

例 The flower smells great.
這花聞起來氣味真好。

3. 單詞動詞 vs. 片語動詞

(1) 單詞動詞

例如：buy 買，love 愛，come 來，go 去，share 分享，receive 獲得，overcome 克服，celebrate 慶祝……

buy 買

例 Please buy some bread on your way home.
請於回家的路上買點麵包。
love 愛

例 She loves singing.
她熱愛歌唱。
come 來

例 Come here whenever you feel like.
你隨時想來這裡都可以來。
go 去

例 You can go home if you are tired.
如果你累了可以回家。
share 分享

例 Children should learn to share things with others.
小孩應該學習與他人分享東西。
receive 獲得

例 Adam received the first prize in the writing competition.
亞當得到了寫作第一名。
overcome 克服

例 Sandy overcame his illness and came back to her work-place.
珊蒂戰勝了她的疾病，回到了工作崗位。
celebrate 慶祝

例 Dru invited us to celebrate his birthday at his place.
杜魯邀請我們到他家去慶生。

(2) 片語動詞

---
a. 二字片語動詞
---

get up 起床

例 She found it hard to get up early in winter.
她感到在冬天要早起很困難。

make sure 確定

例 Make sure you rest well during the holidays.
假期中你可一定要好好休息。

concentrate on 專注於

（例）Please concentrate on one thing at a time.
請一次專心做一件事。

put away 收拾

（例）After the event, nobody stayed behind to put away the trash.
活動結束後沒有人留下來收拾垃圾。

emphasize on/upon 強調

（例）The test emphasizes on/upon reading skills.
這個測驗強調閱讀技巧。

---

b. 三字片語動詞

---

come up with 提出

（例）He came up with a good idea of persuading his father.
他提出了一個説服他父親的好點子。

look up to 尊敬

（例）My mother is much looked up to by many people in our community.
我母親收到我們社區很多人的敬重。

take pride in 引以為榮

⑲ Dennis always takes pride in his work.
丹尼斯總是以他的工作為榮。

be ashamed of 感到恥辱

⑲ Eason is ashamed of his little brother because of his bad
manners.
易森因為他弟弟的無禮感到恥辱。

come across as 顯得

⑲ Nobody would like to come across as rude in a social
occasion.
沒有人會想要於社交場合中顯得無禮。
或：

⑲ Nobody would like to come across as a rude person in
a social occasion.
沒有人會想要於社交場合中顯得像個無禮的人。

4. 與反身代名詞一起用的動詞

behave 舉止, commit 致力, devote 獻出, dedicate 奉獻
……

例如：

behave 舉止端正

例 Behave yourself or you will have to leave the classroom.
守規矩點，不然你得要離開教室。

commit 致力

例 Many international business owners have committed
themselves to environmental issues.
很多國際企業家致力於環境議題。

devote 獻出

例 She has devoted herself to English teaching for decades.
她奉獻於英語教學已有數十年。

dedicate 奉獻

例 He has dedicated himself to the protection of wild dogs.
他獻身於保護野狗。

5. 相互動詞

與 each other 或 one another 連用的動詞稱為相互動詞。
help each other/one another 互相幫助

例 All students should learn to help each other.
所有的學生都應學習互相幫助。

例 No one is an island. We all should help one another.
沒有任何人是一孤島，我們都應互相幫助。
agree with each other/one another 彼此同意

例 The two agreed with each other not to fight again.
他們倆同意不再爭吵。

例 They agreed with one another to do their best to keep peace.
他們同意盡最大力量來保持和平。
fight against each other/one another 與彼此爭吵

例 They do not fight against each other any more. They developed many channels of communication.
他們不再與彼此爭吵，反而發展出很多溝通管道。

6. 使役動詞

使役動詞 (causative verbs) 指的是驅使他人做某事的動詞，主要為：make, have, let...
其結構是：
使役動詞 ＋ 主事者 ＋ 原形動詞

 例句：

例 Our English teacher makes us memorize 10 English words a day.
我們的英語老師要我們一天貝十個單字。

例 The school principle made the bully apologize to the victim.
我們校長要霸凌者向受害者道歉。

比較：

使役動詞 ＋ 受事者 ＋ V-en (過去分詞)

例句：I had my hair cut yesterday.

7. 感官動詞

感官動詞指表示感覺知能的動詞，主要為：
see 看見，watch 注視，hear 聽，feel 感覺，notice 注意，observe 觀察⋯⋯

其結構是：

感官動詞 ＋ 主事者 ＋ 動詞原形或現在分詞

例句：

例 Did you happen to see anyone steal (stealing) in the shop?
你是否碰巧看見有誰在（正在）店裡偷東西呢？

例 At midnight, we heard a baby cry (crying) next door.
凌晨時我們聽見隔壁有嬰兒在（正在）哭。

使用現在分詞較動詞原形更強調此動作現在正在進行

比較：
感官動詞 + 受事者 + V-en (過去分詞)
例句：I saw him hit by a car.

8. 詞彙動詞（主動詞）vs. 助動詞

請見Chapter 18

Exercises 練習題

一、請於空格內填入所提供的動詞加上 oneself, 需要做適當變化。

1. They _____ to bridging the gender pay gap for decades. (commit)

2. She will _____ to girl education. (dedicate)

3. I'll _____ to the environmental protection of my birthplace in the future. (devote)

4. Children should learn to _____ in the public place. (behave)

5. What do you think you should _____ to? (commit)

二、請將下列句中兩個受詞的位置做變化來表達同一句意。

1. He gave me a nice present.

2. She showed me the way to the park.

3. Jason brought me a bottle of wine.

4. Do not tell your teacher lies.

5. I wish all of you great health and a prosperous future.

P a r t 5

三、 請填入適當動詞形式來完成下列句子。

1. Mr. Huang saw his son _____ a bicycle across the street when that accident happened. (ride)

2. Our teacher make us _____ two idioms a day. (memorize)

3. It is very kind of her to let me _____ in her room. (study)

4. His teacher made him _____ English every day. (speak)

5. The boss had all his employees _____ overtime. (work)

6. Nobody likes to be made _____ guilty. (feel)

Key to Exercises 解答

一、

1. have committed themselves

2. dedicate herself

3. devote myself

4. behave themselves

5. commit yourself

二、

1. He gave a nice present to me.

2. She showed the way to the park to me.

3. Jason brought a bottle of wine for me.

4. Do not tell lies to your teacher.

5. I wish great health and a prosperous future for all of you.

三、

1. riding   2. memorize   3. study

4. speak   5. work   6. to feel

TOEIC Exercises 多益題演練

1. By the end of this year, Ms. Han _____ for 2 years with us here.

   (A) works

   (B) will be worked

   (C) will have been working

   (D) is working

2. Ted _____ everything he needed before his mother asked him to do so.

   (A) had packed

   (B) has been packed

   (C) has packed

   (D) had been packed

3. Our boss demanded the project _____ by the end of this week.

   (A) will finish

   (B) was finished

   (C) be finished

   (D) is finished

Questions 4 - 6 refer to the following e-mail.

To: All Customers and Partners

From: David Huang

Subject: Office will be closed

Date: Jan 19, 2019 9:12

Dear Customers and Partners,

　　This is a notice to inform you that the three branch offices in Taiwan will be closed during the Lunar New Year from Feb. 4 to Feb. 10, 2019. It is essential that all urgent business contacts _____ before this period of time.

4. (A) be made

　　(B) is made

　　(C) are making

　　(D) will be made

During the festive time of the year, all employees will not be _____ any e-mails or phone

P
a
r
t
5

5. (A) answer

   (B) answering

   (C) can answer

   (D) are answering

calls. Should you have any questions during this time, please contact Ms. Vicky Dai at vickydai@artworks.com. We look forward to _____ from you in the coming Chinese New Year.

6. (A) hearing

   (B) hear

   (C) can hear

   (D) heard

David Huang

General Manager, Sunrise Apps Store

E-mail: davidhuang@sunrise.com

Address: No. 132, Section 4, Nanjing E Rd, Taipei, Taiwan 104

Key to TOEIC Exercises
多益題解答

1. C

2. A

3. C

4. A

5. B

6. A

看完本章關於各類動詞的解釋，是否感到要掌握英文動詞並不簡單呢？基本的各種時態變化不說，還有種種的分類，除了及物、不及物動詞之外，還有使役動詞、感官動詞等等，種種專有名詞聽起來高深莫測，但是，只要多讀例句就能明白，這些動詞的結構都不難學會，但是如果要能融會貫通並巧妙變化，就只能靠自己多揣摩練習了。

P
a
r
t

5

6

形容詞（Adjectives）

Unit 1

形容詞的定義

修飾名詞的詞稱為形容詞。

1. 形容詞的位置

(1) 前位修飾：形容詞位於所修飾的名詞片語之前，例如：a clever boy（一個聰明的男孩）；後位修飾：形容詞位於所修飾的名詞片語之後，通常用於修飾語較長，大於一個單詞時，例如：a boy clever as you（一個像你這樣聰明的男孩）。

(2) 有些複合詞固定要用後位修飾，特別是法律相關名詞，例如：

- the authorities concerned　　有關當局
- the president-elect　　總統當選人
- the secretary general　　秘書長
- a professor emeritus　　榮譽退休教授

Part 6

(3) 修飾複合不定代名詞時，要用後位修飾，例如：

- anybody interesting　　　　　任何有意思的人
- anything new　　　　　　　　任何新的事
- everybody present　　　　　　在場的所有人
- everything related to Japan　　所有與日本相關的事
- someone special　　　　　　　某個特別的人
- something boring　　　　　　　某件無聊的事
- nothing meaningful　　　　　　沒有任何有意義的事

Unit 2

形容詞的特別用法

1. the ＋ 形容詞 = 具有此形容詞特質的一群人（通常為複數）。

- the rich　　　　　　　　有錢人
- the poor　　　　　　　　貧窮的人
- the weak　　　　　　　　弱者
- the unemployed　　　　　失業的人

比較：

the ＋ 某抽象觀念的形容詞（通常為單數）

例如：

the true 真，the good 善，the beautiful 美

2. 分詞形容詞

(1) 現在分詞：V-ing，意思為主動，未完成，例如：
interesting project 有意思的企劃案，smoking house
冒煙的房子。

(2) 過去分詞：V-ed，意思為被動，已完成，例如：feel
interested 感到有興趣，smoked sausage 煙燻的香腸。

Unit
3

形容詞的種類

形容詞的種類主要分為：

1. 性質形容詞　2. 顏色形容詞　3. 類別形容詞
（依其排列順序）

1. 性質形容詞，例如：big 大的，small 小的，tall 高
的，happy 高興的，positive 正面思考的⋯⋯

2. 顏色形容詞，例如：red 紅的，yellow 黃的，green 綠的……

3. 類別形容詞，例如：golden 黃金的，wooden 木製的，artificial 人工的，medicinal 藥用的……

★ 類別形容詞原則上沒有比較級、最高級。

例如：

- a special green medicinal plant　　一種特殊綠色可作藥用的植物
- a beautiful red artificial flower　　一種美麗的紅色人造花
- the big yellow wooden doll　　一個大型的黃色木製人偶

構造上還有複合形容詞：cold-blooded 冷血的，single-handed 單手的，well-prepared 準備充分的……

Unit
4

形容詞的比較級和最高級

1. 形容詞的等級(degree)可以用比較級和最高級來表示：

原級：形容詞的原來形式。

比較級：兩個人或物當中做比較時，要用形容詞的比較級形式。

最高級：三個或三個以上的人或物當中做比較時，要用形容詞的最高級形式。

2. 形容詞比較級和最高級的形成

(1) 單音節的形容詞，加上 er，形成比較級，加上 est，形成最高級。

(2) 三個或三個以上音節的形容詞，前面加上 more，形成比較級，前面加上 most，形成最高級。

(3) 字尾是 e 時，加上 r 時形成比較級，加上 st，形成最

P
a
r
t

6

高級。

(4) 字尾為子音字母加 y 者，先去掉 y，再加上 ier，形成比較級，加上 iest，形成最高級。

(5) 字尾為母音字母加 y 者，加上 er，形成比較級，加上 est，形成最高級。

(6) 字尾為 ed, en, ing, ly 者，前面加上 more，形成比較級，前面加上 most，形成最高級。

(7) 有些形容詞沒有比較級與最高級，因為為絕對的概念，例如：correct 正確的， horizontal 水平的，parallel 平行的，perfect 完美的，right 正確的，round 圓的 straight 直的，vertical 垂直的，wrong 錯誤的……

(8) 前面加上 more，形成正向比較級，前面加上 most，形成正向最高級；相對而言，前面加上 less，形成負向比較級，前面加上 least，形成負向最高級。

(9) 不規則形容詞的變化

- bad/ill -- worse -- worst　　　　　壞的--更壞--最壞的
- good/well -- better -- best　　　　好的--更好--最好的
- little -- less -- least　　　　　　少--更少--最少
- many/much -- more -- most　　　　多--更多--最多

常見不規則形容詞的變化表

原級	字意	比較級	最高級
good well	好的 健康的，很好地	better	best
bad ill	壞的 有病的	worse	worst
many much	許多	more	most
little	少許的	less	least
old	老的、舊的	older	elder
oldest eldest	遲的 後者的	later latter	latest last
far	遠的 遠的、更多，更進一步	farther further	farthest furthest

3. 表示比較的常用語

原級

★ **as** 原級 **as** 與……一樣……

 例句：

例 Mary did as well as Jenny in school.
瑪莉於學校的表現跟珍妮一樣好。

例 This suitcase is as expensive as that one over there.
這個行李箱跟那邊的那個一樣貴。

例 I hope I can speak English as fluently as you some day.
我希望我的英語有一天能跟你的一樣流利。

★ not as (so) 原級 as 不像……一樣……

例 Her health is not so good as before.
她的健康不若從前那麼好。

例 His memory is not so sound as mine.
他的記憶力不像我的那麼好。

例 The living costs of this city is not so high as that of Tokyo.
這個城市的生活開銷費用不像東京的那麼高。

★ more/less 原級 than 比……更……

例 Rita is more capable in handling suppliers than her colleagues.
麗塔比她同事更擅長於跟供應商打交道。

例 In the meeting I was less talkative than Jennifer.
開會時我説的話比珍妮佛少。

例 Luckily now I was less heavy than I used to be 6 months ago.
幸運的是我的體重比六個月前輕得多。

★ 程度副詞（**far too...** 太……）＋原級

例 He was far too unreasonable.
他太不可理喻。

例 His wife is quite dominant and controlling.
他的太太相當強勢且控制欲很強。

例 Their children are a bit lazy.
他們的小孩有點懶惰。

比較級

★ 比較級＋**than** 比……還……

例 Tiffany is more determined than her to win the position.
蒂芙尼比她還有決心要贏得這職位。

例 Ralf is more suitable than him to receive the scholarship.
羅夫比他還適合得到這份獎學金。

例 Alice is more reliable and trustworthy than any other employees in the office.
愛麗絲比辦公室裡的其他員工都還要可靠，值得信賴。

P
a
r
t

6

> ★ 比較級 + and + 比較級 (more and more 三音節和以上的形容詞原級) 越來越……

（例）This medicine has become darker and darker.
這藥越變越暗。

（例）If you do not learn English grammar step by step, it can get more and more difficult.
如果你不按步就班學習英文文法，就會越來越難學會。

（例）A time goes by, the gap between the diligent students and the less hardworking students would become wider and wider.
隨著時間過去，用功的學生與較不認真的學生之間的差距會越來越大。

> ★ the 比較級…… + the 比較級……　越……就越……

（例）The more I know him, the better I like him.
我越認識他就越喜歡他。

（例）The more I learn English, the easier it becomes.
我越學英語，英語就變得越簡單。

（例）The more I practice playing the guitar, the more fun I get from it.
我越練習，彈吉他就越來越有意思。

★ **no sooner... than** 一‥‥‥就馬上‥‥‥

例 No sooner had I arrived at the bus stop than the bus came.
我一到了公車站牌，公車就來了。

例 No sooner did he heard his mother coming back than he turned off the television.
他一聽見他媽媽回來了就馬上將電視關了。

例 No sooner did she saw the title of the book than she decided to buy it.
她一看見這本書的書名就決定要買了。

★ 程度副詞，如 **a bit** 一點，**a lot** 很多，**any** 任何，**even** 甚至，**far** 更，**much** 很多，**still** 更多‥‥‥＋比較級

例 Mr. Wang visited us yesterday, and still better, he brought gifts for us.
王先生昨天來我們家拜訪，更好的是他為我們帶來了禮物。

例 Taking the lost item on the ground is not a bit better than stealing.
拿取地上的失物比起偷竊沒有好到哪裡去。

例 What you did for us is far more generous and touching than I could imagine.
您為我們所做的事比我能想像的還要慷慨感人。

★ all the 比較級 更加......

(例) Welcome to bring friends with you to the dinner. The more people are all the better.
歡迎帶朋友來參加晚宴，越多人越好。

(例) The English grammar has become all the more difficult since this semester.
英文文法從這學期以來就變得越來越難。

★ no 比較級 (than) 不會更......

(例) His position is no better than a secretary.
他在公司裡的職位與秘書差不多。

(例) Her supervisor treats her no better than an intern.
她的主管對她就像是對實習生一樣多。

★ what is 比較級 更......的是

(例) What is better, you won a free return ticket to Seoul.
更好的是，你贏得了首爾免費來回機票。

(例) What is worse, he often acts as if he were the boss.
更糟的是，他經常表現得像個老闆似的。

(例) What is worse, her father has to undergo a major operation.
更慘的是，她的父親必須接受一個重大手術。

★ 後接介系詞 **to** 的比較級

inferior to 不如的，下級的

例 She has self-confidence and never feels inferior to anybody.
她自信心很充足，從來不覺得比不上任何人。

例 You should never have the feeling that you are inferior to somebody.
你千萬不該有一種不如他人的感覺。

junior to 年輕的，資位較低的

例 Kelly might be junior to you in age, but please treat her like any other new employees in the company.
雖然凱莉可能年紀上比你們小，但是請將她視為跟公司其他新進人員一樣。

senior to 年長的，資位較高的

例 Although he is senior to all of us, he is always very humble and helpful.
雖然他的資位比我們的都高，但是他總是非常謙虛且樂於助人。

最高級

★ 最高級……＋介系詞片語

例 He is the most responsible employee in the company.
他是公司裡最負責任的員工。

例 This is the toughest sport in the Olympics.
這是奧運中最難的運動。

Part 6

例 This is perhaps the hardest problem I have ever encountered in my work.
這或許是我工作遇過最難的問題。

★ **one of the ＋最高級　當中最……**

例 One of the most challenging task is to work in a team made of people from various cultural backgrounds.
當中最有挑戰性的是，在一個由不同文化背景組成的團隊裡工作。

例 One of the best rewards is the students who win in the competition can get the internship in this famous interior design company.
當中最佳獎品是，在這個競賽裡的得獎學生可以於這間出名的室內設計公司裡實習。

例 One of the hardest things is to have to deal with people you have hurt before.
最難的是必須要跟你曾經傷害過的人相處。

★ **almost 幾乎，by far 遠超過於，nearly 幾乎，second 第二個（序數），very 非常……＋最高級**

例 Some say that only the very best and worst people in a country choose to live abroad.
有人說一個國家裡只有最佳和最差的人選擇出國生活。

(例) James' design of architecture is by far the most creative among all the contestants.
詹姆斯的建築設計是所有參賽者當中最有創意的。

★ at (the) + 最高級

at last 最後，at (the) least 至少，at (the) best 最好，......

(例) She was not willing to gave up, and at last she finished the marathon.
她不願放棄，最後跑完了馬拉松。

(例) At least we should send them an e-mail to thank them.
至少我們應該寫封電子郵件來表示對他們的謝意。

(例) At best his left hand can get recovered with lots of Exercises of physiotherapy.
在最好的狀況下，他的左手於非常多的物理治療練習後可以得到復原。

相同屬性的才能比較

相同屬性的形容詞或副詞才能比較

正確

The buildings in Taipei are older than those in Tokyo.

常見錯誤

The buildings in Taipei are older than Tokyo.

Exercises 練習題

一、請用括號內的動詞加上 -ing 或 -ed，填入下列句子的空格。

1. We find that the food in this restaurant is surprisingly good. (amaze···)

1.1 The food in this restaurant is _____ to us.

1.2 We are _____ at the food in this restaurant.

2. I don't like job-hunting. It is very hard to find a suitable job right now. (tire···)

2.1 I am _____ of looking for a new job.

2.2 Currently it is _____ to find a suitable job.

3. Claire has never seen to Europe. It is going to be a new travel experience for her. (excite···)

3.1 The trip to Europe is _____ to her.

3.2 Claire is very _____ about going to Europe.

4. The show last night really made all of us laugh. (amuse···)

4.1 All of us were _____ by the show last night.

4.2 The show last night was really _____ to all of us.

5. This task is a great challenge to us. (challenge···)

5.1 This is a _____ task to us.

5.2 We are _____ by the task.

二、請用比較級的形式來完成下列句子。

1. Joe and I went for a 100-meter run. Joe ran about 14 seconds, and I ran about 13 seconds.

2. The work took them about three hours. We did it in an hour.

3. David and I both did very well in the test. David got A+ while I got A.

4. We expected to finish this work by April 30. In reality we finished the work on May 15.

5. They planned to build this building in 18 months, but in 13 months, they finished building.

6. Usually it is not that hot in summer here. Most people complain about the heat we have in this season.

7. The due date for the baby was on Sep. 7th, but she gave birth to the baby on August 15th.

三、請將下列句子用不同的比較級來表達。

1. Wendy is not as old as she looks.

2. It took you 3 hours to do the homework, but it took me only 1 hour.

3. We used to go to concerts quite often but now not often at all.

4. Unlike your story, my story is quite short.

5. Winnie often does voluntary work, but I seldom do.

四、請用比較級或最高級填入以下句子的空格。

1. The air in a country is usually _____ than that in a big city. (clean)

2. My place is not quiet at night. Do you know any _____ area? (quiet)

3. What is _____ way to get to the main train station? I am in a hurry to catch my train. (fast)

4. You can paint really well. In fact, I think you paint ___ _____ than your teacher. (good)

5. Jenny does not think her job is challenging enough. She now looks for a _____ job. (challenging)

6. She can prepare a nice meal in less than 30 minutes. She is probably _____ cook I've ever known. (fast)

7. Who is _____ singer in your country? (popular)

8. When I travel, I prefer to go the country where _____ tourists do not go to. (many)

9. Her journey to India was exciting, but I think mine was even _____. (exciting)

10. This is probably _____ traveler story I've ever heard. (exaggerating)

Key to Exercises 解答

1.1 amazing　　1.2 amazed　　2.1 tired

2.2 tiring　　3.1 exciting　　3.2 excited

4.1 amused　　4.2 amusing　　5.1 challenging

5.2 challenged

1. I ran 100-meter faster than Joe.

2. We did the work much faster than them.

3. David did better in the test than I did.

4. We finished the work later than we expected.

5. They finished building the building earlier than they planned.

6. This summer is much hotter than usual.

7. She gave birth to the baby earlier than she expected.

三、

1. Wendy is younger than she looks.

2. It took me much less time to do the homework.

3. We do not go to concerts as often as we used to.

4. My story is not as long as yours.

5. I do not do voluntary work as often as Winnie.

四、

1. cleaner   2. quieter   3. the fastest

4. better   5. more challenging

6. the fastest   7. the most popular

8. most   9. more exciting

10. the most exaggerating

TOEIC Exercises
多益題演練

1. A defendant is innocent until proven _____.

    (A) guilty

    (B) guiltily

    (C) guilt

    (D) guiltless

2. Our boss asked us to remain _____ when approached by journalists.

    (A) quietness

    (B) quietude

    (C) quietly

    (D) quiet

3. His recent works of painting are getting much _____ than previous ones.

    (A) good

    (B) better

    (C) well

    (D) nice

Questions 4 - 6 refer to the following e-mail.

To: All Employees

From: Austin Anderson

Subject: Change of Office Notice

Date: April 10, 2019 14:11

Dear Employees,

From April 20, 2019 on, our office will be relocated to a new address in below:

10 F - 5, Dunhua North Rd. Sec 1 Taipei

Our telephone and fax numbers remain _____ so that

4. (A) unchanged

   (B) unchanging

   (C) changing

   (D) changeable

all our customers and partners can reach us without any problems. We apologize if this change of office address would cause any inconvenience to you. We understand this move is _____

5. (A) expecting

(B) unexpected

(C) experienced

(D) inexperienced

and ask for your cooperation.

If you have any _____ questions or concerns regarding the

6. (A) easy

(B) interesting

(C) late

(D) urgent

move, please contact Ms. Wang at the extension number of 10.

Austin Anderson

Manager

Green Home

Key to TOEIC Exercises
多益題解答

1. A

2. D

3. B

4. A

5. B

6. D

結論

形容詞的重點在於其位置有前位與後位修飾之別，如果同時有多個形容詞還需要正確排序，以及形容詞的比較級與最高級，特別是其相關常用片語的用法，都是要花點心思來學習的。能駕馭英文形容詞的結構，遇到要修飾名詞時，就能駕輕就熟，而形容詞的基礎打好了之後，學習起副詞就更能得心應手，這一點容下一章再論。

Part **6**

副詞（Adverbs）

Unit 1

副詞的定義

副詞是用來修飾動詞、形容詞、其它副詞，或是整句的詞類。

Unit 2

副詞的構成

大部分副詞為形容詞字尾加上 ly 而形成，例如：efficient（有效率的）字尾加上 ly 變成 efficiently（有效率地）。

Unit 3

副詞的種類

(1) 時間副詞

tomorrow 明天，yesterday 昨天，then 那時候，
before 之前，after 之後，soon 很快地，later 後來，
at first 起先……

例句：

例 Yesterday Jack got back from his trip to Canada.
昨天傑克從加拿大旅遊回來。

例 At first he was not very interested in English, but soon
he found the language quite fascinating.
起初他對英語不是很感興趣，但是很快地他發覺這個語
言很有意思。

例 Maybe you should work first and take a break later.
或許你該先工作後休息。

例 They never thought they would see each other again.
他們不曾想過會再見面。

例 After sunset, they felt hungry and started to look for a
restaurant.
太陽西下後他們感到餓了，便開始尋找餐廳。

(2) 頻率副詞

always 總是，often 經常地，frequently 經常地，
seldom 很少地，rarely 幾乎不，never 不曾……

 例句：

例 Kelly always has a yearly health check-up in the beginning of a year.
凱莉總是在年初做年度健康檢查。

例 Johnathan usually tries to solve his problems by himself.
強納森通常獨自解決問題。

★ 如果句子是以否定的副詞開始，則需要倒裝，請見以下的例句：

例 Never would I think of hurting others or stealing things.
我從來不曾想過要傷害他人或偷東西。

例 Rarely does the accountant make any mistake.
這個會計幾乎不會犯錯。

例 Seldom did Frank take sick leave in school.
法蘭克幾乎不曾請病假。

(3) 地點副詞

here 這裡，there 那裡，down 下面，up 上面，
near 靠近，out 外面……

 例句：

例 If you haven't climbed the mountain, you can't say you have been here.
如果你還沒有爬過那座山，就不能說你到過這裡。

例 There came one tourist asking for directions.
那邊有個觀光客走來問路。

例 Please don't get too close to that red car.
請不要太接近那輛紅色的車。

例 The black cat appeared out of no where.
那隻黑貓不知從哪裡出現了。

例 Last Christmas they met each other in the flea market.
他們是去年聖誕節在一個跳蚤市場上認識的。

(4) 方式副詞

hard 努力地，well 好地，fast 快速地，quickly 很快地，
gently 溫柔地，rudely 粗魯地，briefly 簡短地，roughly
大略地……

 例句：

例 We all know that Marian studies very hard.
我們都知道瑪麗安讀書很認真。

例 When he gets excited, he often talks so fast that few can
understand him.
他感到興奮時經常說話快到很少人能理解。

例 Could you please go through the rundown roughly?
請你大略講一下行程好嗎？

例 Let me briefly explain the schedule for you.
讓我為你簡短地解釋一下時間表。

例 The doctor listens to his patients carefully.
這位醫師很仔細地聆聽病人。

⑤ 程度副詞

very 很，so 如此，much 非常，enough 夠，little 有點，really 真地，absolutely 絕對地，exactly 正是，entirely 全然地，completely 完全地……

 例句：

例 After the earthquake, this place was completely damaged.
地震後這個地方全毀了。

例 Don't believe what he said to you entirely.
不要完全相信他所說的話。

例 It's a bit hard for me to get up early to exercise every morning.
要我每天早起運動有點困難。

例 Judging from your experiences, you are the exactly the best person we are looking for.
從你的經驗看來，你正是我們所尋找的最佳人選。

例 To them, we are old enough to be considered senior citizens.
對他們來說我們可以算是銀髮族了。

⑥ 否定副詞

no 沒有，not 沒有的，never 不曾，seldom 很少地，
hardly 幾乎沒有地，rarely 非常少地……

 例句：

⑳ There has seldom been such talented musician in our community.
在我們社區很少有這樣有天賦的音樂家。

⑳ This restaurant was so noisy that we could hardly hear each other.
這家餐廳是如此吵雜，以至於我們幾乎聽不見對方的聲音。

★ 如果句子是以否定的副詞開始，則需要倒裝。

 例句：

⑳ Not many landladies would give sweets to their tenants.
沒有很多房東太太會給房客甜點。

⑳ Never have I been late with my homework.
我從來不曾遲交過作業。

⑳ Rarely does she travel overseas.
她很少出國旅遊。

⑦ 不定副詞

somewhere 某地，sometime 某時，somehow 不知怎麼地，
everywhere 到處……

例句：

例 They say he is somewhat eccentric.
他們說他有點神經質。

例 Let's catch up with each other sometime.
我們找個時間來敘舊。

例 When the weather is fine, the place is packed with tourists.
天氣好時這個地方擠滿了遊客。

例 Somehow I have to talk him into giving up smoking.
無論如何我都必須說服他戒菸。

⑧ **全句副詞**

generally 大致來說，fortunately 幸運地，unfortunately 不幸地，apparently 很明顯地，honestly 老實說……

例句：

例 Honestly, this apartment costs far more than we can afford.
老實說這間公寓遠超過我們能負擔的範圍。

例 Mike passed the driving test, and fortunately, his girlfriend passed it, too.
麥克通過了駕照考試，幸運的是，他的女友也通過了。

例 Unfortunately, he passed away this time last year.
不幸地，他在去年的這個時候過世了。

例 Apparently, she is more interested in the house than in the owner.
很明顯地，她對這間房子比對屋主感興趣。

例 Generally, people with fulfilling jobs feel better about themselves than others.
一般來説，擁有充滿意義的工作會讓人比其他人感覺更好。

(9) 連接副詞

therefore 如此一來，nevertheless 然而，furthermore 再者，consequently 因此……

例句：

Most models are skinny; therefore, many young people become obsessive about losing weight.
大部分模特兒都是皮包骨，因此很多年輕人瘋狂減重。

例 Quite a few young people have no knowledge of nutrition; furthermore, they live under huge stress.
很多年輕人沒有營養知識，還有，他們的生活充滿壓力。

例 They should eat properly and slowly; nevertheless, they frequently do quite the opposite.
他們應該均衡飲食並細嚼慢嚥，然而他們經常做恰好相反的事。

例 He lost all his money in gambling; consequently, his wife left him.
他因賭博輸了所有的錢，結果他的太太離開了他。

(10) 焦點副詞

almost 大多，just 剛好，nearly 幾乎，only 唯一……

 例句：

例 In the past almost all graduates from this department wanted to work for the government.
在過去，幾乎所有系上畢業生都想要在公家單位工作。

例 This apartment looks gorgeous and just big enough for both of us.
這間公寓看起來非常好，對我們倆來說剛好夠大。

例 Only narrow-minded people would not want to help new-comers.
只有心胸狹窄的人才不願幫助新來的人。

例 Nearly half of all the marriages end up in divorce.
幾乎所有婚姻有半數會以離婚收場。

例 It will all work out just fine.
一切都會沒問題的。

Unit
4

副詞的位置

副詞通常放於所修飾的動詞、形容詞、副詞附近，修飾整句時通常放於句首。

 例句：

例 He felt terribly sorry for what he said.
他對他說出的話感到非常抱歉。

例 James gets up very early every morning and meditates before he starts the day.
詹姆斯每天早上很早就起床，並且於展開一天活動前冥想。

例 Fortunately, we finished all the tasks before due date, and everyone was pleased.
幸運的是，我們在截止日期前完成了所有任務，大家都很滿意。

例 Generally speaking, most employees here do not work more than two year in this company.
一般說來，這裡大部分員工不會在這家公司待超過兩年。

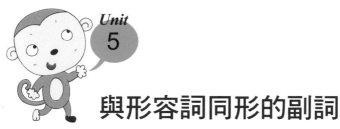

Unit
5

與形容詞同形的副詞

★ **better** 更好

例句：

例 作形容詞：This tea tastes better than that one.
這種茶嚐起來比那種好。

例 作副詞：The assistant works better than the previous one.
這位助理做得比前一位好。

★ **deep** 深

例句：

例 作形容詞：The water of this pond is very deep.
這池塘非常深。

例 作副詞：Don't get deep in the well.
不要到這水井的深處去。

★ extra 多餘

例句：

例 作形容詞：Do you have extra money to lend me?
你有多的錢借我嗎？

例 作副詞：He works extra hard to get a promotion.
他為了獲得升遷而格外努力工作。

★ fast 快

例句：

例 作形容詞：He is a fast eater.
他吃東西吃得很快。

例 作副詞：He walks usually very fast.
他走路通常很快。

★ first 首先

例句：

例 作形容詞：He is the first person to get a raise in this
company.
他是這家公司裡第一個得到升遷的人。

⑩ 作副詞：Finish your meal first before watching TV.
先吃完飯再看電視。

★ high 高

 例句：

⑩ 作形容詞：She got a high score in ice skating.
她在溜冰項目中獲得高分。

⑩ 作副詞：Don't climb so high!　不要爬那麼高。

★ last 最後

 例句：

⑩ 作形容詞：Even on her last day, she still worked very hard.
即使是最後一天，她仍然很努力工作。

⑩ 作副詞：Finish your meal first, and eat the dessert last.
先吃完飯，最後再吃甜點。

★ late 遲

 例句：

⑩ 作形容詞：Do not hand in late assignments.
不要遲交作業。

⑩ 作副詞：This morning he got up very late.
他今早很遲才起床。

★ **next 下個**

 例句：

⑩ 作形容詞：Take the next train.
搭下班火車。

⑩ 作副詞：She first watched the film and read the novel next.
她先看電影然後才看原著小說。

Unit
6

形容詞加上 ly，變成意義不同的副詞

★ **late**

形容詞：遲到的
You are late again.
你又遲到了。

★ lately

副詞：最近

Have you seen him lately?

你最近是否看到過他？

★ hard

hard作形容詞：艱難的

This is a hard task.

這是個艱辛的任務。

hard作副詞：辛苦地

He has worked very hard to get to this position.

他非常努力工作才能得到這個職位。

★ hardly

副詞：幾乎沒有，幾乎不

There was hardly any female medical student at that time.

那個時候幾乎沒有任何女生讀醫學系。

These days there is hardly anyone who does not watch Korean soap opera.

現在幾乎找不到任何沒在看韓劇的人。

特殊

★ pretty

作形容詞：美麗的

She is a pretty girl.

她是個美麗的女孩。

作副詞：非常地

She looks pretty young for her age.

她看起來比實際年紀年輕。

需要注意的副詞片語

(1) not...any longer=no longer 不再

 例句：

(例) He could not put up with it any longer.

= He could no longer put up with it.

他沒辦法再忍受了。

not...anymore=no more 不再

例 He could not work there anymore.
= He could work there no more.
他不再能夠在那裡工作了。

(2) not more than=at most 至多

例 I cannot pay you more than 500 dollars.
= I can pay you 500 dollars at most.
我最多可以付500元給你。

not less than=at least 至少

例 This house would not cost less than 8 million dollars.
= This house would cost at least 8 million dollars.
這間房子至少值八百萬元。

(3) no more than=only 僅僅

例 Right now I have no more than 1500 dollars with me.
= Right now I have only 1500 dollars with me.
現在我身上僅有1500元。

(4) no less than＝as much as 有……那麼多（通常表示多的意思）

例 She has no less than 5,500,000 dollars.

= She has as much as 5,500,000 dollars.

她有550萬元那麼多錢。

••找題目

一、請檢查劃線部分的字是否正確？如果正確請寫 "OK"，如果不正確的話請改正。

1. When I am in the mountain, I walk careful.

2. You look totally different. I can hardly recognize you.

3. Have you run into her late?

4. I work very hardly, like most other employees in this company.

5. Please don't talk so fast. I cannot understand you.

6. Your boyfriend acted very selfish.

7. During the time he worked here, he never arrived lately once.

8. Our new neighbor looks pretty old.

二、請填入括號中正確的字。

1. They work really _____ during the day. (hard / hardly)

2. Jerry behaved very _____ at the party. (childish / childishly)

3. Have you seen him _____? (late / lately)

4. The more you know him, the _____ you will like him. (well / better)

5. Do not climb so ___. (high / highly)

6. I think ___ of this man. (high / highly)

7. We agree that whoever arrives _____ has to pay for the dinner. (late / lately)

8. _____ there have been several cases of campus shooting in the States. (Late / Lately)

Key to Exercises
解答

1. carefully   2. OK   3. lately

4. hard   5. OK   6. selfishly

7. late 8. OK

1. hard   2. childishly 3. lately

4. better   5. high   6. highly

7. late 8. Lately

TOEIC Exercises
多益題演練

1. The debate about _____ modified? food has been ongoing for a long time.

   (A) genetically

   (B) genetical

   (C) gene

   (D) general

2. The boss thinks the employee should put _____ more effort into the project.

   (A) just

   (B) very

   (C) much

   (D) quite

3. All her staff members have _____ been late for work.

   (A) well

   (B) almost

   (C) seldom

   (D) even

Questions 4 - 6 refer to the following e-mail.

To: Head of the DaCheng Hospital

From: Deming Chen

Subject: About the hospital

Date: April 30, 2019

Dear Head of the DaCheng Hospital,

I have been a loyal patient of your hospital for more than ten years. Generally speaking, I am _____ satis.

4. (A) quite

(B) even

(C) nearly

(D) far

fied with the excellent services provided in the hospital. One thing that has been bothering me for a long time is the overcrowded patients. A visit to a doctor there can _____ be accomplished without waiting for

5. (A) hard

(B) hardly

(C) also

(D) later

more than 3 hours. In fact, I have _____ complained

6. (A) never

(B) much

(C) however

(D) already

to my doctor many times, but he told me there was nothing he could do about it.

Deming Chen

A senior citizen

Key to TOEIC Exercises
多益題解答

1. A

2. C

3. C

4. A

5. B

6. D

結論

副詞在句中的位置可以視情況來調整變化，要看副詞是用來修飾動詞，還是形容詞或其它副詞，或是修飾整句。除此之外，副詞也可以像形容詞一樣作比較，有比較級與最高級。有了副詞，句子就得以變得生動活潑起來，有時用對了副詞，對整個句子就達到了畫龍點睛的效果。

8

介系詞（Prepositions）

Unit
1

Part
8

介系詞的作用

置於名詞或代名詞（受格）前面，構成形容詞性介系詞片語修飾名詞，或副詞性介系詞片語修飾動詞、形容詞、副詞。

1. 形容詞性介系詞片語

 例句：

例 The jewelry in the box is gone.
這個盒子裡的珠寶不見了。

2. 副詞性介系詞片語

 例句：

例 He put the money into the red envelop.
他將錢放進紅包袋裡。

Unit **2**

介系詞的種類

1. 表示地點與方向的介系詞

表示在某個地方通常用 "in"；若是地點較小，為某一特定地點則用 "at"；若是在某地點上方則用 "on"。

(1) 在什麼地方的介系詞

| in　在某個較大地點 |

例 As time went by, he felt more and more at home living in a big city.
隨著時間過去，他感到越來越習慣住在大城市。

| at　在某個較小地點 |

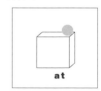

例 We met each other at a language school.
我們是在一間語言學校認識的。

| on　在某地點上方 |

例 Have you been on the top of Taipei 101?
你曾經到過台北101頂端嗎？

(2) 在什麼地方之正上、之正下的介系詞

| over　在什麼地方之正上方 |

例 He planted orange trees all over his farm.
他在農場上種滿了柳丁樹。

under 在什麼地方之正下方

例 They are having a picnic under cherry flowers.
他們在櫻花下野餐。

(3) 在什麼地方上方、下方的介系詞

above 在什麼地方上方

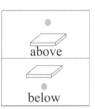

例 Above the mountain, there is a statue.
在山頂上有座雕像。

below 在什麼地方下方

例 Do you like the oil painting below this drawing?
你喜歡這素描下方的油畫嗎？

我們使用over表示在某物正上方，under表示在某物正下方；above表示在某物上方範圍，below表示在某物下方範圍，因此可知用over的情形也可用above來描述，用under的情形也可用below來描述。

(4) 表示地點的介系詞：in front of、behind

in front of 在……之前

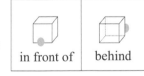

例 In the line there were 13 people standing in front of me.
排隊隊伍中有13個人排在我前面。

behind 在……之後

Do you know the guy sitting behind you?
你認得在坐在你後面的人嗎？

⑤ 表示地點的介系詞：near、against、inside、outside

> near　靠近

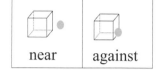

near｜against

例 There are many pine trees near the house.
靠近屋子處種了很多松樹。

> against　靠著

例 Tom leaned against the wall for support.
湯姆靠著牆支撐身體。

> inside　在⋯⋯之內

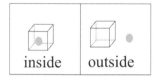

inside｜outside

例 Most people are afraid of going inside the haunted house.
大部分人都不敢進入這間鬼屋。

> outside　在⋯⋯之外

例 Please wait for us outside the gallery.
請在藝廊外面等我們。

⑥ 表示相對位置的介系詞：opposite、between、among

> opposite　在⋯⋯對面

The sales manager sat opposite to me during the meeting.
在⋯⋯之間

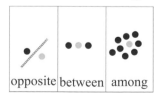

opposite｜between｜among

> between　在⋯⋯之間（兩者之間）

例 There are some low trees between the two houses.
兩個屋子間種了些小樹。

例 The two sisters decided to share the food between themselves.
這兩姊妹決定兩個人來分享食物。

> among 在……之間（三者或三者以上）

例 The teacher always sits among his students in class.
那位老師上課時喜歡和學生坐在一起。

例 Among all students in the class, Amy did best in her research paper.
在班上所有學生當中，艾美的研究報告寫得最好。

(7) 進出什麼地方的介系詞：into、out of

> into 進入

例 We have never walked into the forest.
我們從來沒有進入這座森林過。

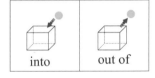

> out of 出來

例 Out of nowhere, a shadow suddenly appeared.
不知從哪裡來的一個陰影突然出現於前。

(8) 表示沿著或穿過的介系詞：along、across、over

> along 沿著

例 We enjoy walking along the river after dinner.
我們喜歡於晚飯後沿著河岸散步。

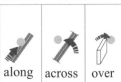

> across　穿過

（例） When walking across street, you should pay attention to the coming cars.
穿越馬路時要注意來車。

> over　過

（例） Go over the bridge and you will see us.
走過橋就可以看見我們。

⑼ 表示向上，向下的介系詞：up、down

> up　向上

（例） He went up to the mountain almost every morning.
幾乎每天早上他都去山上。

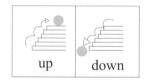

> down　向下

（例） The teacher has never come down from the podium.
那個老師不曾從講台走下來。

⑽ 前往或離開某地點的介系詞：from、to、for

> from　從什麼地方離開

（例） The flight from Tokyo to Taipei was delayed for almost 1 hour.
從東京到台北的班機延誤了將近一小時。

to　前往什麼地方

⑩ He decided to fly to Tokyo to have a meeting with the client in person.
他決定飛往東京去與一位客戶親自會面。

for　前往什麼地方

⑩ He left for Korea for skiing.
他前往韓國滑雪。

2. 表示時間的介系詞

(1) 於什麼時間的介系詞

in

⑩ The lucky winner will be drawn in this week.
幸運得主會於本週抽出。

on

⑩ On Friday, many staff leave early in this company.
星期五很多員工都提早離開公司。

⑩ On New Year's Day, he made up his mind to lose weight.
在新年那一天他下定決心減重。

at

⑩ He always finishes his work at sharp 5 pm.
他總是下午五點準時下班。

(2) 於什麼時間之前或之後的介系詞

before 於什麼時間之前

例 All tasks have to be finished before the deadline.
所有的任務都要在截止期限之前完成。

after 於什麼時間之後

例 No garbage will be collected after 18:00.
18:00後不會收任何垃圾。

(3) 有一段時間的介系詞

for 有一段時間

例 I have known this young salesman for almost 5 years.
我認識這個年輕的業務專員已經有五年之久。

during 在什麼期間

例 During your stay here, you can always stay at our place.
你待在這裡的期間都可以住在我們家。

(4) 直到什麼時間的介系詞

until 直到

例 People often only cherish something until it is lost.
人們通常直到失去才懂得珍惜。

by 最遲什麼時候

例 By this time of next year, I'd like to be able to buy a new house.
到明年的這個時候，我希望能夠買間新房子。

3. 其它介系詞

★ 由什麼製成

be made of 物理變化（本質不變）

例 The desk is made of wood.
這個桌子是木材做的。

be made from 化學變化（本質已變）

例 The wine is made from organic grape.
這個酒是有機葡萄做的。

★ with & without

with 帶有

例 We went home with many sweets.
我們帶了很多甜點回家。

without 沒有

例 Without her help, we could not have finished the project.
如果沒有她的幫忙，我們不可能完成這個企劃案。

4. 與一些形容詞、名詞、動詞搭配的特定介系詞

(1) 與一些形容詞搭配的特定介系詞

about

careless about

happy about

worry about

for

sorry for

at

angry at

with

familiar with

to

married to

similar to

of

afraid of

aware of

capable of

fond of

jealous of

made of

proud of

sure of

tired of

in

interested in

(2) 與一些名詞搭配的特定介系詞

answer to

approval of

awareness of

attitude toward/towards

belief in

cause of

concern for

confusion about

confusion about

decrease in

demand for

desire for

difference between

difficulty in/with

example of

fall in

fondness for

grasp of

hatred of

hope for

increase in

invitation to

interest in

love of

need for

participation in

picture/photograph of

reaction to

reason for

respect for

relationship with/between

reply to

rise in

success in

solution to

understanding of

(3) 與一些動詞搭配的特定介系詞

ask about

ask for

belong to

bring up

care for

find out

give up

grow up

look for

look forward to

look up

make up

pay for

prepare for

study for

talk about

think about

trust in

work for

worry about

動詞後面接受詞，之後再接介系詞

apologize to somebody for something

accuse somebody of something

blame somebody for something

blame something on somebody

borrow something from somebody

complain to somebody about something

congratulate somebody on doing something

explain something to somebody

invite somebody to something

remind somebody about/of something

tell somebody about something

warn somebody about something/somebody

秒懂！
關鍵 英文 Fast! Easy
文法 輕鬆學 English Grammar

Exercises 練習題

一、請於下列句子的空格中填入 at 或 on 或 in。

1. Our flight will be ___ July 29, 2018.

2. The concert tonight starts ___ 7:30 pm.

3. My friends and I usually meet up ___ weekends.

4. Do you like to exercise ___ the early morning?

5. It is not easy to find a job because many graduates are looking for a job ___ the moment.

6. I only have piano lessons ___ Saturdays.

7. David is looking forward ___ his birthday.

8. Where do you see yourself ___ five years?

9. Many people stay up ___ New Year's Eve.

10. Are you going to bring your little sister ___ the party?

二、請於下列句子的空格中填入 for 或 during。

1. I have worked in this company ____ 6 years.

2. Recently I have been so busy that I haven't worked out ____ a week.

3. We seldom have time to go to the movies ____ the week.

4. He will go on a business trip _____ three weeks.

5. _____ the time I was in the temple, I meditated every day.

6. You are welcome to stay with us _____ the time you are in this city.

7 . I have been waiting for the result of my job interview _____ one whole week.

8. You should go into nature _____ your stay in this region.

9. We haven't seen each other _____ nine years.

10. You haven't contacted me at all _____ the time you were in the army.

三、請於下列句子的空格中填入 by 或 until。

1. Jerry will stay with us _____ next Monday.

2. _____ the time you get this postcard, I will be in Boston already.

3. The teacher asked his students to hand in assignments _____ Friday.

4. The library is open only _____ 5 pm on Sundays.

5. The worker is supposed to finish his work _____ the end of this week.

6. _____ the time you finish high school, you can decide if you want to continue studying.

7. Why don 't we wait ＿＿ midnight and see if they are back.

8. You have to pay the bill ＿＿ the end of this month.

9. Don 't rush to make a decision. You can think about it ＿＿ next Friday.

10 The deadline is next Friday. You have to apply ＿＿ then.

四、請於下列句子的空格中填入 at 或 on 或 in。

1. How many people are there ＿＿ the room?

2. I have been waiting ＿＿ the bus stop for twenty minutes and the bus still hasn't come.

3. Please register ＿＿ the reception, and somebody will lead you to your seat immediately.

4. Did you see my keys ＿＿ the table?

5. Most people here learn how to swim ＿＿ a swimming pool.

6. Look up and you will see the stars ＿＿ the sky.

7. Have you noticed her painting ＿＿ the wall?

8. It is usually very crowded ＿＿ this area at this time.

9. Jeremy enjoys living ＿＿ a big city.

10. There seems to be a fly ＿＿ his nose.

五、請於下列句子的空格中填入 from 或 of。

1. This wine is made ＿＿ the local grape.

2. Do you like the table made ＿＿ pine wood.

3. How about putting some cooking rice wine, made ＿＿ the best rice here.

4. This basket is made ＿＿ paper.

5. Do you like this sculpture made ＿＿ brass?

6. This flower arrangement is made ＿＿ roses and daisies.

Key to Exercises 解答

一、

1. on	2. at	3. on
4. in	5. at	6. on
7. to	8. in	9. on
10. to		

二、

1. for	2. for	3. during
4. for	5. During	6. during
7. for	8. during	9. for
10. during		

三、

1. until	2. By	3. by
4. until	5. by	6. By
7. until	8. by	9. until
10. by		

四、

1. in	2. at	3. at
4. on	5. in	6. in
7. on	8. in	9. in
10. on		

五、

1. from	2. of	3. from
4. of	5. of	6. of

TOEIC Exercises
多益題演練

1. Many visitors are afraid of walking _____ the suspension bridge.

    (A) toward

    (B) backward

    (C) across

    (D) of

2. The audience were fascinated _____ the presentation.

    (A) in

    (B) on

    (C) at

    (D) by

3. Do you know the meanings attached _____ the Lunar New Year?

    (A) at

    (B) to

    (C) in

    (D) on

Questions 4 - 6 refer to the following e-mail.

To: Owner of Red Stone Restaurant

From: Debbie Chang

Subject: An Honest Waiter: Jack

Date: April 30, 2019 15:11

Dear Owner of Red Stone Restaurant,

Yesterday I went to your restaurant and unfortunately left behind me an envelope with 100,000 TWD inside. When I went back, _____ my surprise,

4. (A) to

   (B) too

   (C) for

   (D) at

someone told me that a waiter named Jack had picked up the money and gave it to his manager. Jack told the manager he would not want any reward _____ the person who lost the money.

5. (A) for

(B) against

(C) at

(D) from

I hope you can let the other employees know what Jack did and he can be a great example _____ the rest of the company.

6. (A) for

(B) from

(C) at

(D) on

Debbie Chang

A loyal patron of Red Stone Restaurant

Key to TOEIC Exercises
多益題解答

1. C

2. D

3. B

4. A

5. D

6. A

結論

小小的介系詞可以表達出非常不同的意思，用對了介系詞可以為整個句子加分不少，但是如果不小心用錯了介系詞，可能就會讓人誤解了意思。介系詞並不需要死記，因為還是有邏輯可以遵循，如果平常學習介系詞的時候就是有系統地學習，那麼遇到類似的詞句一定就能舉一反三，以此類推。

9

連接詞
（Conjunctions）

Unit 1

連接詞的定義

連接詞 (conjunctions) 是用來連接相同詞類與子句的詞類。

Unit 2

連接詞的分類

1. 對等連接詞：分為單詞對等連接詞 & 片語對等連接詞

單詞對等連接詞：

and 然而，but 但是，or 或，yet 卻，for 因為，so 所以……

(1) and 和，而且

★ 連接對等詞類

例 All staff members, new and old ones, have to submit English proficiency certificates within 2 months.

所有員工，新舊皆然，都要於兩個月內交英語程度檢定
證書。

例 You have to hand in your photos, homework, and term
paper.
你們必須交相片、功課、期末報告。

例 On this market you can find cherries, oranges, and apples
and so on.
在這個市場上你可以找到櫻桃、柳丁、蘋果等等。

★ 連接對等子句

例 Jeremy is always on time, and his assistant is the same.
傑瑞米不曾遲到，他的助理也一樣。

例 The teacher has never lost his temper, and he is gentle
and kind to his students.
這位老師從來不曾發脾氣，而且他對學生溫柔又仁慈。

例 Catherine has never thought about retirement, and neither
does her husband.
凱撒琳從未想過要退休，她的先生也一樣。

(2) but 但是

★ 連接對比詞類

例 My doctor is gentle but firm.
我的醫師溫柔而堅定。

例 Monica is old but fit.
莫妮卡雖然年紀大但很健康。

例 He works hard but not smart.
他雖然工作很努力，但是方法卻不聰明。

★ 連接對比子句

例 They are not rich, but they always share things with others.
他們並不富有，但是總會與別人分享。

例 His first son works very hard, but the second son is quite lazy.
他們的第一個兒子工作非常勤奮，但是第二個兒子很懶惰。

例 This business model sounds promising, but it does not work in this region.
這個企業模式聽起來很有前景，但是在這個地區卻不成功。

(3) or 或

★ 連接可供選擇的名詞

例 The guests can choose chocolate or banana flavor.
客人可以選擇巧克力或香蕉口味。

例 In the end of the semester, students can choose to do a presentation or to write a paper.
在學期結束後，學生可以選擇做簡報或寫一篇論文。

例 In this company, male or female workers have to do the same amount of physical work.
在這家公司無論男性或女性員工都要做同樣份量的勞力工作。

例 For this cooking competition, you can prepare within half an hour a western dish or an Asian one.
在這個烹飪比賽，你在半小時內，可以準備一道西式菜餚或一道亞洲菜。

★ 連接可供選擇的子句

例 Employees can apply for overtime pay, or they can take make-up leave.
員工可以申請加班費或補休。

例 All employees have to learn this software well soon, or they cannot work with their colleagues in other Asian countries.
所有員工都要快點學會這個軟體，不然會無法跟其他亞洲國家的同事一起工作。

例 Sometimes we just have to adapt to the market, or our business will not be viable.
有時候我們就是要順應市場，不然我們的企業會無法繼續運作下去。

④ yet 儘管，然而

★ 連接對比詞類

simple yet effective

簡單但有效的
brief yet impressive
簡短但是令人印象深刻的
knowledgeable yet modest
有智識但謙虛的

★ **連接對比子句**

(例) His wife is always nagging, (and) yet somehow, he does not complain about it.
他太太總愛嘮叨，儘管如此他從未抱怨過。

(例) They haven't met each before, yet they feel like old friends when they just meet up.
他們未曾相識，但是他們一見如故。

(例) This task was a bit too demanding for someone like him, yet he embraced this challenge.
這個任務對像他這樣的人來說有點要求過份，不過他正面迎向這個挑戰。

(5) for 因為，相當於 because, as。

(例) We are all very sad, for our mother passed away.
我們都非常難過，因為我們的母親逝世了。

(例) They had to go back without reaching the top of the mountain, for they had run out of food.
他們必須折返，無法攻頂，因為他們的食糧已經吃完了。

㊀ Andrew always wrote an e-mail to his high school teacher at Christmas, for the teacher helped him out when his family had financial problems.

安德魯總會在聖誕節時寫封電子郵件給他的高中老師，因為這位老師在他家經濟有困難時幫助了他。

⑥ so (that) 所以，因此

㊀ The employee worked very hard, so (that) he could get a raise.

這名員工為了能獲得加薪，非常努力工作。

㊀ Jim studies hard, so (that) he may pass the exams to be a pharmacist.

吉姆為了通過考試成為藥師，非常用功讀書。

㊀ They have saved up for many years, so (that) they can afford this new apartment in this city.

他們為了能在這城市裡買下這間新公寓，存了很多年的錢。

片語對等連接詞：

both... and ... ; not ... but ... ; not only ... but (also) ... ; either ... or ... ; neither ... nor ...

原則：句中的動詞要與最靠近的名詞一致

(1) both... and... 和

例 Both Harry and Sally are single at that time.
哈利和莎莉那時都單身。

例 Adam wants to both study and work at the same time.
亞當想要一邊讀書一邊工作。

例 This chef can both cook authentic Italian cuisine and bake cake and biscuits in Italian style.
這位主廚能夠做正統的義大利料理，也能烘焙義大利風格的蛋糕和餅乾。

(2) not ... but ... 並非……而是……

例 He is not a salesman but an entrepreneur.
與其說他是個業務專員，不如說他是位創業家。

例 Winnie is not an administrator but a coordinator.
與其說維妮是個行政人員，不如說她是協調專員。

例 This is not a cybercafe but a capsule hotel.
與其說這是一間網咖，不如說這是間膠囊旅館。

(3) not only ... but (also) ... 不但……而且……

例 To me, she is not only a good teacher but (also) a nice friend.
對我而言，她不但是良師而且也是益友。

例 Anthony is not only the owner of this bed & breakfast but also the tour guide and the minibus driver.
安東尼不但是這間民宿的主人，同時也是導遊兼迷你小巴駕駛。

(4) either ... or ...　或（二擇一）

例 You can bring either a dish or beverage to the picnic.
你可以帶一道餐點或飲料來野餐。

例 James has either forgotten or chosen to forget that he should bring some wine for the dinner this evening.
詹姆斯可能忘了或是他選擇忘記，今晚要帶紅酒來晚餐。

例 To apply for this master program, the students have to either have done internship for at least 6 months or have won major awards in related fields.
要申請這個碩士學程，學生必須要具有六個月實習經驗，或是於相關領域中得到過大獎。

(5) neither ... nor ...　**既不……也不……**

例 We should neither forget nor repeat this lesson.
我們不能忘記或是重覆這個教訓。

例 Imprisonment can neither rectify the perpetrators nor compensate the victims for their loss.
受監服刑不但無法矯正犯罪者，也不能彌補受害者的損失。

2. 從屬連接詞：從屬連接詞所引導的子句為從屬子句，而無從屬連接詞引導的子句為主要子句，藉此表達出目的或因果的邏輯。

(1) although & though & even though / in spite of & despite
雖然

表示雖然有某種條件存在，但是還是發生了這樣的結果，例如：

(例) Although he had much work to do, he did not complain about it.

(= He had much work to do, but he did not complain about it.)

雖然他有很多的工作要做，但是他沒有抱怨。

（於此中文翻譯當中可見，「雖然」與「但是」經常連在一起用，不過在英文，"although" 與 "but" 不會用於同一個句子，只能擇一來使用。）

上句也可用 "in spite of (despite)" 表達：

(例) In spite of (Despite) much work to do, he did not complain about it.

注意：in spite of 與 despite 後要加名詞（代名詞）或動名詞。

 例如：

例 In spite of the heavy workload, he is very polite to all customers.

例 Despite the heavy workload, he is very polite to all customers.
雖然工作量大，他還是對所有客人很有禮貌。

例 He looks all right in spite of the fact (that) he just lost his job.

例 He looks all right despite the fact (that) he just lost his job.
即使他剛丟了工作，他看起來好好的。

★ 有時會用 **though** 來代替 **although**，在口語中常常放在句末。例如：

例 We could not go to Spain this summer though we had enough money.
雖然我們有足夠的錢，但是今年夏天我們還是不能去西班牙。

上句也可以這樣表達：

例 We could not go to Spain this summer. We had enough money though.

★ **"Even though"** 則比 **"although"** 又更加強語氣。

例 Even though we had saved up for the trip to Spain for a long time, we could not go there at the last minute.
即使我們為了去西班牙存錢存了很久，但是最後一刻我們還是不能成行。

(2) in case
由 in case 所引導的子句表示「以防萬一」，例如：

例 You should take an umbrella in case it rains.
你應該帶把傘以防萬一下雨。
請注意 in case 後面用現在式來代替未來式，it rains，而非 in will rain。
過去的時態也可以使用 in case，例如：

例 Yesterday I got up one hour earlier than usual to get to school in case there was a traffic jam.
昨天我比平常還早起一個小時，以免萬一被困在堵塞的交通中。

(3) unless / as long as / provided & providing

★ **unless** 表示「除非」，例句：

例 You cannot go in the basketball game unless you have a ticket.
= You cannot go in the basketball game except if you have a ticket.
= You cannot go in the basketball game only if you have a ticket.

意思等同於：If you don't have a ticket, you cannot go in the basketball game.

上面的句子意思皆相同：除非你有票，否則不能進入棒球賽場。

★ **as long as & so long as** 與 **provided (that) & providing (that)** 都表示條件，等同於 **"if "** 或 **"on condition that"**。

 例句：

例 You can borrow my book as long as you return it by the end of this month.
要是你在月底會還書才能向我借書。
請注意從屬子句中要用現在式來代替未來式，例如：

例 We will not go to a picnic unless it stops raining tomorrow.
除非雨停了，我們不會去野餐。

例 I can lend money to you as long as you return it tomorrow.
要是你明天還我錢，我就可以借錢給你。

(4) as
當兩件事同時發生，我們可以用 **"as"** 來連接這兩個子句，例句：

例 As she was a student, she always had a part-time job at night.

她在求學時，晚上一直都有兼差。

例 Kevin slipped as he was looking at his smartphone.
凱文在看手機時滑倒了。

例 Just as I went out, it started to rain.
我才剛出門就開始下雨了。

★ **"as"** 作為從屬連接詞還有 **"because"** 與 **"since"** 的意思

例 The host introduced him to me as I had never met him before.
= The host introduced him to me because / since I had never met him before.
因為我不曾見過他，主人介紹他給我認識。

例 We should meet up with each other more often as you just moved here.
= We should meet up with each other more often because / since you just moved here.
既然你剛搬到這裡，我們應該多見面。

例 It took me 5 years to finish my studies as I had to work part time.
= It took me 5 years to finish my studies because / since I had to work part time.
我花了五年完成學業因為我必須半工半讀。

⑨ You should work harder than before as your supervisor is not satisfied with your performance.

= You should work harder than before because / since your supervisor is not satisfied with your performance

你要比從前更努力工作因為你的主管對你的表現不滿意。

⑤ like & as

> ★ **like** 當作介系詞，後面要接名詞（代名詞）或動名詞，意思是「如同、就像」的意思。不可以用 **"as"** 來替代。

例如：

⑨ The place where you live is like an office.
你住的地方像個辦公室。

⑨ I like gentle sport, like swimming.
(= such as)
我喜歡溫和的運動，例如游泳。

> ★ **as** 作為從屬連接詞有「以此方式」的意思。

例如：

⑨ You should tidy up this room as I showed you.
= You should tidy up this room like I showed you.
（口語中可以用like代替as。）
你應該用我示範給你的方式來整理這房間。

★ **as** 作關係代名詞，有「如同」的意思，常見於下面的例子當中：

as you like / as you promise / as you know / as I said / as he thought / as they expected, etc.

例 Make yourself at home. You can do as you like. (= do what you like)
把這裡當成自己的家，做任何你想做的事。

例 As you know, the deadline of this project is coming. (= You know this already)
如同你所知的，這個專案的截止日期快要到了。

例 As we expected, he spent all the money his had. (= We expected this before)
如同我們預料的，他花光了所有的錢。

(6) as if / as though
如果要表示「好似」，則可以用 "as if" 或 "as though"，因為與事實相反，後面要接假設法，例如：

例 He acts as if he knew her. （與現在事實相反）
他表現出他認識她的樣子。

例 He acted as though he had known her. （與過去事實相反）
那時他表現出他認識她的樣子。
與現在事實相反的 "as if"，"as though" 後用 "were" 或 "was" 來代替 be 動詞。

例如：

例 Why do you talk about him as if he were (was) dead?
為什麼你把他當作過世的人來討論呢？

例 Don't act as if you were (was) innocent.
不要裝作你是無辜的。

(7) while

while 是用來連接同時發生的動作，例如：

例 I fell down while I was walking home yesterday.
昨天我在走路回家的路上跌倒了。
While my mother cooked the dinner, I did my homework.
我媽媽在做晚餐時，我在做功課。

例 Louisa baked bread while her son watched television.
露易莎在烤麵包時，她的兒子在看電視。

例 We found many lovely shops while we were taking a walk.
我們在散步時發現了許多家可愛的店家。

例 The students were having a great time while the teachers were busy coordinating the excursion.
學生玩得正開心時，老師們忙著聯絡事情。

例 The band members were playing music while the guests were starting to sing.
樂團演奏音樂時，客人唱起歌來。

★ 如果 **while** 後面接的是未來時態則必須用現在式代替未來式，例如：

（例） What will you do while you take a year off from college studies?
你休學一年要做什麼？

（例） While you stay in the city, Jessica will drop by at your hotel.
你待在這個城市時，潔西卡會順道到妳飯店拜訪妳。

Exercises 練習題

一、請於空格內填入一個適當的對等連接詞。

1. This town is famous not only for the scenery ____ also for its hot spring.

2. Please choose ____ pork or beef for your main dish.

3. He is good at playing not ____ the piano but also the flute.

4. He is very picky with food. ____ continental breakfast nor English breakfast suits him.

5. ____ his parents and his friends will attend his birthday party.

6. Not only his work ____ also his family life was deeply affected by his illness.

7. He has never been to school one day, but he taught himself ____ reading and writing.

8. Either this black tie ____ that red one will do.

9. Hurry up ____ we will miss the bus.

10. He is ____ a writer and a publisher.

二、請用括號內的字將下列兩個句子合併為一句。

1. Einstein was very famous. Einstein was very humble. (although)

2. They do not have much money. They like to share with thers. (in spite of)

3. I am not very well-paid. I like my job very much. (even though)

4. We used to study together. We seldom contact each other now. (despite)

5. We should not look down at others. We know much better than them. (although)

三、請於下列兩項中選擇正確的用法。

1. You should not worry too much unless / as long as you have enough money.

2. You should not cancel the picnic tomorrow afternoon unless / as long as it rains.

3. This shoud not be an issue unless / as long as you are really bothered by it.

4. Unless / As long as you work hard, you will get a raise soon.

5. You cannot rent a car in this company unless / as long as you are over 18 years old and have a valid driving license.

四、請用 "as if" 或 "as though" 將下列兩個句子連接起來。

1. You look pale. You seem to be very sick.

   _____

2. James sounded very cheerful. He seemed to have won lottery.

   _____

3. Jason acts like the smartest person in the world. The teacher says to him:

   _____

4. We were all scared after listening to the ghost story. We felt like we had seen the ghost.

   _____

5. You are totally starving and you feel like you could eat a horse.

   _____

一、

1. but	2. either	3. only
4. Neither	5. Both	6. but
7. both	8. or	9. or
10. both		

二、

1. Although Einstein was very famous, he was very humble.

2. In spite of not having much money, they like to share with others.

3. Even though I am not very well-paid, I like my job very much.

4. Despite that we used to study together, we seldom contact each other now.

5. We should not look down at others, although we know much better than them.

1. as long as   2. unless   3. unless

4. As long as   5. unless

四、

1. You look as if you were very sick.

2. James sounded as though he had won lottery.

3. Stop acting as if you were the smartest person in the world.

4. We felt as though we had seen the ghost in the ghost story.

5. I felt as if I could eat a horse.

TOEIC Exercises
多益題演練

1. In the end of the year, the manager asked the employees to write _____ one's own evaluation of the past year and his or her expectation for the next year.

   (A) neither

   (B) both

   (C) so

   (D) either

2. Visitors to the musuem are told neither to make noises _____ to take photos.

   (A) or
   (B) too
   (C) nor
   (D) also

3. For this project, all employees have not only brainstormed in advance _____ also worked hard as a team.

   (A) and
   (B) but
   (C) too
   (D) therefore

Questions 4 - 6 refer to the following notice.

Sun Food

"Sun Food", a new restaurant of Southeastern Asian cousins is going to open from Feb. 12, 2019 on. The menu features not _____ traditional Asian dishes, like rice

4. (A) also

 (B) only

 (C) and

 (D) well

and noodles, but also western ones, like burgers and pizzas. Customers who dine here during the first week can get _____ a free drink

5. (A) both

 (B) neither

 (C) either

 (D) or

or a complimentary dessert of their choice. In addition ____

6. (A) on
    (B) in
    (C) at
    (D) to

_____ the menu, the chefs can provide dishes at guests' request for special events held in the restaurant if there are more than 10 diners. Why out come and check it out? You will be pleasantly surprised.

Key to TOEIC Exercises
多益題解答

1. B
2. C
3. B
4. B
5. C
6. D

結論

讀完本章後是否會不禁讚嘆連接詞的功用呢？除了單詞的連接詞，還有許多片語，都可以大大增加句子的豐富性，畢竟一整篇都是由單句所構成的英文文章不免顯得太像初學者的作文，也顯得太幼稚，如果適當運用連接詞將句子的前後、因果合併起來，寫出來的文章馬上就會顯得更加流暢，更為生動，讀者的閱讀興致也就更提高了。

10

感歎句
（Exclamations）

Unit 1

感歎句的定義

感歎句是用很短的字或片語加上驚嘆號，以較高的音調來表達特別的情緒，例如驚訝、讚賞、憤怒等等。

Unit 2

常用的感歎詞

感歎詞後面常接驚嘆號，於句中則可以接逗號。
常用的感歎詞如下：

★ **what** 什麼

例 What! You mean you spent all the money on the computer games?
什麼！你是說你把所有的錢花在買電玩了？

★ yuck 噁

> Yuck! Look at what our tenants have done to our apartment!
> 真噁心！你看看我們房客把我們公寓搞成什麼樣子！

★ damn 可惡

> Damn! Our bread was bitten by a rat again.
> 可惡！我們的麵包又被老鼠咬了。

★ aha 啊哈

> Aha, I see you are trying to take advantage of me.
> 啊哈，我看你是要佔我便宜。

★ cool 酷

> Cool, you won the first prize again.
> 酷，你又得到第一名了。

★ ouch 哎呦

> Ouch! My right wrist hurt from too much typing.
> 哎呦！我的右手腕因為打太多字而受傷了。

★ wow 哇

> Wow, your son is studying at the prestigious medical school.
> 哇，你的兒子在著名的醫學院就讀。

★ **bravo** 好棒

Bravo! Your term paper is finally done.
好棒！你的期末報告總算寫完了。

★ **god** 天啊

God, my workload this month is so heavy.
老天，我這個月的工作量是如此大。

★ **gosh** 天哪

Gosh! Have you seen where my smartphone is?
天哪！你是否看到我的智慧型手機？

★ **oh** 喔

Oh! How nice it would be if I could travel around the world!
喔！要是我能環遊世界該有多好！

★ **oops** 糟了

Oops, I forgot today is my girlfriend's birthday.
糟了，我忘了今天是我女朋友的生日。

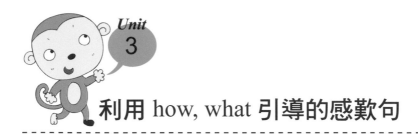

Unit
3

利用 how, what 引導的感歎句

How ＋形容詞／副詞 ＋ 主詞 ＋ 動詞 ＋！

例句：

例 How adorable the girl is!
如此可愛的女孩！

例 How optimistic he is right now!
他現在是如此樂觀！

例 How fast Nick ran!
尼克跑得如此快！

例 How patiently the customer service clerk talks on the phone!
客服專員在電話中講話是如此有耐心！

What ＋形容詞 ＋ 名詞＋ 主詞 ＋ 動詞 ＋！

例句：

例 What an adorable girl she is!
她是如此可愛的女孩！

例 What adorable girls they are!
她們真是可愛的女孩！

Unit 4

其他詞類的感歎句，常接驚嘆號

其他詞類也可當作感歎句，句尾常接驚嘆號。

1. 名詞！

例如：

例 Nonsense! Don't tell me you have a cold again.
胡扯！別說你又感冒了。

例 Rubbish! You are lying to me, aren't you?
廢話！你在跟我說謊，對吧？

例 What a bullshit!
真是胡說八道！

2. 動詞！

例如：

例 Fuck! Our boss gave us so much to do during the holidays.
幹！我們老闆在假期中給我們這麼多工作。

例 Damn! Another typhoon is coming this summer.
可惡！今年夏天第二個颱風將來襲。

例 Go away! We don't want to see your face again.
滾開！我們不想再看到你的臉。

例 Get lost! Never come back again.
滾！不要再回來。

3. 形容詞！

例如：

例 Enough! Stop making fun of your little brother.
好了！不要再嘲笑你弟弟。

例 Fantastic! You made huge progress in English.
太棒了！你的英文進步很多。

例 Awesome! Our team won another gold medal in the winter Olympics.
太好了！我們團隊又得到一面冬奧金牌。

4. 副詞！

例如：

例 Absolutely! We agree with what you said.
完全正確！我們同意你的看法。

例 Totally! Go ahead!
確實如此！就這麼去做吧。

例 Exactly!
確實是這樣！

5. How + 直述句

 例句：

例 How I love writing!
我是如此熱愛寫作！

例 How she enjoys learning English!
她是如此熱愛學英文！

6. so, such, quite

 例句：

例 So good!
真好！

例 Such a good friend!
真是好朋友啊！

例 Quite a friend!
相當好的朋友！

7. 否定疑問句作為感歎句

句尾要用感歎號。

 例句：

例 Isn't it beautiful weather today!
今天天氣真是好啊！

例 Wasn't the old man's life miserable!
這個老人的生活真是悲慘啊！

例 Hasn't it all worked out for you!
你不是一切都沒事了！

Exercises 練習題

一、請於下列句子的空格中填入 How 或 What。

1. _____ a heavy box it is!

2. _____ heavy the box is!

3. _____ a meaningful movie! Don't you want to know who wrote the script?

4. _____ intelligent students they are!

5. _____ intelligent these students are!

6. _____ quickly the IT specialist solved the technical problem!

7. _____ a coincidence! I've never thought of bumping into you here.

8. _____ different we are!

9. Maybe you haven't noticed it. _____ a serious mistake it is!

10. _____ fast she has recovered!

二、請於下列句子的空格中填入 So 或 Such。

1. _____ tasty!

2. _____ a tasty meal!

Part 10

3. _____ a long way to go!

4. _____ far away from here!

5. _____ a rewarding job!

6. _____ easy it is to judge others!

7. _____ tough challenges!

8. _____ nice the weather is!

9. _____ a lovely day!

10. _____ a win-win solution!

Key to Exercises 解答

一、

1. What	2. How	3. What
4. What	5. How	6. How
7. What	8. How	9. What
10. How		

二、

1. So	2. Such	3. Such
4. So	5. Such	6. So
7. Such	8. So	9. Such
10. Such		

TOEIC Exercises
多益題演練

1. Even the most demanding customer praised Darren:
   " _____ a capable salesperson he is! "

   (A) So

   (B) Such

   (C) That

   (D) How

2. _____ a busy day in the office it is today!

   (A) How

   (B) So

   (C) That

   (D) What

3. Our boss gave us _____ a headache!

   (A) such

   (B) so

   (C) that

   (D) this

Questions 4 - 6 refer to the following notice.

Jupiter

To celebrate Valentine's Day, "Jupiter", the most famous online dating agency in this city, will give special offers for those who are seeking true love. Whoever signs up for membership in the month of February will receive free gifts, ranging from free holidays to free airline tickets. Don't miss _____ a great occasion!

4. (A) so

   (B) such

   (C) that

   (D) this

In February, we will also interview several married couples who met each other through our agency, and share their stories online with all members free of charge. _____ a special and rare offer!

5. (A) That

   (B) This

   (C) What

   (D) So

Why don't you give it a try and become a member with us on: http://www.jupiter.com/ . We have dating coaches to provide you with assistance. Soon you will not be complaining: _____

6. (A) Such

(B) That

(C) What

(D) How

hard it is to find a soul mate.

Carol Smith

"Jupiter" Dating Agency

Key to TOEIC Exercises
多益題解答

1. B
2. D
3. A
4. B
5. C
6. D

結論

感歎句特別能夠於英語口語中為情緒表達增添色彩，無論
是喜、怒、哀、樂，或是讚歎、感傷，甚至咒罵，如果能
夠用對感歎詞與感歎句，搭配適當語調，不但可以有利於
與人溝通，更可以顯示出自己的英語非常道地，不信的話
你試試看！

句子的5種型式
（5 structures of sentences）

句子有下列的5種型式：

英語句子主要是由主詞 (subject)、動詞 (verb)、受詞 (object)、主詞補語 (object complement)、受詞補語 (object complement) 等成分構成。

句型一：主詞＋不及物動詞 (＋介系詞片語)

 例句：

例 Susan walks to school every day.
　　蘇珊每天騎腳踏車上學。

例 Every morning Amy swims in the pool.
　　艾美每天早上在泳池游泳。

例 Several years ago, we shopped in the department store.
　　幾年前我們在這家百貨公司購物過。

例 Next year we will move to a bigger house.
　　明年我們會搬到一個比較大的房子。

句型二：主詞＋及物動詞＋受詞 (＋副詞片語)

 例句：

例 Judy bought the house immediately.
　　茱蒂馬上買了這間房子。

例 Bill enjoys learning new skills.
　　比爾喜愛學習新技能。

例 Many medical students did internships in this hospital.
很多醫學系學生在這家醫院當實習生。

例 All work and no play makes Jack a dull boy.
只用功不玩耍，聰明孩子也變傻。

例 His words made his mother very upset.
他說的話使得他母親非常難過。

句型三：主詞 + 連綴動詞 + 主詞補語

這些連綴動詞有：be動詞 (am, is, are)、look 看起來、seem 看來、appear 顯得、sound 聽起來、smell 聞起來、feel 感覺起來、taste 嚐起來、get 變得、grow 變得、turn 變得、become變成、remain 保持、hold 保持、stand 保持、keep 保持、stay 保持。

 例句：

例 The patient looked very tired.
這位病人看起來很累。

例 The woman appeared to be a beggar.
這個女人看似乞丐。

例 Now we are in the museum.
現在我們在博物館內。

例 My homework in the winter vacation is to interview 10 users of this tablet.
我的寒假作業是要訪問十位這種平板的使用者。

句型四：主詞 + 及物動詞 + 雙受詞 (間接受詞和直接受詞)

 例句：

囫 My teacher gave me this English novel.
我的老師給我這本英文小説。

囫 Vicky showed me how to solve this problem.
維琪示範如何解決問題給我看。

囫 Sue reads her daughter a fairy tale every night.
蘇每晚都為她女兒讀一篇童話故事。

囫 Donald made Gloria a necklace.
丹諾德為葛莉亞做了一個項鍊。

囫 Joe convinced himself to stay in this company.
喬伊説服自己待在這家公司。

句型五：主詞 + 及物動詞 + 受詞 + 受詞補語

★ 受詞補語跟在直接受詞後面，修飾直接受詞，受詞補語可以是名詞或形容詞，少數副詞也可作受詞補語。

1. 受詞補語是名詞

 例句：

囫 Many people consider her the best piano player in the world.
很多人認為她是世上最佳鋼琴家。

例 That's what we call meddling in politics of another country.
那正是我們所謂的干涉外國政治。

例 Dave reckons Debby an angel.
戴夫將黛比視作天使。

例 We call our English teacher a walking dictionary.
我們稱我們英語老師活字典。

2. 受詞補語是形容詞。

 例句：

例 Our English teacher often keeps us busy by giving us lots of assignments.
我們英文老師經常給我們很多作業，讓我們很忙碌。

例 His family members thought him dead.
他家人以為他已死了。

例 They consider him incapable of doing the job.
他們認為他沒有做這份工作的能力。

3. 受詞補語是副詞。

 例句：

例 In summer, we always have the air conditioner on.
夏天我們總是開冷氣。

（例） At night Sherry usually keeps a small light on.
晚上雪莉通常開著一盞小燈。

4. 受詞補語為動詞原形或動詞加上 -ing。

a. 感官動詞，受詞補語為動詞原形或動詞加上 -ing。

hear

 例句：

（例） I heard John cry.
我聽見約翰在大喊。

（例） I heard John crying.
我聽見約翰正在大喊。

see

（例） He saw his child fall down.
他看見他的小孩往下掉。

（例） He saw his child falling down.
他看見他的小孩正往下掉。

b. 使役動詞，受詞補語為動詞原形。

 例句：

（例） His mother makes him read newspaper every day.
他的母親要他每天都要看報紙。

（例） Paul made his son save 100 dollars a week.
保羅要他的兒子每星期存一百元。

Exercises 練習題

請於兩個選項當中選出正確的項目。

1. They made the employees _____ (to overwork / over work).

2. My boss seldom asked us _____ (to overwork / over work).

3. Did you see the teacher _____ (coming / to come)?

4. He was seen _____ (to hand in / hand in) his I.D. card.

5. I've never heard him _____ (talk / to talk) like that.

6. Keep _____ (talk / talking). I'm listening.

7. I've never seen him _____ (dress/ dressed) like that.

8. Those who fail in the exams are made _____ (to leave / leave) the room.

9. His mother asked him to have his hair _____ (cut / to cut) short.

10. We've never heard him _____ (singing / sang).

11. You made me totally _____ (confuse / confused).

12. The students were made _____ (to rewrite / rewrite) their composition.

13. If you see someone _____ (approaching/ to approach), call the police.

14. When he returned, he saw his seat _____ (take / taken).

15. Do you hear the birds _____ (sing / to sing) in the morning?

16. Mandy had her little brother _____ (do / to do) house work for her.

17. Why don't you hire an assistant _____ (to do / do) the administrative work for you?

18. Ask your children help _____ (do / doing) housework.

19. Maybe we should have this place (clean / cleaned) up soon.

20. We will try to make your dream _____ (happen / happened).

Key to Exercises 解答

1. overwork	2. to overwork	3. coming
4. to hand in	5. talk	6. talking
7. dressed	8. to leave	9. cut
10. singing	11. confused	12. to rewrite
13. approaching	14. taken	15. sing
16. do	17. to do	18. do
19. cleaned	20. happen	

TOEIC Exercises
多益題演練

1. The manager regard him _____ best customer service clerk in the company.

   (A) a

   (B) the

   (C) that

   (D) what

2. Have you heard him _____ the piano?

   (A) playing

   (B) was playing

   (C) to play

   (D) played

3. The boss taught her _____ to save budget.

   (A) what

   (B) how

   (C) if

   (D) that

Questions 4 - 6 refer to the following e-mail.

To: Debbie Dai

From: Ashley Liu

Subject: Business trip

Date: July 1, 2019 13:19

Dear Ms. Dai,

  I am writing to apply to go on the business trip to trade fair in Texas in October. _____ I am an IT engineer,

 4. (A) That

   (B) Even

   (C) If

   (D) Although

not a salesperson as requested, it is important for all staff members to keep informed with the latest developments of all products in our field. Besides, I can demonstrate _____

5. (A) how

   (B) what

   (C) whether

   (D) that

_____ to use our electronic products extremely well because I am familiar with them better than anyone else. Last year, I was _____ the

 6. (A) award

    (B) awarded

    (C) awarding

    (D) to award

Prize of the Best Designer in our company. Please take a look at the attached application letter and documents.

Ashley Liu

IT engineer
Eagle Electronics Co., Ltd.
E-mail: Ashleyliu@eagle.com.cn
Tel: 0571-88084168
Address: No. 203, Jianghan Rd, Dayun,
Jiashan, Zhejiang 314113 China

Key to TOEIC Exercises
多益題解答

1. B

2. A

3. B

4. D

5. A

6. B

結論

學習句子的基本句型結構有什麼好處呢？最大的好處是在閱讀時有助於解析較為複雜的句構，經過層層拆解後，原先可能難解的句意也就變得清楚明白，因此不要小看本章的內容與例句，這些都像是基本功，也像是在為將來的閱讀與寫作打地基。

12

特殊句型
（special structures of sentences）

特殊句型主要有強調句、倒裝句、省略句。

Unit
1

強調句

★ 強調句中某部分

例一：

例 Early this year I found a good job.
今年初我找到了份好工作。

--> It was early this year that I found a good job
就在今年初，我找到了份好工作。【強調今年初】
--> It was I that found a good job early this year.
我就是那個在今年初找到了份好工作的人。【強調是我】
--> It was a good job that I found early this year.
今年初我找到的是份好工作。【強調是份好工作】

例二：

例 They will go on a school excursion to the museums in Tokyo this summer.
他們今年夏天會去東京博物館做校外教學。

P
a
r
t
12

-->It was a school excursion to the museums in Tokyo that they will to go on this summer.

他們今年夏天去東京博物館要做的是校外教學。【強調校外教學】

-->It was to the museums in Tokyo that they will to go on a school excursion this summer.

東京博物館是他們他們今年夏天的校外教學的目的地。【強調東京博物館】

-->It was this summer that they will go on a school excursion to the museums in Tokyo.

他們去東京博物館做校外教學的時間是今年夏天。【強調今年夏天】

例三：

例 While Justin was in high school, he made up his mind to be a fashion designer in the future.

賈斯汀在高中時下定決心未來要成為服裝設計師。

-->It was Justin who in high school made up his mind to be a fashion designer in the future.

在高中時下定決心未來要成為服裝設計師的是賈斯汀。【強調是賈斯汀】

-->It was while in high school, Justin made up his mind to be a fashion designer in the future.
賈斯汀下定決心未來要成為服裝設計師是在高中時。
【強調是在高中時】

-->It was a fashion designer that Justin in high school made up his mind to be in the future.
賈斯汀在高中時下定決心未來要成為的是服裝設計師。
【強調是服裝設計師】

★ 強調動詞

> do 真的

例 I do love my country.
我真的熱愛我的國家。

例 She does look much like her father.
她真的看起來很像她父親。

例 Jeff did do his homework, but he forgot to bring it.
傑夫真的做了功課，但是他忘了帶來。

例 This school does put so much emphasis on music education.
這所學校的確很強調音樂教育。

例 Their products of this store do look ingenious.
這家商店的產品真的看起來很精巧。

P a r t *12*

★ 強調疑問詞

on earth, in the world 到底

(例) What on earth did you tell her?
你到底告訴了她什麼？

(例) What in the world were you thinking at that time?
你那個時候到底在想什麼？

(例) What in the world made you think your business would work?
究竟是什麼使你覺得你的生意做得起來？

(例) How on earth are you going to pay all the bills?
你究竟要如何付這些帳單？

★ 強調否定

not 後面加上 at all, for (all) the world

(例) He is not trustworthy at all.
他一點也不值得信賴。

(例) I would not move any where for the world.
無論如何我都不會想搬離這裡。

(例) This is not what I mean at all.
這完全不是我的意思。

(例) I would not take part in triathlon for all the world.
我無論如何不會參加鐵人三項。

例 Many teenagers do not listen to their parents at all.
很多十幾歲的青少年根本不聽父母的話。

★ 強調名詞

very

例 This is the very guide book I was looking for.
這正是我在找的導覽書。

例 He is the very person for this position.
他正是符合這職位要求的人。

例 The very venue for the event is your garage.
最適合活動的地點就是你的車庫。

例 This gym is the very place for you to spend the evening after work.
這間健身中心正是你下班後消磨傍晚時光的好地方。

秒懂！
關鍵 **英文**
文法 輕鬆學
Fast! Easy
English Grammar

Unit
2

倒裝句

1. 否定詞倒裝

否定詞 + 動詞 + 受詞

例 Little did I notice the change of his tone of voice.
我沒什麼注意到他語調有變化。

例 Not until we lose our health do we realize its importance.
若非我們失去了健康，就不會明白健康的重要性。

例 Hardly would I say something like that to her.
我幾乎不會對她說這樣的話。

例 Never should you take things which do not belong to you.
不屬於你的東西絕對不要拿。

例 Rarely would she say something bad behind someone's back.
她幾乎不會在別人背後說壞話。

例 Seldom would Peter talk about the financial situations in his family.
彼得非常少會談到他家裡的經濟狀況。

例 Under no circumstances must you leave the office without locking the door.
你絕對不可以沒鎖門就離開辦公室。

2. 受詞倒裝

受詞 ＋ 主詞 ＋ 動詞

受詞置於句首時，通常主詞和動詞不對調，但如果受詞帶有否定詞則必須對調。

例 The dreams we all had when we were young.
我們年輕時都有過的夢想。

例 The house all people would want to purchase.
人們都想要買的房子。

例 Not a single word of apology did Ian say to his wife.
伊安沒有跟他太太說任何一個道歉的字眼。

3. 補語倒裝

補語 ＋ 動詞 ＋ 受詞

補語置於句首時，主詞若為一般名詞，則要使用倒裝法，句型為：補語 ＋ 動詞 ＋ 主詞，主詞若為代名詞時，則不使用倒裝，句型為：補語＋代名詞＋動詞 。

例 Blessed are the people who help others.
幫助別人的人有福報。

P
a
r
t
12

例 Happy are the people who are contented.
知足常樂。

例 Afraid and worried he is feeling right now.
他現在感到害怕又擔心。

4. 副詞倒裝

副詞置於句首時，主詞若為一般名詞，則要使用倒裝法，句型為：副詞 + 動詞 + 主詞，主詞若為代名詞時，則不使用倒裝，句型為：副詞 + 代名詞 + 動詞。

例 Right opposite to his house is an artificial lake.
他房子對面有個人造湖。

例 In front of him is a huge birthday cake.
在他前面有個大型生日蛋糕。

例 Down he jumped into the river.
他就這樣跳下河去。

例 There came the bus.
巴士從那兒來了。

例 There he came.
他從那兒來了。

Unit
3

省略句

★ 從屬子句中省略主詞與 be 動詞

(例) Finish the task by 18:00 Friday if (it is) possible.
盡可能在下午六點前完成這個任務。

(例) Take one sleeping pill if (it is) necessary.
需要的話服用一顆安眠藥。

(例) Please reply the messages on the answering machine if (it is) possible.
請盡可能回覆電話答錄機裡的所有留言。

★ 省略不定詞

(例) I spoke up because nobody wanted to (do it).
因為沒有人願意說，我說了。

(例) Never mind calling back if you don't have time to (call back).
要是你沒有時間回電的話就不用回了。

★ 省略重覆單字

例 He is good at playing the violin, and she (is good at) singing.
他擅長小提琴，她專長於唱歌。

例 Robert loves seafood, and his mother (loves) steak.
羅伯特愛吃海鮮，他母親則喜歡牛排。

例 Jean enjoys reading poems, and Owen (enjoys reading) short fictions.
珍喜歡讀詩，而歐文則喜歡讀短篇小說。

★ 省略比較語句

例 Sally is as diligent as her colleagues (are diligent).
莎莉和她的同事一樣勤奮。

例 His father is not as patient as his mother (is patient).
他父親不像他母親一樣有耐心。

★ 省略其他

感歎句

例 What a wonderful world (it is)!
這個世界真美妙！

例 What an unbelievable football game (it is)!
這場足球賽真令人不可置信！

省略 that

例 It is amazing (that) what a wonderful world it is!
精彩的是這個世界真美妙！

例 Do you recall the story (that) the teacher told us in the beginning?
你還記得老師剛開始時告訴我們的故事嗎？

告示語中的省略

例 No fishing (is allowed).
禁止釣魚。

例 No smoking (is allowed).
禁止吸菸。

Exercises 練習題

一、請將下列句子依照括號內所要強調的部分做改變。

1. Larry wrote a short science fiction when he was in the army.

a. 強調 Larry：_____

_____

b. 強調 a science fiction：_____

c. 強調 in the army：_____

2. I finished my homework yesterday.

強調動詞 finished：_____

3. What were you thinking about when you did that?

強調疑問語氣：_____

4. Kevin did not win the contest, but he did not feel bad.

強調否定：_____

5. This young man is the right person for the position available.

強調 "的確是"：_____

二、請將下列句子依照指示改成倒裝句。

1. Many people do not cherish what they have until they lose it.

   改為：Not until _____

2. He seldom comes to school late.

   改為：Seldom _____

3. There is a river in front of her house.

   改為：In front of her house _____

4. Those with faith are blessed.

   改為：Blessed _____

5. We hardly know this new comer.

   改為：Hardly _____

6. This place has never been so crowded with tourists.

   改為：Never _____

7. Little girls all love to have the Barbie doll.

   改為：The Barbie doll _____

8. You should take things through customs for people you do not know well under no circumstances.

   改為： Under no circumstances _____

9. The bus came from that corner.

   改為：From that corner _____

10. After e-mail was invented, most people nowadays rarely write a letter.

改為：Rarely _____

Key to Exercises
解答

一、

1.

a. It was Larry that wrote a short science fiction when he was in the army.

b. It was a short science fiction that Larry wrote when he was in the army.

c. It was when Larry was in the army that he wrote a short science fiction.

2. I did finish my homework yesterday.

3. What on earth were you thinking about when you did that?

4. Kevin did not win the contest, but he did not feel bad at all.

5. This young man is the very person for the position available.

二、

1. Not until they lose it do many people cherish what they have.

2. Seldom does he come to school late.

3. In front of her house is a river.

4. Blessed are those with faith.

5. Hardly do we know this new comer.

6. Never has this place been so crowded with tourists.

7. The Barbie doll little girls all love to have.

8. Under no circumstances should you take things through customs for people you do not know well.

9. From that corner came the bus.

10. Rarely do most people nowadays write a letter, after e-mail was invented.

TOEIC Exercises
多益題演練

1. It is the latest developments of digital technology _____
_____ make it possible for the government to monitor its citizens.

(A) that

(B) the

(C) so

(D) such

2. Little did Mary _____ that she was going to become the controversial person in the office.

(A) knew

(B) know

(C) to know

(D) had known

3. Finish all the projects before Christmas holidays _____
_____ possible.

(A) that

(B) when

(C) if

(D) so

Questions 4 - 6 refer to the following e-mail.

To: Ted Zheng

From: Gloria Lai

Subject: Yearly Meeting in Taipei

Date: August 15, 2019 13:19

Dear Mr. Zheng,

    As announced by our manager, it is in Taipei _____

4. (A) this

   (B) that

   (C) what

   (D) which

____ this yearly meeting will take place in on August 30, 2019. I am the coordinator who is responsible for taking care of all issues related to the meeting. Hardly _____ I think of

5. (A) could
   (B) might
   (C) would
   (D) should

anything that is not on the Internet these days. Nevertheless, I am glad to help you arrange things such as transportation and accommodation. Please let me know if you will attend the meeting as early _____ you can so that we can order

6. (A) so
   (B) that
   (C) as
   (D) and

the catering for dinner in time.

Gloria Lai
Coordinator

Dolphin Language School
E-Mail: glorialai@dolphinlg.com.tw
http://www.dolphinlg.com.tw
Address: 89 Cueihua Road, Zuoying District, Kaohsiung 81354 Taiwan
Tel: +886 7 586 3300

Key to TOEIC Exercises
多益題解答

1. A

2. B

3. C

4. B

5. A

6. C

結 論

本章所列的特殊句型，無論是強調句、倒裝句、省略句，
其實於日常英文中都非常常見，因此都要好好學習，務必
要能熟悉每種用法，掌握其中的巧妙，這樣表達方式才會
更加豐富，才不會從頭到尾都是平鋪直述，而且還能當下
聽懂別人所提問題的重點所在。

13

時態（Tenses）

英語的時態非常嚴格，不僅常會使用時間副詞點明時間點，動詞也必須要做相關變化，因此在學習時，要對時態建立起觀念，分門別類學好各時態的基本形式與適用情形。

時態共有以下幾類：

現在式、過去式、未來式
現在進行式、過去進行式、未來進行式
現在完成式、過去完成式、未來完成式
現在完成進行式、過去完成進行式、未來完成進行式

Unit
1

現在式

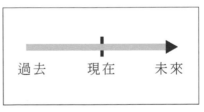

過去　　　現在　　　未來

現在式的形式

大部分動詞的現在式為動詞原形，第三人稱字尾要加上 -s, -es, -ies；have的第三人稱為has；be動詞的現在式是 am, are, is。

現在式適用情形

1. 描述真理或事實。

例 No one is an island.
沒有人是一座孤島。

例 There is no place like home.
沒有別的地方像家一樣。

例 Silence is golden.
沉默是金。

例 Doing sport regularly is vital to your health.
規律運動對你的健康很重要。

例 Every child is entitled to education in this country.
在這個國家每個小孩都有受教育的權利。

2. 描述現在的狀態或動作。

例 Laura is now divorced.
蘿拉目前是離婚狀態。

例 Lucy is currently single and lives with 3 cats.
露西目前單身，跟三隻貓同住。

例 Jerry is right now very rich because he just won the lottery.
傑瑞現在很有錢，因為他剛贏了樂透。

例 At present he is bankrupt because his business failed.
目前他破產了，因為他做生意失敗了。

例 They are not rich, but always helpful to others.
他們雖不富有但總是樂於助人。

3. 描述經常的習慣。

例 He gets up at 5:30 every morning.
他每天早上五點半起床。

例 Our boss never show up at the office before noon.
我們老闆中午前不會到辦公室。

例 The first thing Ivy does after she wakes up every morning
is Tai Chi.
艾維每早一起床做的第一件事就是打太極拳。

例 Every year Darren's parents organize a family trip abroad.
每年戴倫的父母都會安排一次全家海外旅行。

例 Irene goes swimming with her son almost every Saturday
afternoon.
幾乎每星期六下午艾琳都會和她兒子一起去游泳。

4. 口語中表示預計將要發生的事。

例 Tomorrow is a public holiday.
明天是國定假日。

例 Next month our headquarter in Germany has a month
off.
下個月我們位於德國的總公司休息一個月。

例 Their wedding is on the first Sunday of next month.
他們的婚禮會於下個月的第一個星期日舉行。

5. 副詞子句中必須用現在式來代替未來式。

例 Let's leave this place before it's too late.
讓我們在尚未太晚前離開這個地方。

例 When I finish the research, I'll take a short break.
我完成研究後會短暫休息一下。

例 If the weather is nice tomorrow, we will go hiking.
如果明天天氣好的話，我們會去健行。

例 After I finish this task, I'll reward myself with a weekend trip.
完成了這個任務之後，我會給自己來趟周末旅遊作為獎勵。

例 When you are in need, you can always contact me.
當你有需要的時候，隨時都可以聯絡我。

6. 意思為「來、去」、「開始」的動詞常用現在式加上未來時間副詞表示未來。

go/come/leave/arrive/start ＋ tomorrow/next month/next year

例 Jason leaves here tomorrow evening.
傑森明天傍晚會離開這裡。

例 Next month Teresa goes to work.
　下個月德瑞莎會去上班。

例 My work starts next Monday.
　我的工作下星期一開始。

例 Tomorrow afternoon our guests arrive in Taipei.
　明天下午我們的客人會到達台北。

例 The day after tomorrow the delegation from Japan comes to the city hall.
　後天日本代表團會來到市政廳。

Unit 2

過去式

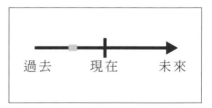

過去　　現在　　未來

過去式的形式

be動詞的過去式為was（am與is的過去式）；were（are 的過去式）；其他動詞的過去式通常於字尾加上 -ed, -d，其餘為不規則變化過去式。

過去式適用情形

1. 描述過去的狀態或動作

例 Back then he was not that interested in English.
那時候他還沒有對英語那麼有興趣。

例 My English teacher asked us to keep a diary in English, but I never really did it.
我的英文老師要我們用英語寫日記，但是我從來沒有真的那麼做。

例 In high school Rory developed a strong interest in reading science fictions.
在高中時羅里發展出閱讀科幻小說的強烈興趣。

例 During the time Carolyn worked for Ms. Howard, she made a huge progress in communication.
卡羅琳在為霍華德女士工作期間，她的溝通能力進步良多。

例 Mrs. and Mr. Johnson always went jogging together in the early morning when they lived in the country a couple of years ago.
強森夫婦兩三年前住在鄉下時，每天一大早總是一起去慢跑。

2. 描述過去的習慣

例 Susan was always late for all appointments.
不論什麼約會，蘇珊總是會遲到。

例 During high school, he borrowed at least 5 books a month from the city library.
高中時期他一個月至少向市立圖書館借五本書。

例 Whenever he had time, he would visit his parents living in the countryside.
只要他有時間就會去看住在鄉下的父母。

例 Helen always took notes whenever she was in a meeting.
只要是開會，海倫總會記筆記。

例 In the past when Mr. Li had breaks from work, he frequently did voluntary work for the disadvantaged children in isolated rural areas.
在過去李先生工作有放假時，他經常當志工為偏鄉弱勢兒童服務。

3. 描述歷史

例 From 1895 to the end of World War II in 1945, Taiwan was a Japanese colony for 50 years.
從 1895 到 1945 年台灣是日本殖民地有五十年之久。

例 The American Civil War was a civil war that was fought in the United States from 1861 to 1865.
美國南北戰爭是1861 至 1865年在美國發生的內戰。

例 In 2008 Obama rose to power as US's first African American president and stepped down as US president in 2017.
在 2008 年歐巴馬以第一位美國非裔總統獲得政權，於 2017年結束美國總統任期。

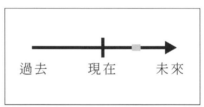

Unit 3 未來式

未來式的形式

| will/shall ＋ Verb |

| be going to ＋ Verb |

未來式的形式是於原形動詞前加上will/shall 或 be going to。

| 未來式適用情形 |

1. 描述未來發生的動作或狀態

will ＋ Verb

例 By the time of next year, the construction of this building will have to be completed.
到明年的這個時候，這棟建築將會完工。

例 These children will go on a hiking tour to the mountain in summer.
這些小孩在夏天會去山上健行。

例 Modern technology will develop at such a high speed that we cannot imagine.
現代科技會以我們無法想像的速度來發展下去。

例 Some thoughtful words will be remembered forever.
有些體貼的話能為人永遠記住。

be going to ＋ Verb

例 Are you going to study abroad after graduation?
畢業後你會去留學嗎？

例 We are not going to give up just because of some minor problems.
我們不會因為一些小問題就放棄。

例 If there is a severe earthquake, what are you doing to do?
如果發生嚴重地震，你會怎麼辦？

例 Many people are going to see fireworks on the New Year's Eve.
跨年夜很多人都要去看煙火。

例 What are you going to cook for so many guests coming to our place?
你要為來我們這裡的這麼多客人煮些什麼呢？

例 Whatever is going to happen will happen, whether we worry or not. (Ana Monnar)
不論我們擔憂不擔憂，該發生的就是會發生。（安娜‧摩納）

2. 表達說話者或聽者的意志，使用 will, shall。

will

例 Will you come with me to the business lunch?
你要跟我一起吃午餐嗎？

例 I will finish the task as soon as I can.
我會儘快完成這項任務。

例 We will not give in.
我們不會屈服。

例 Love will conquer all.
愛會戰勝一切。

shall

傳統原則：第一人稱代名詞（亦即 I, we）與 shall 連用
來形成未來式，其他的人稱代名詞（亦即 you, he, she,
it, they）則用 will 來形成未來式，但是在現代英語中，
通常一切人稱都習慣用 will。另外，如果要表達強烈的
決心，則 I, we 要與 will 連用。

例 Shall we dance?
我們一起跳舞吧？

例 Shall we work on this together?
我們一起工作吧？

例 We shall wait and see.
我們等著瞧。

例 Let's go, shall we?
我們一起走吧？

例 I shall thank you for the second chance.
我感謝你給我第二次機會。

例 I shall never forget her.
我將永遠不會忘記她。

比較：

例 I will never forgive him.
我絕對不會原諒他。

秒懂！
關鍵 **英文** Fast! Easy
文法 輕鬆學 English Grammar

Unit 4

過去　　現在　　未來

現在進行式

現在進行式的形式

am/are/is ＋ V-ing

現在進行式是於be動詞的現在式（am/are/is）後加上現在分詞（V-ing）。

現在進行式適用情形

1. 表示目前正在進行的動作

例 At this moment, almost all people are enjoying reunion dinner with their family members.
在這個時刻幾乎所有的人都在享受團圓飯。

例 At the moment Vivian is having lunch with her colleagues.
現在薇薇安正和她同事一起吃午餐。

例 The kettle is boiling.
水壺的水燒開了。

例 The listeners are waiting for his answer to this question.
聽眾正在等著他對這問題的答覆。

例 The talk show host was making all sorts of jokes to entertain the audience.
脫口秀主持人說各種的笑話來娛樂觀眾。

2. 表示預計不久就要發生的動作，主要用於 go, come, arrive, leave, start。

例 Our new secretary is coming tomorrow morning.
新秘書明天早上將會來到。

例 The books you ordered online are arriving this afternoon.
你在線上訂的書今天下午會到。

例 They are leaving for Dublin tomorrow morning.
他們明天一早就要出發去都柏林。

例 The bride and the bridegroom are starting a new chapter of life.
新娘和新郎正要開始人生新的一章。

例 Next Monday we are leaving for a famous resort town with hot spring.
下個星期一我們要去一個著名的渡假溫泉小鎮。

Unit
5

過去進行式

| 過去 | 現在 | 未來 |

過去進行式的形式

| was/were ＋ V-ing |

過去進行式是於be動詞的過去式（was/were）後加上現在分詞（V-ing）。

| 過去進行式適用情形 |

過去進行式表示過去某時刻正在進行的動作。

（例） Judy was talking to someone on the phone when the doorbell rang.
門鈴響時茱蒂正在講電話。

（例） When Matthew entered the room, everybody was too busy talking to notice him.
馬修進門時，每個人都忙著說話而沒注意到他。

（例） Allison was preparing the dinner while her children were watching TV.
艾麗森在準備晚餐，而她的小孩正在看電視。

例 Anna was mopping the floor and listening to music through earphone at the same time.
安娜一邊拖地一邊聽耳機裡的音樂。

例 Many gadgets can record the physical conditions of the users while they are doing sport.
很多器材可以在使用者運動時記錄他們的生理狀況。

Unit 6

未來進行式

未來進行式的形式

| will (shall) be + V-ing |

未來進行式是於 be + V-ing 之前加上 will (shall)，表示未來某時刻正在進行的動作。

| 未來進行式適用情形 |

未來進行式表示某一行為會於未來某一時刻或某一時段進行。

（例）Tomorrow morning, my husband will be receiving treatment from his dentist.
明天一早我先生要看牙醫。

（例）Next summer, I will be staying at my friend's farm.
明年夏天我會待在我朋友的農場。

（例）We shall be landing New York in ten minutes.
我們十分鐘後會降臨紐約。

（例）Our boss believes that our company will be making huge profits this year.
我們老闆認為我們公司今年會賺大錢。

（例）This farm will be attracting flocks of visitors after we put the advertisement online.
我們在網路廣告後，這個農場將會吸引成群的遊客。

★ 請特別注意：have, know 和感官動詞（feel, see, hear, notice）不可用於進行式。

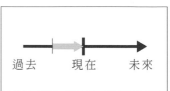

過去　　　現在　　　未來

現在完成式

現在完成式的形式

| have/has ＋ V-ed |

現在完成式的形式為 have (has) 加上過去分詞。

| 現在完成式適用情形 |

1. 表示從過去持續至現在的動作或狀態

例 Mary has played the piano for years, and she wants to be a piano teacher someday.
瑪莉彈鋼琴多年，她想要將來成為鋼琴老師。

例 Nilson has always been very interested in designing, and he is now enrolled in university to study architecture.
一直以來尼爾森都對設計非常感興趣，現在他在大學專攻建築。

例 The boy has played computer games for the whole day.
這個男孩已經玩一整天電玩了。

Part
13

例 Anderson has learned Japanese for quite some time since he started university.
自從開始唸大學以來，安德森已經學日語學了一段時間。

例 Recently Paul has been stable after being not so well in previous years.
幾年前保羅健康不太好，最近穩定了。

2. 表示至今的經驗

例 Have you been to Japan?
你到過日本沒有？

例 I have been to Japan once and that was to visit Tokyo.
我曾經去過日本一次，是去東京旅遊。

例 Have you had any experience with martial arts before?
你是否接觸過武術？

例 I have tried Judo and have become quite good at it.
我曾嘗試過柔道，也變得相當內行。

例 I have never heard her saying something like that.
我從來沒有聽過她說過這種話。

例 You have made much progress in English learning.
你在英語學習上進步良多。

過去 現在 未來

過去完成式

過去完成式的形式

had ＋ V-ed

過去完成式的形式為 had 加上過去分詞。

過去完成式適用情形

1. 表示於過去某一時刻之前已發生的動作

例 He had cleaned up the room when his mother got back home.
他母親回到家時，他已經將房間整理好。

例 Andy had seen the face of the pickpocket before he tried to steal his wallet.
安迪在扒手偷他錢包之前，已經看見了他的臉。

例 Albert had packed everything long before the shuttle bus arrived.
亞伯特在接駁車到達前，老早就將所有行李收好了。

Part 13

例 No sooner had we arrive at the train station did our train left.

我們一到火車站，我們的火車就離開了。

〔no sooner 為否定詞，所以要倒裝〕

2. 表示於過去某一時刻之前的經驗

例 Tim had never left his home country before he visited Japan.

在堤姆去日本前他從未出國過。

例 Mark had changed many companies before he finally settled down in that trading company.

馬克在那家貿易公司穩定工作之前換了好幾家公司。

例 Martin had worked in the company for a year when Angel started to apply for a position there.

安琪兒開始申請那家公司的工作時，馬汀已經在那兒工作了一年。

例 Before Ken became really fluent in English, he had tried many various methods of learning.

在肯恩的英語變得非常流利之前，他曾經試過很多不同的學習方式。

例 Before Tracy published her first book, she had been rejected by many publishing companies.

在崔西發表第一本書之前，她曾經被多家出版公司拒絕。

Unit
9

未來完成式

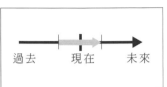

| 過去 | 現在 | 未來 |

未來完成式的形式

will (shall) have + V-ed

未來完成式的形式為 will (shall) have 加上過去分詞。

未來完成式適用情形

未來完成式表示於未來某一時間之前已完成的動作或經驗。

(例) By next June, they will have learned English for 5 years.
到了明年六月，他們學英語就有五年之久了。

(例) They will have been to China twice after this trip to Shanghai.
這次上海之行後，他們就去過中國兩次了。

(例) By this time of next year, I shall have had the experiences of doing Yoga for one and a half years.
到明天的這個時候，我就會累積有練瑜珈一年半的經驗。

例 Usually children of a bilingual family will have become fluent in both languages before they start schools.
通常雙語家庭的小孩會在開始讀小學前，就能夠流利地說這兩種語言。

例 Kent will have passed the exam when this summer arrives.
在今年夏天來臨時，肯特將已經通過考試。

Unit **10**

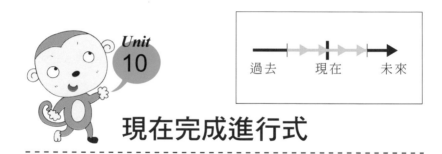

過去　　現在　　未來

現在完成進行式

現在完成進行式的形式

have(has) been ＋ V-ing
現在完成進行式的形式為 have(has) been 加上現在分詞。

現在完成進行式適用情形
現在完成進行式表示過去某時間開始的動作，通常還要再進行下去。

例 Jim has been watching TV the whole afternoon.
傑姆已經一整個下午都在看電視。

例 Since retirement, we have been living in the countryside.
自從退休後我們一直都住在鄉下。

例 Celine has been talking about quitting his job for a long time, but she still hasn't done it.
賽琳一直說要辭職，但是仍然沒有這麼做。

例 Since Jenny started the work in February, she has been putting a lot of effort into everything.
自從珍妮於二月開始工作後，她就非常努力把一切事做好。

Unit
11

過去　　現在　　未來

過去完成進行式

過去完成進行式的形式

had been + V-ing

過去完成進行式的形式為 had been 加上現在分詞。

過去完成進行式適用情形

　過去完成進行式表示表示過去某時間開始的動作，通常持續到過去某一時刻。

例 Tom had been cooking before his girlfriend got back.
湯姆的女友回來前，他都在做飯。

例 Jill had been learning English in a wrong way before she met her current English teacher.
潔兒在遇見她目前的英文老師前，都是用一種錯誤方法在學英語。

例 Our business had not been working until a new CFO was appointed.
我們的生意直到新的財務長上任後才順利運作。

例 Tony had been complaining about his job all the time before he talked to his supervisor of the company.
湯尼在跟公司主管談之前，一直不停抱怨他的工作。

例 Our business had been booming before the competitor opened a similar shop next corner.
在競爭對手在下個街角開了間類似商店前，我們的生意一直發展蓬勃。

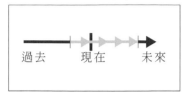

過去　　　現在　　　未來

Unit
12

未來完成進行式

未來完成進行式的形式

will have been + V-ing
未來完成進行式的形式為 will have been 加上現在分詞。

未來完成進行式適用情形
未來完成進行式表示動作於未來某時刻之前開始，持續
至某時為止。

例 By next Autumn we will have been living in this district
for 3 years.
到了下個秋天，我們就已經在這一地區住滿了三年。

例 Next June when Dan's contract is terminated, he will have
been working in this bed & breakfast for one year.
明年六月契約到期時，丹就已經在這間民宿工作滿一年
了。

P
a
r
t

13

例 By the end of this May, they will have been building this structure for more than three years.
到了今年五月底，他們就已經建了這棟建築物超過三年。

例 The two brothers will have been studying in the school for one whole year by the end of this year.
到今年底為止，兩兄弟就會在這個學校上學滿一年了。

例 James will have been staying in this country for more than two years by this Christmas.
到今年聖誕節為止，詹姆斯就會在這個國家待超過了兩年了。

請見附錄：動詞過去式 & 過去分詞的不規則變化

Exercises 練習題

■、請於下列空格中填入動詞的簡單現在式或現在進行式。

1. Your suitcase looks heavy. _____ a hand? (you / need)

2. Scott _____ (study), please turn down the music.

3. Please don't throw the clothes away. Why not _____ (give / them) away to the poor.

4. Why _____ (they / stare) at us right now? We look just like them.

5. Please _____ (think) twice before you act.

6. What _____ (you / think) at this moment?

7. John _____ (get up) early every morning to exercises.

8. They _____ (dance) right now at the party.

9. Many children _____ (dislike) green vegetables.

10. Many people _____ (not / know) English grammar rules.

二、請於下列空格中填入動詞的簡單過去式或過去進行式。

1. Last evening I _____ (slip) on the road when I _____ (use) my smartphone.

2. They _____ (have) a meeting when I _____ (arrive).

3. My dog _____ (run) across the street when the accident _____ (happen).

4. During the trip he _____ (take) many photos of people while they _____ (not / look).

5. What _____ (you / do) at the time when earthquake happened?

6. At this time yesterday, my friends _____ (play) basketball, I was studying in the library.

7. Nobody _____ (notice) that the child _____ (bleed) at that time.

8. When Jack _____ (hear) the bad news on the radio, he _____ (drive) home.

9. Nina _____ (call) while Ted _____ (do) his homework yesterday.

10. On that night our neighbor upstairs _____ (play) the piano when we _____ (ring) the bell.

三、請於下列空格中填入動詞的現在完成式或現在完成進行式。

1. It smells really great. What _____ (you / cook) the whole afternoon?

2. My mother is a writer. She _____ (write) several books.

3. Listen! Our neighbor's kid _____ (make) noise for a while.

4. My watch is missing. _____ (you / see) it somewhere?

5. Look! The mother carrying her little child _____ (wait) for a seat on the train for a long time.

6. See over there! They _____ (build) the dome day and night.

7. Do you have some money to lend me? I _____ (spend) all my money.

8. Liz _____ (paint) for many hours and she just cannot stop it.

9. If you _____ (find) side effects, contact the nurse at any time.

10. His health _____ (improve) continuously since he moved to the southern part of the country.

四、請將下列兩句按照時間順序邏輯連接起來，視需要使用過去完成式。

1. I called her many times this morning.

   Susan left early.

   Susan didn't get my phone calls.

   Answer: Susan ＿＿＿＿＿＿ before I called her many times in the morning. Susan didn't get my phone calls.

2. Somebody broke into our apartment.

   We found some of our money missing.

   We called the police.

   Answer: We found some of our money missing, and we knew somebody ＿＿＿＿＿＿ into our apartment. We decided to call the police.

3. Thomas Edison invented the light bulb in the end.

   Thomas Edison's many ideas to invent the light bulb failed.

   Answer: Thomas Edison's many ideas to invent the light bulb ＿＿＿＿＿＿ before he invented the light bulb in the end.

4. We did not go on a business trip.

   We were invited by our partner in Boston.

   Answer: Before we were invited by our partner in Boston, we ＿＿＿＿＿＿ on a business trip.

5. They finally became parents.

   They expected to be parents for a long time.

   Answer: They _____ to be parents for a long time, and finally they _____ parents.

Key to Exercises 解答

一、

1. Do you need   2. is studying   3. give them

4. are they staring   5. think   6. are you thinking

7. gets up   8. are dancing   9. dislike

10. do not know

二、

1. slipped, was using   2. were having, arrived

3. was running, happened   4. took, were not looking

5. were you doing   6. were playing

7. noticed, was bleeding   8. heard, was driving

9. called, was doing   10. was playing, rang

三、

1. have you been cooking   2. has written

3. has been making   4. Have you seen

5. has been waiting   6. have been building

7. have spent   8. has been painting

9. have found   10. has been improving

四、

1. had left   2. had broken   3. had failed

4. had never gone   5. had expected, became

TOEIC Exercises
多益題演練

1. No sooner had the supervisor _____ the office than the custom service clerks started chatting.

   (A) left

   (B) leave

   (C) had left

   (D) have left

2. By this time of next year, I will _____ been working on the project for two whole years.

   (A) have had

   (B) had

   (C) have

   (D) has

3. By the time the executive finished doing her presentation, her staff members had _____ taking all notes needed.

   (A) be

   (B) been

   (C) do

   (D) being

Questions 4 - 6 refer to the following e-mail.

To: Hong Kong Tourism Board

From: Mindy Liu

Subject: 2019 Taipei International Travel Fair

Date: Jan 10, 2019 11:12

To whom it may concern,

On behalf of the committee of the 2019 Taipei International Travel Fair, I would like to invite the travel agencies based in Hong Kong to participate in the event. Over the past decades, there _____ been numerous cultural

4. (A) had

   (B) have

   (C) has

   (D) have been

exchange activities between Hong Kong and Taiwan. The Taipei Travel Fair has become the best place to launch new products and services in the travel industry. If any company _____ early, it will be

5. (A) register

(B) registered

(C) registers

(D) registering

able to pick its favorite spot in the venue. Please understand we only have limited spaces, and first come, first served! All comments and suggestions are _____.

6. (A) appreciated

(B) be appreciated

(C) appreciating

(D) appreciation

Mindy Liu

Director

Committee of the 2019 Taipei International Travel Fair

P.O. Box 201 XinYi District Taipei Taiwan

e-mail: mindyliu@gov.com.tw

Key to TOEIC Exercises
多益題解答

1. A

2. C

3. B

4. B

5. C

6. A

結論

時態變化是英文的一大特色，中文可能只需要加上一兩個時間副詞就能夠表達出時態，但是在英文中幾乎所有的動詞形式都要隨之做變化，還有一些常見的片語，都會決定動詞的時態變化。難怪有人說，學會了動詞，文法也就學會了一大半，希望讀者能多加體會其中道理。

P a r t **13**

疑問詞
（Interrogative Words）

疑問詞主要分為疑問代名詞和疑問副詞。

Unit
1

疑問代名詞

★ **who** 作為人稱的疑問代名詞主格。

例 Who is he? He is William.
他是誰？他是威廉。

例 Who won the lottery? He did.
誰贏了樂透？是他。

例 Who wrote this piece of article in the newspaper? Jackie did.
報上這篇文章是誰寫的？賈姬寫的。

例 Who will be leaving this company? Melody will.
誰會離開這家公司？美樂蒂。

★ whose 所有格代名詞

whose = whose + 名詞　（所有格，表示 "誰的"）

例 Whose is the money? = Whose money is this?
這錢是誰的？

例 Whose is that book? = Whose book is that?
那本書是誰的？

★ whom

whom 是 who 的受格，口語中常以 who 代替。

例 Whom (Who) is the teacher talking about?
老師在談的是誰？

例 Whom (Who) will you go out with tonight?
你今晚會跟誰出去呢？

例 Whom (Who) was elected to be the next CEO?
誰被選為下一個執行長？

★ what

what 為疑問代名詞，用來詢問人或事物。

例 What did you see?
你看見了什麼？

例 What is the meaning of this word?
這個字的意思是什麼？

例 What was his purpose of doing this to his girlfriend?
他對他女朋友這麼做的目的是什麼呢？

例 What do people carry with them when they go to a temple?
人們到佛寺都帶些什麼呢？

> what（疑問形容詞）＋ 名詞

例 What work does your father do?
你父親是做什麼的？

例 What food do people usually prepare on such an occasion?
人們在這樣的日子通常會準備什麼樣的食物呢？

例 What clothes do people wear in a wedding in a church?
人們會穿什麼樣的衣服去參加教堂的婚禮呢？

例 What color is associated with luck in the Lunar New Year?
什麼顏色代表農曆新年的好運呢？

★ which

which是用來詢問是「哪一個」。

(例) Which is the better product?
哪一個產品比較好？

(例) Which is your favorite subject when you were in school?
你在學校裡最喜歡的科目是哪一個？

(例) Which do you prefer? Orange or apple?
你比較喜歡哪一個？柳丁或蘋果？

(例) Which makes sense to you? A, B, or C?
哪一個對你來說是正確的？A 或 B 或 C？

which（疑問形容詞）＋ 名詞

(例) Which day is the Lunar New Year this year?
今年農曆新年是哪一天？

(例) Which boy do you think is the best among them?
那些男孩子當中哪一個你認為最好？

(例) Which movies are you going to see these days?
這陣子的電影你要去看哪幾部？

(例) Which books should I read to prepare for the exam?
我應該要讀哪些書才能為這個考試做準備呢？

Unit
2

疑問副詞

疑問副詞即是疑問詞作副詞用。

★ **why** 為什麼

例 Why was Dawn so exhausted?
為什麼彤恩這麼疲憊？

例 Why did you disappear without saying good-bye?
為何你不說聲再見就離開？

例 Why didn't you come in when you walked past our place?
為何你經過我們家卻不進來呢

例 Why don't you like your job? Is it because of your supervisor or your colleagues?
你為什麼不喜歡你的工作？是因為你的主管或是你的同事嗎？

★ where 什麼地方

(例) Where did you meet him?
你在哪兒遇見他的？

(例) Where can I buy souvenirs?
哪裡有賣紀念品？

(例) Where have you met this tall guy with a beard?
你是在哪裡認識這個高個子留鬍鬚的男子呢？

(例) Where did you put your wedding ring?
你把結婚戒放在哪裡了呢？

(例) Where shall we meet after we arrive in the big city?
我們到了這個大城市之後要在哪裡會面呢？

★ when 什麼時候

(例) When will you hand in your project?
你什麼時候可以交這個專案？

(例) When is the next train coming?
下班車什麼時候會來？

(例) When is your baby due?
你的預產期是什麼時候？

(例) When and where was this book published?
這本書是在何時何地出版的呢？

例 When will this building be finished?
這棟建築物什麼時候會建好？

★ **how 怎麼樣**

例 How have you been?
你最近過得怎麼樣？

例 How does Henry learn Japanese?
亨利是怎麼學日語的呢？

例 How well can Emily cook?
艾默莉的菜燒得有多好呢？

例 How good was the president's inauguration speech?
總統的就職演講有多好呢？

Exercises 練習題

一、請選出正確的答案。

1. ( ) _____ is that girl? (a) Whose (b) Who (c) Whom

2. ( ) _____ do you like better? Apple or orange? (a) Whose (b) Which (c) Who

3. ( ) _____ book is this? (a) Whose (c) Who (c) Whom

4. ( ) _____ were you doing at that time? (a) Which (b) What (c) Whose

5. ( ) _____ color do you prefer for the car? Black or blue? (a) Whose (b) Whose (c) Which

6. ( ) _____ you need is patience. (a) Which (b) What (c) When

7. ( ) Do you know _____ won the chess game? (a) what (b) who (c) whose

8. ( ) This is _____ would happen when children play too much video games. (a) what (b) who (c) which

9. ( ) This is not the time to talk about _____ fault it is. (a) who (b) which (c) whose

10. ( ) No matter _____ happens, I will support you. (a) what (b) which (c) when

二、請選出正確的答案。

1. _____ were you last night when I was looking for you? (a) When (b) Where (c) Who

2. _____ did you tell a lie? Is it because you are afraid of being blamed? (a) Why (b) What (c) When

3. _____ do you think you can finish this work? (a) What (b) Which (c) When

4. Please tell us _____ you got the idea to create this art work. (a) what (b) who (c) how

5. Nobody knows exactly the time _____ he dropped out of high school. (a) how (b) which (c) when

6. Do you remember the place _____ we first met? (a) where (b) when (c) which

7. The fortune teller wants to know the day _____ my child was born. (a) when (b) which (c) whose

8. _____ do most people learn a foreign language? (a) What (b) Which (c) Why

9. _____ is English first taught in school in your country? (a) When (b) Where (c) Whether

10. My grandmother can remember the time _____ she was little, but she cannot remember what happens recently. (a) which (b) what (c) when

Key to Exercises 解答

一、

1. b	2. b	3. a	4. b	5. c
6. b	7. b	8. a	9. c	10. a

二、

1. b	2. a	3. c	4. c	5. c
6. a	7. a	8. c	9. a	10. c

TOEIC Exercises
多益題演練

1. _____ umbrella is it at the door?

   (A) Who

   (B) Whose

   (C) Whom

   (D) Which

2. _____ have you been in the past few months?

   (A) When

   (B) What

   (C) Which

   (D) Where

3. _____ did you do right after you graduated from college?

   (A) Where

   (B) When

   (C) What

   (D) Which

Questions 4 - 6 refer to the following memo.

To: All Employees

From: Jerry Livingston, CEO

Date: March 2, 2019

Subject: Spring Get-together

Dear all,

J & H Accounting, Inc. invites all our employees and associates for a get-together to celebrate the start of work in the spring. Please cast your vote and help us decide on: _____ _____ is the best venue?

4. (A) When

   (B) Whose

   (C) Where

   (D) Whom

1. Golden Seafood Restaurant

2. Hot Spot Steak House

3. Judy's Hong Kong Style Restaurant

Please take your time and let us know _____ is your

  5. (A) which

   (B) whom

   (C) whose

   (D) when

favorite choice. If you have special dict requests, please let us know _____ they are. Plese RSVP to this memo by March 9, 2019.

  6. (A) when

   (B) who

   (C) whom

   (D) what

Thank you very much.

Jerry Livingston, CEO

J & H Accounting, Inc.

Key to TOEIC Exercises
多益題解答

1. B
2. D
3. C
4. C
5. A
6. D

結論

疑問句或許看起來很容易，但是要注意的細節還是不少，
例如：目前以 "who " 取代 "whom " 的趨勢。只要多聽
多記，仿效實際生活中所聽到的常用疑問句句型，那麼就
不會有太大問題了。

附加問句
（Tag Questions）

Unit 1

附加問句的定義

附加問句是接於直述句尾的簡短問句，用來確認或詢問某事，有時也用來請求同意，相當於中文的「對不對？」或「是不是？」。附加問句於英式英語較美式英語常見。

Unit 2

附加問句的要點

★ 肯定句後面要接否定附加問句，否定句後面要接肯定附加問句；否定附加問句通常要用縮寫，例如 **didn't you? wasn't it?** 等。

 例句：

附加問句為否定

例 You eat all sorts of food, don't you?
你什麼食物都吃，對吧？

附加問句為肯定

例 Kevin doesn't like eating seafood, does he?
凱文不喜歡吃海鮮，對不對？

附加問句由助動詞（be, have, can, will, shall...）
和代名詞（I, you, he, she, it...）構成；如果句子
裡有be動詞、have或其它助動詞，附加問句就用
該be動詞、have或其它助動詞；如果句子裡沒有
be動詞、have或其它助動詞，附加問句就用do,
does, did...。

例句：

例 You've been to the United States before, haven't you?
你曾經到過美國，對不對？

例 Sam can find his way home, can't he?
薩米能找到回家的路，對不對？

例 Vicky is not fond of the new teacher, is she?
維琪不喜歡這個新老師，是不是？

例 Michelle had a good day today, didn't she?
蜜雪兒今天過得不錯，對不對？

例 Bill isn't coming to Taiwan this year, is he?
比爾今年不會來台灣，是吧？

(例) Jessica just won the lottery, didn't she?
傑西卡剛中了樂透，是嗎？

(例) Susan enjoys learning foreign languages, doesn't she?
蘇珊喜歡學習外語，對不對？

(例) You watch mainly western movies, don't you?
你主要是看西洋片，對不對？

★ **I am** 的否定附加問句是 **aren't I?**（主要用於英式用法。）

例句：

(例) I am a successful businessman, aren't I?
我是個成功的商人，對吧？

★ 用 **it** 為主詞的主句，或是用動名詞、不定詞、**that / this**、**nothing**、**everything** 為主詞，附加問句要用 **it**。

例句：

(例) It is important to stay fit, isn't it?
保持健康很重要，對不對？

(例) Keeping a balanced diet is vital, isn't it?
飲食均衡很重要，是吧？

例 To care for the elder people takes training, isn't it?
照顧長者需要受過訓練，對吧？

例 That is your wishful thinking, isn't it?
那只是你一廂情願的想法，是不是？

例 Everything seems so real in this painting, doesn't it?
這幅畫裡的每樣東西都如此逼真，對不對？

例 Nothing is more important than health, is it?
沒有比健康更重要的東西，對不對？

★ 主句中含有否定詞，例如：**never, seldom, hardly, rarely, scarcely, nobody, nowhere...**後面的附加問句要用肯定附加問句。

 例句：

例 The new assistant never complains about her workload, does she?
新助理從未抱怨工作量過重，對不對？

例 The English teacher seldom gives us homework, does he?
新老師很少給我們出作業，是不是？

例 There is hardly any evidence supporting this, is it?
根本沒有什麼支持這個的證據，對不對？

例 Nowhere is better than this place, is it?
沒有比這裡更好的地方，是不是？

Ｐ
ａ
ｒ
ｔ
⑮

㉗ Simon rarely went on a business trip, did he?
賽門很少出差，對吧？

★ **疑問句後面不要接附加問句。**

疑問句本身就是問句，因此後面不要再有附加問句。

I, we ＋ think/believe/suppose/assume/expect/guess...＋
受詞子句
附加疑問句要與子句的主詞與動詞一致。

例句：

㉗ I think Katherine is a person who likes challenge, isn't she?
我認為凱撒琳是個喜歡挑戰的人，對不對？

㉗ We believe this is the best way to solve this problem, isn't it?
我們相信這是解決問題的最好方法，是不是？

但如果是以否定開頭：

I, we don't/didn't ＋ think/believe/suppose/assume/expect/ guess... ＋ 受詞子句
附加疑問句則要用肯定式。附加疑問句仍要與子句的主詞與動詞一致。

 例句：

㉘ I don't think it is for you to decide on this matter, is it?
我不認為你有權利決定這件事，對不對？

㉘ We don't think he is to blame, is he?
我們不認為他該被罵，是不是？

㉘ We didn't expect they would give in so soon, would they?
我們沒有料到他們會這麼快就退讓，對不對？

★ **let's/let us...**的附加問句通常用 **shall we?**

 例句：

㉘ Let's dance, shall we?
我們來跳舞吧？

㉘ Let us not give kids too much pressure, shall we?
我們不要給小孩太大壓力，好不好？

㉘ Let's forgive those young students, shall we?
我們就原諒這些年輕學生好不好？

★ 如果 **let us**（此處不用縮寫 **let's**）**...** 指的是 **you let us**，因為對象為「你、你們」，附加問句通常用 **will you?**

 例句：

例 Let us go, will you?
　讓'我們走好不好？

例 Let us have a day off, will you?
　你就讓我們放一天假好不好？

例 Let us have the air condition on, will you?
　你讓我們開冷氣好不好？

★ 祈使句的附加問句

1. 要求、命令、告知，附加問句要用：will/won't/
can/can't/could/would you?

例 Don't believe what he says to you, will you?
　不要相信他所説的話好嗎？

例 Listen to what he has to say, won't you?
　聽聽他有什麼要説的好嗎？

2. 客氣的請求，附加問句要用： won't you?

例 Be more patient to others, won't you?
　對他人要多點耐心好嗎？

3. 否定祈使句，附加問句要用：will you?

例 Do not dump garbage here, will you?
不要倒垃圾到這裡好不好？

例 Don't repeat the same mistake, will you?
不要犯同樣的錯誤行不行？

> 肯定句可以接肯定附加問句來達到確認或強調的效果，但是也有的情形是在聽到別人的肯定句後，講話者重複並且附上肯定附加問句以表示驚訝或懷疑，甚至是諷刺，此時並非真正要提問，因此語調不上揚。一般來說，如果回話者是真的要詢問，語調要上揚；如果是要表示驚訝或懷疑，甚至諷刺，並非真要提問，則語調不上揚。

例 God helps those who help themselves, does He?
天助自助者，對不對？

例 A healthy mind resides in a healthy body, does it?
健全的心智需要健全的身體，是不是？

例 Your husband said he could get a raise next month, did he?
你先生說他下個月能加薪，是嗎？

例 Maria will go on a business trip to Mexico next Monday, will she?
瑪麗亞下星期一要去墨西哥出差，是嗎？

P
a
r
t
15

例 Recently Rodney goes to the gym every day, does he?
最近羅德尼每天去健身中心，是嗎？

★ 回答附加問句時用 **yes / no** 來回覆，答案不要受到附
加問句的影響。

例 A：That is your own problem, isn't it?
那是你個人的問題，是不是？

例 B：Yes, it is. 或 No, it isn't.
是的（不是）。

例 A：It's not my fault, is it?
這不是我的錯，對不對？

例 B：Yes, it is. 或 No, it isn't.
對（不對）。

★ 以附加問句來回覆

原句是肯定句時要以肯定附加問句來回覆；原句是否定
句時則要以否定附加問句來回覆。

 例一：

例 A：Ted just gave his keynote speech.
泰德剛發表了主題演講。

例 B：Did he? Now he must feel relieved.
真的嗎？現在他一定鬆了口氣。

 例二：

例 A：Kate can't use a computer.
　　凱特不會使用電腦。

例 B：She can't?（美式英語）
　　不會吧。

例 Can't she?（英式英語）
　　不會吧。

請選出最適合的附加問句。

1. There is no place like home, _____?

   (a) is it (b) isn't it (c) was it

2. I am a rich man, _____?

   (a) was I (b) is it (c) aren't I

3. He never speaks ill of others, _____?

   (a) doesn't he (b) did he (c) does he

4. Everything happens for a reason, _____?

   (a) does it (b) doesn't it (c) do they

5. Let's take a break, _____?

   (a) should we (b) shall we (c) shouldn't we

6. Let us have a day off, _____?

   (a) shouldn't you (b) will you (c) should you

7. Don't talk while I am talking, _____?

   (a) will you (b) don't you (c) do you

8. Clean up the room after the party is over, _____?

   (a) do you (b) won't you (c) don't you

9. It has not rained for quite a long time, _____?

(a) hasn't it (b) isn't it (c) has it

10. This cannot be true, _____?

(a) can it (b) does it (c) cannot it

11. Nothing can compare to a wonderful reunion, _____?

(a) does it (b) can't it (c) can it

12. I don't think it is for you to decide on this matter, _____? (a) is it? (b) isn't it (c) don't I

13. I think you do not have to worry about it for her, _____?

(a) do you (b) don't you (c) do I

14. We barely know this new employee, _____?

(a) don't we (b) do we (c) did we

15. He could hardly understand anything in English, _____?

(a) couldn't he (b) could he (c) could it

16. The new semester has just started, _____?

(a) does it (b) has it (c) hasn't it

17. Never should we judge others before we know the facts, _____?

(a) should we (b) shall we (c) shouldn't we

18. It is never too late to learn a new skill, _____?

    (a) isn't it (b) is it (c) is this

19. Do unto others as you would have them do unto you, _____?

    (a) will you (b) won't you (c) won't they

20. He has so many excuses for not doing his job, _____?

    (a) does he (b) do they (c) doesn't he

Key to Exercises 解答

1. a	2. c	3. c	4. b	5. b
6. b	7. a	8. b	9. c	10. a
11. c	12. a	13. a	14. b	15. b
16. c	17. a	18. b.	19. b	20. c

TOEIC Exercises
多益題演練

1. He's never come to office late, _____ he?

   (A) has

   (B) have

   (C) had

   (D) has had

2. Let's dance to the music, _____ we?

   (A) can

   (B) let

   (C) shall

   (D) should

3. Jack has many certificates that he didn't mention, _____ _____ he?

   (A) does

   (B) do

   (C) don't

   (D) doesn't

Questions 4 - 6 refer to the following advertisement.

Han & Soong Skiing Resort

Are you still wondering where to spend your vacation this winter? You know you don't have to stay indoors and be bored during snowy days, _____ you? Whether you

4. (A) do

(B) don't

(C) aren't

(D) are

have tried to learn skiing or not, Han & Soong Skiing Resort is perfect for you. We have the best skiing coaches and standard equipment for rent. If you haven't skied before, give it a try now, _____

5. (A) have

(B) haven't

(C) don't

(D) won't

you? Please do book in advance at http://www.hansoongski-ing.com.kr/. because winter vacation is generally the peak season. Come to us and make skiing the best experience of this winter, _____ you?

6. (A) are

 (B) aren't

 (C) won't

 (D) shall

Han & Soong Skiing Resort

E-Mail: hansoongkiing.com.kr

Website: http://www.hansoongskiing.com.kr/

Tel: 82 2-6128 6362

Address: 88, Oak Valley 2-gil, Wolsong-ri,Jijeong-myeon, Wonju-si, Gangwon-do, Republic of Korea

Key to TOEIC Exercises
多益題解答

1. A

2. C

3. D

4. B

5. D

6. C

結論

附加問句雖然只是附隨著主要句子的簡短問句，但是為句子增加了不少韻味，有時真的在期待對方回覆，但是有時卻只是在表達懷疑、諷刺等等的語氣，端看情境為何，才能決定是否要回答，以及如何回答。

16

祈使句
（The Imperative Sentences）

Unit 1

祈使句的定義

祈使句即是用祈使語氣的句型，用來表示命令、請求、號召等作用，通常以句號結尾，但如果是一個強烈命令則以驚歎號結尾。

Unit 2

祈使句的構成

基本上祈使句的即是省略了第二人稱代名詞 you（單數或複數依情形而定）的命令句。

例如：

(You) be seated. 坐下。

(You) take this document home.
把這些文件帶回家。

(You) don't talk too much in this meeting.
在這會議上不要太多話。

(You) do not use others' data without citing the source.
不要使用別人的數據而不註明出處。

點出主詞的祈使句

有時為了強調主詞，可以將主詞明白寫出來，也就是句中 you 所指的對象。

例如：

例 Class, be quiet!
全班安靜！

例 All of you, never make the same mistake!
全部人聽好，不要犯同樣的錯！

例 Carol, be here on time tomorrow.
卡羅，明天要準時到。

例 You take care.
你多保重。

例 Kids, keep eating properly.
孩子們，繼續好好吃飯。

例 Jeremy, make sure you clean up the mess in the living room.
傑瑞米，你一定要收拾好髒亂的客廳。

肯定或否定的祈使句

肯定祈使句 (Affirmative Imperatives)
肯定祈使句用原形動詞。

例句：

例 Get the work done by this Friday!
這星期五前要完成工作！

例 Have more patience.
要耐心點。

例 Stay optimistic and think positively!
保持樂觀，正向思考！

例 Solve this problem immediately!
馬上解決這問題！

★ 如果要顯得有禮貌，可以於祈使句前或後加上 **please**。

例句：

例 Please make some tea for us, Ms. Huang.
黃小姐，請為我們泡點茶。

例 Lower the volume of your stereo, please.
請將你的音響音量調低點。

例 Please wear loose clothes when you practice Tai Chi.
練習太極時請穿寬鬆衣服。

例 Focus on one thing at a time, please.
請一次專注於一件事。

例 Please concentrate on problem solving.
請專注於解決問題。

★ 如果要加強語氣，也可以於句尾加上附加問句。

例如：

例 Lower the volume of your voice, won't you?
講話小聲一點好不好？

例 Be a bit reasonable, won't you?
理智點好不好？

例 Think positively, won't you?
樂觀一點好不好？

否定祈使句 (Negative Imperatives)

否定祈使句表示不要去做什麼事，通常於句首加上：Do not, Don't, Never （不曾）。

 例句：

例 Do not arrive late for the meeting.
開會不要遲到。

例 Don't forget your jacket!
不要忘了你的夾克！

例 Never upset your wife in front of your kids.
不要在小孩面前讓你太太不開心。

例 Don't embarrass your colleagues in the public.
不要在公眾場合讓你的同事難堪。

例 Do not talk so loudly in the library.
在圖書館不要那麼大聲說話。

強調祈使句 Emphatic Imperatives

如果想要強調或加強祈使句的語氣，則於祈使句前加Do
（助動詞）或Please（請）或Always（總是）。

例如：

例 Do bring your laptop with you!
一定要帶筆記型電腦來！

例 Do make sure you pay the bills in time.
一定要及時付帳單的費用。

例 Always take your laptop with you when you are in the
library.
在圖書館要隨時帶著你的筆記型電腦。

例 Please try to see the good in everyone.
請試圖去看每個人的優點。

例 Do work hard!
好好認真工作！

例 Do reward your employees when they do something
especially well.
當你的員工將某事做得特別好時，要好好獎勵一下。

例 Do make him pay for it!
一定要他付出代價！

例 Do talk to him about this issue.
一定要跟他談這件事。

被動祈使句 Passive Imperatives

被動祈使句表示要某人去促使某件事完成。
句型通常用： get/have ＋ 受詞 ＋ 過去分詞

 例句：

例 Get your hair cut soon!
快去剪髮！

例 Have your homework done by dinner!
晚餐前要做完功課！

例 Get the paper finished by the end of August!
在八月底前要完成論文！

例 Have new keys cut immediately!
馬上去打新鑰匙！

Let引導的祈使句

於祈使句開頭使用 let 表示提議、建議、請求、命令。

★ **let us**

如果 let us = you let us，則意思是「請你讓我們……」。

例如：

⟨例⟩ Let us take you to the speech hall.
說話對象為 you（你或你們），意思為「讓我們載你（你們）到演講廳」。

比較：

⟨例⟩ Let's walk to the speech hall.
可能說話對象沒有 you（你或你們），只有我們，意思為「讓我們一起走到演講廳」；如果說話對象有我們和 you（你或你們），則意思為「讓我們（包含說話者和說話對象）一起走到演講廳」。

★ **let me** ＋原形動詞，准許我做某件事。

例如：

⟨例⟩ Let me see. Have I mentioned it before?
讓我看看，我從前提過這件事嗎？

⟨例⟩ Let me stress the issues once again.
讓我再次強調這件事。

★ **let him/her** （第三人稱）＋原形動詞，准許他人做某件事。

例如：

⟨例⟩ Let Laura do whatever she wants to do.
讓羅拉做任何她想做的事。

Part 16

例 Let patients go outside for a walk.
讓病患到外面散散步。

★ **let's** 的否定

1. 第一人稱的否定：do not let us=don't let us 或 let us not=let's not

 例句：

例 Let's not forget (Do not let us/Don't let us forget) our handbags in the train. 我們可不要忘了將火車上的手提行李帶下火車。

例 Let's not forget (Don't let us forget) terrorists can be active everywhere in the world.
我們不要忘了恐怖份子可能在世界到處活動。

2. 第三人稱的否定：do not let/don't let him/her/them

 例句：

例 Do not let/Don't let Jonathan skip washing dishes tonight.
不要讓強納森躲過今晚的洗碗工作。

例 Do not let/Don't let small children walk across the street by themselves.
不要讓小小孩自己過馬路。

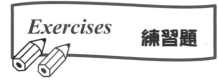

Part **16**

一、請翻譯下列句子成英文。

1. 請快進到車子裡。

   Please _____ into the car.

2. 要多保重啊。

   Do _____!

3. 小孩在旁邊不要抽菸。

   _____ while children are around.

4. 永遠不要放棄！

   Never _____!

5. 你的頭髮太長了，去剪頭髮吧。

   Your hair is too long. Get your hair ____.

6. 不要浪費錢買沒有用的東西。

   _____ on useless things.

7. 機會來臨時隨時要準備好。

   Always _____ when opportunity knocks.

8. 不要以為你什麼都知道。

   Do not _____ everything.

9. 將你的所有文件帶到辦公室蓋章。

Take all your documents to the office and have them
____. (stamp)

10. 你來我家就把這裡當成自己的家。

_____ when you are at my place.

11. 你好瘦，多吃點好嗎？

You are so thin. _____, won't you?

12. 不要相信任何你所聽到的，好不好？

Don't believe whatever you hear, _____?

Key to Exercises
解答

1. get

2. take care

3. Don't smoke

4. give up

5. cut

6. Do not waste money

7. be ready

8. think you know

9. stamped

10. Make yourself at home

11. Eat a bit more

12. will you

TOEIC Exercises
多益題演練

1. _____ in the data of the survey questionnaires.

   (A) Key

   (B) Keying

   (C) Keyed

   (D) Entering

2. Sign up for the charity event, _____ you?

   (A) shall

   (B) won't

   (C) do

   (D) don't

3. Don't _____ to call the customer, will you?

   (A) forgetting

   (B) forget

   (C) to forget

   (D) forgot

Questions 4 - 6 refer to the following advertisement

Hotel for Lovebirds

To promote the love industry of Kaohsiung, the Hotel for Lovebirds

offers exclusive suite discounts for all couples who are coming during February this year. _____ now to get

4. (A) Book

   (B) To book

   (C) Booked

   (D) Booking

limited red wine and chocolates in the suites for free. Around Valentine's Day, there will be special events of the love program along the Love River. _____ invite all your loved ones,

5. (A) Don 't

　(B) Does

　(C) Do

　(D) To do

including your family members and relatives, to visit
Kaohsiung. _____

6. (A) Keeping

　(B) Kept

　(C) To keep

　(D) Keep

informed with the coming events designed by the
government and private tourism industry. Welcome to
Kaohsiung, welcome to love!

Hotel for Lovebirds

E-Mail: lovebirds@hotel.com.tw

Website: http://www.lovebirds.com.tw/

Tel: 886 07 3422567

Address: 30 Liouhe 2nd Rd, Kaohsiung Xinxing District,

Kaohsiung 80049 Taiwan

P
a
r
t
16

Key to TOEIC Exercises
多益題解答

1. A

2. B

3. B

4. A

5. C

6. D

祈使句又可稱為「命令句」，因為我們用祈使句時，就如同是向對方下命令，要求對方做某事，因為這個概念在中文中也有類似的表達方式，因此對學習者來說並不難，例如：「站起來」、「坐下」，不過，有時祈使句比較是在請求對方做某件事，例如：「請保重」（"Please take care."），這裡並不是在命令對方，而比較像是祈求對方做某事，所以本書採用「祈使句」這個專有名詞。

17

假設法
（The Subjunctive Mood）

Unit
1

假設法的種類

1. 與現在事實相反

If + 主詞 + were/動詞過去式，主詞 + would (should, might, could) + 動詞原形

 例句：

例 If I were you, I might take sick leave.
要是我是你，我可能會請病假。

例 If Leo could control his temper, he would be a successful businessman.
要是利歐能控制他的脾氣，他可能會是個成功的企業家。

例 If I knew it, I would tell you.
要是我知道的話，我就會告訴你。

例 If it were not raining right now, we would be enjoying picnicking.
要是現在沒有在下雨的話，我們就會在享受野餐了。

2. 與過去事實相反

If ＋ 主詞 ＋ had ＋ 過去分詞 ， 主詞 ＋ would (should, might, could) ＋ have ＋ 過去分詞

例句：

（例）If I had known it, I would have told you.
我那時要是知道的話，我就會告訴你。

（例）If it had not been raining at that time, we would have been enjoying picnicking.
若非那時在下雨，我們就可享受野餐。

（例）If Stacy had saved money, she could have afforded a trip to Paris.
若非那時崔西放棄學鋼琴，或許她就能上台演奏。

（例）If Tracy had not given up learning the piano, she might have performed on stage.
要是崔西沒有放棄學鋼琴的話，她或許就能在舞台上表演。

★ **If ＋與過去事實相反 ，與現在事實相反**

If ＋ 主詞 ＋ had ＋ 過去分詞 ， 主詞 ＋ would (should, might, could) ＋ 動詞原形

例 If I had taken up the position, I would be the manager of the company now.
要是那時我接受這個職位，現在我或許就是這家公司的經理。

例 If I had worked harder, I could be on vacation right now.
要是那時我更努力工作，現在我可能就在渡假了。

3. 表達未來萬一的情形

If + 主詞 + should (were to) + 動詞原形 , 主詞 + will, shall, can, may (would, should, might, could) + 動詞原形

 例句：

例 If I should win the lottery, I shall purchase a mansion with a garden.
要是我中了樂透，我就要買一棟附有花園的豪宅。

例 If you should decide to leave the company, please do not take any items in the office with you.
要是你決定要離開公司，請不要將辦公室內的任何東西帶走。

例 If it should get extremely cold tomorrow, you had better buy a new heater.
要是明天天氣變得非常冷，你最好買一台新暖器。

Unit
2

假設法的特殊用法

1. I wish

例句：

(例) I wish I were a successful entrepreneur.
但願我是個成功的企業家。

(例) I wish I had been a successful entrepreneur.
但願我那時是個成功的企業家。

2. as if / as though

例句：

(例) He acts as if / as though he didn't know me.
他表現得好像不認識我。

(例) He acted as if / as though he had not known me.
他那時表現得好像不認識我。

3 but for/without

(例) But for her help, I would not be working in this company now.
要不是有她的幫忙，現在我不可能有辦法在這裡工作。

(例) Without Simon's support, I would not have made it to the end.
那時要不是有賽門的幫忙，我不可能有辦法完成工作。

4. 省略 if

省略了 if，則需要將 be 動詞 (were), had, 助動詞 (should) 放置句首。

例一：

If I were you, I would quit the job.

--> 省略 if

Were I you, I would quit the job.
要是我是你，我就會辭職。

例二：

If I had the money, I would travel around the world.

--> 省略 if

Had I the money, I would travel around the world.
要是我有錢，我就會環遊世界。

例三：

If it should snow, the event will not take place.

--> 省略 if

Should it snow, the event will not take place.

萬一下雪的話，這個活動就不會舉行。

例四：

If I had had the time, I would have talked to him about it.

--> 省略 if

Had I had the time, I would have talked to him about it.

要是那時我有時間的話，我會跟他談這件事。

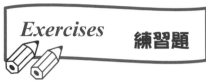

一、請完成下列句子。

1. If you _____ (are) me, what would you do?

2. If I _____ (live) in the country, I would be able to have many chances to enjoy the nature.

3. If I _____ (have) the money, I would have lent you some.

4. If we hadn't got on this train, we _____ not be in the meeting now.

5. Should you _____ (need) help, just call me.

6. What would you do if you _____ (lose) your pass port?

7. What would you do if you _____ (are) retired now?

8. My parents _____ disappointed if you could not be our guest tonight.

9. If I had not told her that news, she _____ (not be) sad.

10. She _____ (forgive) you if you apologized to her.

二、請用假設法來改寫下列的句子。

1. Right now I can not show you around because I am busy.

2. The old man slipped because there was a banana on the road.

3. I do not have the money, and that is why I cannot travel around the world.

4. They could buy the house with a garden because they took a mortgage from the bank.

5. He is not hungry so he does not order a big steak.

6. You do not go jogging every morning, and because of that, you cannot keep fit.

7. I did not take my mother's suggestion, and that is why I am not a teacher now.

三、請參照例句寫出在下列情形下,用 ”I wish” 開頭的句子。

1. You do not have days off and that is why you cannot go on a trip.

   I wish _____

2. You did not learn Japanese. Many job openings now re quire Japanese conversation skills. You regret this now.

   I wish _____

3. You did not dry your hair, and you caught a cold last night.

I wish _____

4. Your friend Jeremy is a freelance photographer and does not have to work in an office like you.

   I wish _____

5. You did not work out when you were in school, and you got sick very often at that time.

   I wish _____

6. You chose to major in philosophy, and you now have difficulty finding a well-paid job.

   I wish _____

7. You asked your teacher for advice, and you did not follow her advice. Now you regret this.

   I wish _____

8. You started a business, and that business was not doing well. Now you think that decision was wrong.

   I wish _____

9. You married your first boyfriend right after you graduated from university. Now you regretted it.

   I wish _____

10. You promised to babysit your neighbor's little kids. Now you regret that.

    I wish _____

Key to Exercises 解答

1. were   2. lived   3. had had

4. would   5. need   6. lost

7. were   8. would be

9. would not have been

10. would forgive

1. If I were not busy, I could show you around.

2. If there had not been a banana on the road, the old man would not have slipped.

3. If I had the money, I would travel around the world.

4. If they had not taken a mortgage from the bank, they could not have bought the house with a garden.

5. If he were hungry, he would order a big steak.

6. If you go jogging every morning, you would keep fit.

7. If I had taken my mother's suggestion, I would been a teacher now.

三、

1. I wish I had days off.

2. I wish I had learned Japanese.

3. I wish I had dried my hair.

4. I wish I could be a freelance photographer.

5. I wish I had worked out when I was in school.

6. I wish I had not majored in philosophy.

7. I wish I had followed my teacher's advice.

8. I wish I had not started that business.

9. I wish I had not married my first boyfriend right after I graduated from university.

10. I wish I had not promised to babysit my neighbor's little kids.

TOEIC Exercises
多益題演練

1. _____ I you, I would tell the truth now.

   (A) Was

   (B) Am

   (C) Were

   (D) Are

2. _____ you written him an e-mail to inform him, he would have attended the workshop.

   (A) Should

   (B) If

   (C) Have

   (D) Had

3. If you _____ told the truth, you wouldn 't be in such a big trouble.

   (A) have had

   (B) had

   (C) have

   (D) did

Questions 4 - 6 refer to the following e-mail.

To: Davc Wang

From: Rebecca Baker

Subject: Your application for leave-taking

Date: April 1, 2019 14:22

Dear Dave,

　　Regarding your application for leave-taking, I as Human Resource Officer can explain here why it was turned down. _____ you applied two week earlier, you would

4. (A) Have

　(B) Had

　(C) If

　(D) When

have been able to take three-week leave last month. If you had told me that your mother was ill, I _____ have let you work

5. (A) will

   (B) won 't

   (C) would

   (D) wouldn 't

from home as you already applied for. If I _____ you, I would study

6. (A) were

   (B) am

   (C) had been

   (D) been

our company 's rules on leave-taking much more carefully.

Rebecca Baker

Human Resource Officer

Winner Energy

12 F, No 85, Duhua North Rd, Taipei, Taiwan 105

Tel: (02) 2751 1043

E-mail: hr@winnerenergy.com

http://www.winnerenergy.com/

Key to TOEIC Exercises
多益題解答

1. C

2. D

3. B

4. B

5. C

6. A

如果英文假設法也如同中文一樣，那麼就不會那麼令人頭痛了（注意到了嗎？上句也用到了假設法。），最主要的是因為英文假設法的時態需要變化，還是根據「與現在事實相反」或是「與過去事實相反」來變化，還有條件句與主要子句「混搭」的情形層出不窮，所以務必要多加研讀本章內容，讓假設法深深烙印於腦海中。

18

助動詞
（Auxiliary Verbs）

Unit 1

助動詞的定義

助動詞本身並沒有詞義，它是用來幫助主要動詞（Main Verb）形成各種時態、語氣、語態、疑問句、或否定句。最常使用的助動詞有：do (do, does, did)、have (have, has, had)、be (am, are, is, was, were, be, being, been)、will, shall, can, may (would, should, could, might) 等等。

Unit 2

助動詞的分類

助動詞的種類：

1. 一般助動詞：do, have, be, will

用來形成：(1) 疑問句 (2) 附加問句 (3) 否定句
(4) 加強語氣

(1) do

第三人稱單數：does

過去式：did

㊐ Do you review the lessons every day?　疑問句
你是否每天複習功課？

㊐ He does not believe in God.　否定句
他不相信上帝。

㊐ At that time, most schools did not have facilities for the people with disabilities.　過去式
在那個時候，大部分學校沒有身心障礙設施。

㊐ They do work hard for the future.　簡單現在式的強調
為了未來他們真的很拚。

㊐ The students did try their best to save up for their school outing this summer.　簡單過去式的強調
這些學生為了夏季校外教學真的很盡力存錢。

---

do除了當助動詞外，也可以做行為動詞。例如：

My mother does the cooking, and my father does the washing up.

---

(2) have

與過去分詞一起構成各種完成式。

第三人稱單數：has

過去式：had

⑨ Have you ever been to Europe? 疑問句
你曾經去過歐洲嗎？

⑨ We have never seen such a brilliant student. 否定句
我們從來沒見過這樣聰明的學生。

⑨ His mother told the teacher that he had been terribly ill.
過去完成式
他的母親告訴老師他有一陣子得了重病。

⑨ He has been lying to his teacher since the beginning.
現在完成進行式
他一開始就對老師撒謊。

⑨ Having told one lie, he has to make up another one.
分詞完成式
說了一個謊之後，他只得再撒一個謊。

(3) be
與現在分詞一起構成各種進行式
與過去分詞一起構成被動式
am/is/are
was/were
being
been

⑨ The substitute teacher is writing the topic of English
composition on the blackboard. 現在進行式
代課老師在黑板上寫下英文作文的題目。

例 We were making progress in English. 過去進行式
我們英文進步很多。

例 Nobody likes to be scolded. 簡單現在被動式
沒有人喜歡挨罵。

(4) will

與動詞原形一起構成未來式

現在式：will

過去式：would

例 Quite a few people believe that she will win the champion. 簡單未來式
非常多人認為她會贏得冠軍。

例 Contrary to what we expected, Linda would not work for her company any more. 過去未來式
出乎我們意料之外，琳達不會再為她公司工作。

2. 情態助動詞

(1) can

> a. 表示能力 = be able to

例 Can you speak English?
你會說英語嗎？

例 Mark cannot study because it is too noisy.
馬克無法讀書，因為太吵了。

例 We can demonstrate it for you.
我們能為您示範。

---
b. 表示准許

例 Nobody can see him without making an appointment.
沒有人能不預約就與他會面。

例 Can I smoke here?
我可以在這裡抽菸嗎？

---
c. 表示可能性

例 I don't know who has been here. Can it be your landlord?
我不清楚誰到過這裡，會是房東嗎？

例 Can this language school offer courses of European languages?
這所語言學校提供歐語課程嗎？

---
d. 表示請求（常與 please 連用）

例 Can I please take a look at the room in the bed & breakfast?
我可以看看這間民宿的房間嗎？

例 Can you open the door for me?
你可以幫我開門嗎？

例 Can you please stop making noise?
你可以停止製造噪音嗎？

(2) could

> a. 是 can 的過去式

例 We could not afford many items back then.
我們那時無法負擔很多事物。

> b. 表示過去的能力

例 Misha could speak a bit Russian in high school.
米夏在高中時會説一點俄語。

> c. 表示容許，比 could 委婉

例 Could you please stop smoking?
你可以戒菸嗎？

(3) may

> a. 表示准許

例 May I leave classroom and go home?
我可以離開教室回家嗎？

例 May I tell you my answer later?
我可以晚點再告訴你我的答案嗎？

> b. 表示可能性

例 This typhoon may come or may not come.
這個颱風可能會來也可能不會來。

> c. 表示祈願

例 May all your wishes come true!
但願你的願望都能成真！

d. 與 not 連用，表示禁止

🦉 You may not take the items here away.
你不能拿走這裡的東西。

(4) might

a. 是 may 的過去式

🦉 This might not be a good idea.
這或許不是個好點子。

b. 表示比 may 更小的可能性

🦉 We might not be able to find this parcel ever again.
我們可能無法再找到這個包裹。

(5) will

a. 表示單純未來

🦉 It seems we will finish this project in time.
看來我們似乎可以及時完成這個專案。

🦉 It will rain tomorrow.
明天會下雨。

b. 表示意願、承諾

🦉 Will you marry me?
你願意嫁給（娶）我嗎？

🦉 Will you look after your sick mother?
你願意照顧你生病的母親嗎？

c. 表示請求

(例) Will you please clean up this room?
可以請你清理一下這間房間嗎？

(例) Will you please turn down the volume a bit?
可以請你將音量調低一點嗎？

d. 表示主張、決心

(例) I will never trust any man again.
我不會再相信任何男人。

e. 表示習慣

(例) We will eat desserts after dinners.
我們是在晚飯後吃甜點的。

(例) They will travel abroad when they have holidays.
他們放假時會出國渡假。

(6) would

a. 是 will 的過去式

(例) Rita would go mountain climbing when she had time off in high school.
麗塔高中放假時會去爬山。

b. 表示比 will 更委婉的請求，常用於問句

(例) Would you please quit smoking?
請你戒菸好嗎？

c. 表示過去的習慣

例 At that time, he would smoke a cigarette after meals.
他那時會在飯後抽一根菸。

d. 表示意願，常與 like, love 連用

例 I would like to teach children English.
我想要教小孩英語。

例 I would go to Japan for vacation.
我想要去日本渡假。

例 I would like to study abroad.
我想要出國留學。

例 I would love to go in nature.
我想要去大自然走走。

★ **would rather** （常與 **than** 連用）

表示比較喜歡

例 I would rather go in nature than staying home.
比起待在家裡，我比較喜歡去大自然走走。

否定式，用 would rather not

例 She would rather not return to her home country.
她寧願不回她自己的國家。

(7) must

a. 表示義務

例 Almost all young men in this country must do military service.
在這個國家幾乎所有年輕男生都要服兵役。

> b. 表示必然

例 It must be you.
一定是你。

> c. 表示重要性

例 One must lock the door before leaving this place.
離開這裡前一定要鎖門。

> d. 過去式時要用 had to

例 She had to call her husband because she needed his computer.
她必須要打電話給她先生，因為她必須要用他的電腦。

> e. 與 not 連用表示禁止

例 You must not complain to your boss.
你不該向你的老闆抱怨。

(8) need

> a. 當助動詞時，用於否定句及疑問句

例 You needn't worry too much for your child.
你不需要為你小孩太過擔心。

例 Need we bring some food to your place?
我們需要帶什麼食物到你家嗎？

> b. 當主要動詞時，變化如同一般動詞

 例句：

例 Maybe there is nothing we can do in this situation.
或許在這個情形下沒有什麼我們可以做的。

(9) shall

a. 常用於第一人稱的問句

 例句：

例 Shall we go?
我們該走了嗎？

例 Shall I make tea for you?
需要我為你泡杯茶嗎？

b. 用於第一人稱，表示決心

例 I shall come back.
我會回來的。

c. 用於第二或第三人稱，表示絕對與義務

例 You shall come here on time tomorrow morning.
你明早要準時到這裡。

d. 用於附加問句表示邀請

例 Let's go to the movie, shall we?
我們一起去看電影好嗎？

(10) should

a. 是 shall 的過去式

例 Lisa should be able to provide you with the information you need.
麗莎會提供你所需要的資訊給你。

b. 表示義務，等於 ought to

例 We should not forget the lesson of WWII.
我們不該忘記第二次世界大戰的教訓。

c. 與 why 連用於問句中，表示驚奇

例 Why should we do so much for our children?
我們為何要替小孩做這麼多事？

(11) ought to

a. 表示義務 = should

例 People ought to care for the aged.
人們應該照顧長者。

b. 表示建議

例 We ought to tell him about this.
我們應該告訴他相關事項。

例 We ought to be getting ready now.
我們現在應該要準備好了。

c. 表示期待

例 They are unsure what they ought to do.
他們不確定該做什麼事。

d. 否定式

例 People ought not to take everything for granted.
人們不該將所有事視為理所當然。

e. 疑問句

例 Ought she to see a dentist?
她該去看牙醫嗎？

(12) used to

a. 表示過去的習慣

例 When Tim was working, he used to get up very early to learn English.
提姆還在工作時，他總是每天很早起床來學習英語。

b. 否定式 used not to

例 Jerry used not to talk to so many people in English.
傑瑞那時不習慣在這麼多人面前說英語。

c. 口語中否定式可用 did not use to

例 Jerry did not use to talk to so many people in English.
傑瑞那時不習慣在這麼多人面前說英語。

be/get used to ＋ NP/V-ing （此處的 to 為介系詞）

 例句：

例 She got used to getting up in the early morning.
她習慣每天早起。

例 He is used to working so many hours a week.
他習慣一星期工作這麼多時數。

Exercises　練習題

一、請用 couldn't 或 couldn't have 來完成下列句子。

1. This book _____ (be) Larry's. He never reads love stories.

2. Have you heard that our basketball team won champion? This _____ (be) better.

3. Somebody left a message for you this afternoon. Jennifer was here so it _____ (be) Jennifer.

4. We _____ (make) it in the contest without our teachers' support.

5. Many students _____ (spell) because they depend too much on software.

6. Without social media, I _____ (find) my fellow students in high school.

7. Many young mothers _____ (manage) to work if their parents do not babysit their children for them.

8. You _____ (finish) your studies if your teacher didn't assist you.

9. This photo _____ (not be taken) by her. She had never been to Mexico.

10. This signature _____ (be) his because he is left-handed.

二、 請用 must have 或 can't have 來完成下列句子。

1. She has not called me back for more than a week. (she / busy)

   Answer: _____

2. Tod did not show up at our place. (he / get / invitation)

   Answer: _____

3. The necklace you made is really pretty. (take / you / a long time)

   Answer: _____

4. The police came to ask if we knew our neighbor was a thief. (Our neighbor / be a thief)

   Answer: _____

5. Ted looked so happy after the teacher announced the result of the test. (He / pass the test)

   Answer: _____

6. We have not seen Jim for three days. (He / ill)

   Answer: _____

7. Yesterday I saw Jim with his dog in the park. (He / ill)

   Answer: _____

8. The teacher called Alan's name, but he didn't hear it. (he / asleep)

   Answer: _____

9. Kevin has been away the whole week. (he / on a business trip)

   Answer: _____

10. She cannot afford to pay the rent anymore. (she / buy the house)

    Answer: _____

■ 三、請用 might t not have 或 couldn't have 來完成下列句子。

1. A：Do you think Jack got the message?

   B：No, he would have been in the meeting. _____
   _____

2. A：I wonder if they know the airport is closed because of a strike.

   B：I doubt it. _____

3. A：Have you been to Europe recently?

   B：I _____ Europe recently because I have had any holidays at all.

4. A：Do you think the dairy products you bought are really from Australia?

B：I am not sure. _____

5. A：I am surprised our manager is here. Does he know our company has been merged?

   B：I have no idea. _____ _____

6. A：Do you know the burglars in the photos?

   B：I have never seen them, but the police say _____ _____ this place so well if they are not local people.

7. A：Have you met this doctor on television?

   B：It's possible, but I _____ him if I have seen him.

8. A：I visited your high school. Could Ms. Chen have been your English teacher?

   B：I don't think so. You _____ my English teacher because she was retired long time ago.

9. A：I got a message that said I won the lottery.

   B：Watch out. It _____ true.

10. A：Do you know that Prof. Wang was in Boston attending a conference last October?

    B：I don't think so. Last October he was teaching here. He _____ at two places at the same time.

四、請用 shouldn't have 來完成下列句子。

1. Last night we went to the night market and I ate too much. I _____ so much.

2. We went shopping again, and I spent half of my salary on clothes. I _____ so much money.

3. We had a party last night and made a lot of noise. We _ _____ so much noises.

4. Mr. Wang worked so hard that he did not have time for his family. He _____ so hard.

5. Mr. Richardson won the lottery, and his friends wanted to borrow money from him. He _____ his friends know he won the lottery.

6. She was caught for using other' data in her research. She _____ others' data without their permission.

7. Lily's little brother asked her friends to lend him money. Now she thinks she _____ him to her friends.

8. Jessie agreed to check Jerry's essay for him, but it turned out to be full of mistakes. Now she regrets this. She thinks she _____ to help him.

9. This evening I invited some guests over for dinner, but some got so drunk that they could not drive home. They asked me to let them stay overnight. I _____

_____ to my guests.

10. This morning Mr. Li interviewed somebody for the position of salesperson, but he kept talking about himself. Maybe Mr. Li _____ too much about himself.

Key to Exercises 解答

1. couldn't be
2. couldn't be
3. couldn't have been
4. couldn't have made
5. couldn't spell
6. couldn't have found
7. couldn't manage
8. couldn't have finished
9. couldn't have been taken
10. couldn't be

1. She must have been busy.

2. Tod can't have got my invitation.

3. It must have taken you a long time.

4. Our neighbor can't have been a thief.

5. Ted must have passed the test.

6. He must have been ill.

7. He can't have been ill.

8. He must have been asleep.

9. He must have been on a business trip.

10. She can't have bought the house.

三、

1. He couldn't have got it.

2. They might not have known about it.

3. couldn't have been to

4. They might not have been from Australia.

5. He might not have known about it.

6. they couldn't have known

7. might not have remembered

8. couldn't have met

9. might not have been

10. couldn't have been

四、

1. shouldn't have eaten

2. shouldn't have spent

3. shouldn't have made

4. shouldn't have worked

5. shouldn't have let

6. shouldn't have used

P
a
r
t
18

7. shouldn't have introduced

8. shouldn't have agreed

9. shouldn't have given wine

10. shouldn't have talked

TOEIC Exercises
多益題演練

1. All workers in the company _____ wear
   uniforms. It is stated in the company's Code of
   Conduct.

   (A) can

   (B) must

   (C) may

   (D) have

2. This document _____ have been produced by
   him. He does not even know how to use a computer.

   (A) wouldn't

   (B) shouldn't

   (C) mustn't

   (D) can't

3. You _____ bought that fax machine. There is now
   an end-of-year sale in the shop.

   (A) shouldn't have
   (B) couldn't have
   (C) wouldn't have
   (D) cannot have

P
a
r
t
18

Questions 4 - 6 refer to the following e-mail.

To: Eileen Chen

From: Ted Miller, Sales Manager

Subject: Your presentation

Date: May 13, 2019 13:44

Dear Eileen,

   I am writing to confirm that it is your turn to give a presentation next Wednesday. For the subject, it _____ _ be

4. (A) couldn't

   (B) can't

   (C) shouldn't

   (D) should

about ways to boost sales in our company. You _____ want to

5. (A) can

   (B) could

   (C) might

   (D) should

discuss it with other salespeople in our team. The time cannot be more than five minutes. You _____ heard the

6. (A) have had

   (B) must have

   (C) shouldn't have

   (D) can have

presentation given by Michael last time, and that could be a good example for your short speech. Do your best and you will be fine.

Ted Miller

Sales Manager

J & J Department Store

10 F, No 15, Zhongxiao W. Rd, Taipei, Taiwan

Tel: (02) 2764 7880

E-mail: tedmiller@jjstore.com

http://www.jjstore.com/

Key to TOEIC Exercises
多益題解答

1. B
2. D
3. A
4. D
5. C
6. B

結論

助動詞的功能是輔助主要動詞，通常是放在主要動詞之前，用來表達時態、被動語態，構成疑問句或否定句，這樣聽來似乎非常簡單，不過，不同的助動詞之間都有微妙的差異，還是要靠經驗法則才能純熟掌握助動詞的運用。

19

被動語態
（The Passive Voice）

Unit
1

被動語態的定義

被動語態的作用被動語態是用來表示對「承受」某動作的人或物的關注，而不是關注「執行」某動作的人或物。換句話說，最重要的人或物變成句中的主詞。

適合使用被動語態的情況

1. 被動語態適合用於強調句中動作的受詞，有別於強調動作的執行者的主動語態。

 例句：

P
a
r
t
19

例 His work of photography was awarded the first prize in the competition of visual art.
他的攝影作品得到視覺藝術比賽的第一名。

例 Mark's invention was highly praised for its wide application in medical equipment.
馬克的發明因為可以大量用於醫療器材而廣受好評。

例 My grandfather was taken away by the policeman that night.
那晚我祖父被警察帶走了。

例 You can borrow the books if they are not ordered by someone online.
如果線上沒有別人預定的話，您就可以借這些書。

例 The money she just borrowed was stolen on a bus.
她剛借來的錢在巴士上被偷了。

2. 動作的行為者為泛指且不重要或顯而易見。

例句：

例 This medicine is taken before sleep (by patients).
這藥是睡前服用的。〔省略了病人〕

例 He was sentenced to life in prison without parole (by the judge).
他被宣判無期徒刑不得假釋。〔省略了法官〕

例 She was chosen as the winner (by the jury) in the Eurovision Song Contest this year.
她被選為今年歌唱大賽的得主。
〔省略了評審團〕

3. 被動語態用於轉述常理。

例句：

★ **It is said that ... = people say ...**

 例句：

例 It is said that there is a will, there is a way.
常聽人說有志者事竟成。

It is said that job hunting is getting harder and harder.
= People say that job hunting is getting harder and harder.
聽說工作變得越來越難找。

★ **It is believed that ... = people believe that ...**

 例句：

例 It was once believed that women were not capable of running for government.
從前婦女一度被認為沒有從政的能力。

4. 為了避免責任歸屬問題

 例句：

例 The garbage was not taken out yesterday.
昨天垃圾沒有拿出去。

例 The plants have not been watered for a month.
這些植物已經有一個月沒人澆水。

5. 為求句子結構的平衡

 例句：

例 Her decision to move to Shanghai with her boyfriend from China to work as a doctor over there shocked her mother.
她決定跟隨著中國男友搬到上海並且在那裡當醫師，這讓她母親非常震驚。

使用被動語態使句子結構平衡

---> Her mother was shocked by her decision to move to Shanghai with her boyfriend from China to work as a doctor over there.
她母親非常震驚，因為她決定跟隨著中國男友搬到上海並且在那裡當醫師。

Unit
2

被動語態的構成

主動語態句子中的主詞於被動語態句子中變成 by ＋ 受詞，或省略。

主動語態句子中的動詞於被動語態句子中變成 be ＋ 過去分詞。

主動語態句子中的受詞於被動語態句子中變成主詞。

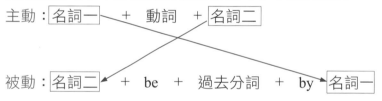

主動：名詞一 ＋ 動詞 ＋ 名詞二

被動：名詞二 ＋ be ＋ 過去分詞 ＋ by 名詞一

例如：

主動：She loves him.　她愛他。

被動：--> He is loved by her.　他為她所愛。

主動：She loved him.　她愛過他。

被動：--> He was loved by her.　他曾為她所愛。

要多注意主動語態和被動語態句子裡的動詞式態變化，以下為主詞是第三人稱單數，動詞是take，所整理出的被動語態一覽表。

P
a
r
t
19

時式與時態	主動語態	被動語態
現在簡單	takes	is taken
過去簡單	took	was taken
現在完成	has taken	has been taken
過去完成	had taken	had been taken
現在進行	is taking	is being taken
過去進行	was taking	was being taken
現在完成進行	has been taking	has been being taken
過去完成進行	had been taking	had been being taken

Unit
3

被動語態的用法

★ 句中有直接受詞與間接受詞時，直接受詞與間接受詞都可以當被動語態句子的主詞。

例如：

例 We gave him a room.
我們給他一間房間。

改為被動：

(1) A room was given to him by us.

一間房間由我們提供給他。

〔直接受詞作為主詞〕

(2) He was given a room by us.

他從我們這兒得到一間房間。

〔間接受詞作為主詞〕

★ 否定句

(1) do not (did not) + 動詞 ==> be + not + 過去分詞
例如：

例 He did not call her.

他沒有打電話給她。

改被動--->

例 She was not called by him.

她沒有接到他的電話。

(2) 助動詞 + 動詞 ==> 助動詞 + not + be + 過去分詞
例如：

例 She cannot call him.

她不能打電話給他。

改被動--->

例 He cannot be called by her.

他不能接她的電話。

★ 祈使句 ==> Let + 受詞 + be + 過去分詞

例如：

例 Don't forget this lesson.
不要忘了這個教訓。

改被動--->

例 Don't let this lesson be forgotten.
不要讓這個教訓被遺忘。

★ 疑問句

例 Did you find your passport?
你找到了護照嗎？

改被動--->

例 Was your passport found by you?
你護照找到了嗎？

★ 當行為者為泛指的時候，可以省略 " by + 受詞 "

例句：

例 He was given two months for improvement (by the authorities).
他被（有關單位）給予兩個月時間做改進。

例 She was fined for 500 USD for not keeping her restaurant clean enough.
她因為餐廳不夠清潔而被罰了 500 美元。

★ 用介系詞 **by** 或 **with** 引導動作執行者或方式

1. 介系詞 by 是最常見的被動語態用法。

 例句：

例 She will be missed by all of us.
我們都會懷念她。

例 The singer was much admired by many teenage girls.
很多十幾歲的女孩都非常仰慕這個歌星。

例 This way of running a business is not accepted by society.
這種經營企業的方式不為社會所接受。

2. 用介系詞 by 引導執行動作的方式，後接名詞或動名詞。

 例句：

例 In this company, all employees can only get ahead by hard work.
在這家公司裡，所有員工都只能靠努力工作才能向上爬。

例 The new accountant made a huge mistake by reporting to the wrong person.
這個新來的會計因為向錯誤的人報告而鑄下大錯。

例 He made a good impression on the interviewer by presenting his work portfolio.
他因為帶了作品集而讓面試官留下良好印象。

3. 用介系詞 with 引導執行動作的方式或工具。

例 This lock can be easily opened with an iron wire (by the robber).
這種鎖（強盜）可以輕易用鐵絲打開。

例 Nothing can be achieved without great effort (by us).
沒有任何事情（我們）可以不勞而獲。

4. 有些固定片語要用特定的介系詞

例 He is interested in the position.
他對這份職缺很感興趣。

例 She is surprised at the result.
她對這個結果很訝異。

例 This bottle was filled with tea.
這個瓶子裝滿了茶。

例 His mind is preoccupied with her.
他的心裡都是她。

5. 非正式的口語中常見到 get 加上過去分詞，特別是在美式英語。

例句：

例 After one semester, the students got totally confused.
一學期下來，學生都感到非常困惑。

例 Russel got arrested for taking bribery.
羅素因為收賄而被收押。

Exercises 練習題

一、請將下列句子的空格填入動詞的正確形式，請注意可能是主動或被動句型。

1. This morning when I woke up, I found our balcony _____ (cover) by leaves.

2. Her parents _____ (die) when she was a teenager.

3. The library _____ (close) at 9 pm during week days.

4. Do you know where this parcel _____ (send) to last Christmas?

5. Who _____ (write) the letter for her grandmother?

6. These grammar rules are complicated to me. I _____ (confuse) when I do the Exercises.

7. This morning somebody _____ (order) 50 pizzas to be delivered.

8. In this test, all the content of this book will _____ (cover).

9. During the whole time she was away, her house _____ (take care) of by her neighbor.

10. A person who _____ (hire) workers is called an employer.

二、請將下列句子省略 somebody 或 they，改寫成被動句型。

1. Somebody saw the pickpocket stealing wallets.

   _____

2. They are fixing the water pipe on the road.

   _____

3. Somebody heard an explosion at midnight.

   _____

4. They sent the best students to study abroad.

   _____

5. Someone must have called the police.

   _____

6. They are building a tennis court on campus.

   _____

7. I didn't realize that somebody was video recording my interview.

   _____

8. They immediately hired her for the position of art director.

_____

9. Somebody told the journalist the true story of what happened.

_____

10. They are not following the rules of making traditional bread.

_____

●●●找題目

三、請用下列劃線的單字來改寫句子。

1. It is expected that children look after their parents when parents are old.

_____

2. It is supposed that the employees of this company retire at the age of 65.

_____

3. It is reported that a little girl in red in the village went missing.

_____

4. It is thought here that when a baby is already one year old when it is born.

_____

5. It is alleged that the man does not know the woman.

_____

6. It is reported that the movie star is retired in Canada.

_____

7. It is believed that the old man has moved out of his family.

_____

8. It is expected that she will go back to the university and finish her studies someday.

_____

9. It is believed that she overcame her illness.

_____

10. It is said that their company will make a huge profit this year.

_____

Key to Exercises
解答

、

1. was covered

2. died

3. is closed

4. was sent

5. wrote

6. am confused

7. ordered

8. be covered

9. was taken care

10. hires

二、

1. The pickpocket was seen stealing wallets.

2. The water pipe is being fixed.

3. An explosion at midnight was heard.

4. The best students were sent to study abroad.

5. The police must have been called.

6. A tennis court is being built on campus.

7. I didn't realize that my interview was being video recorded.

8. She was immediately hired for the position of art director.

9. The journalist was told the true story of what happened.

10. The rules of making traditional bread are not being followed.

、

1. Children are expected to look after their parents when parents are old.

2. The employees of this company are supposed to retire at the age of 65.

3. A little girl in red in the village was reported to have gone missing.

4. A baby is thought here to be already one year old when it is born.

5. The man is alleged to not know the woman.

6. The movie star is reported to be retired in Canada.

7. The old man is believed to have moved out of his family.

8. She is expected to go back to the university and finish her studies some day.

9. She is believed to have overcome her illness.

10. Their company is said to make a huge profit this year.

TOEIC Exercises
多益題演練

1. This book is _____ to be a bestseller.

    (A) consider

    (B) considering

    (C) considered

    (D) be considered

2. By next Friday, this project _____ totally completed.

    (A) will be

    (B) is going to

    (C) has

    (D) has to

3. If all factors are _____ into consideration, this event can be called a success.

    (A) take

    (B) took

    (C) taken

    (D) be taking

Questions 4 - 6 refer to the following e-mail.

From: Clara Wang <clarawang@fitness.com.hk>
April 4 15:34

To: peterchen@compex.com.tw

Dear Peter,

　　Let me begin by expressing our gratitude for the excellent training programs you have offered our company these years. Your company is widely _____ to be the

4. (A) believe

　　(B) believed

　　(C) believing

　　(D) be believed

leading training institute of leadership. As to your request to conduct the training workshops at your place instead of our company, our manager think it is a great idea. In fact, a team will _____ to receive training over there.

5. (A) chosen
   (B) choose
   (C) be choosing
   (D) be chosen

All materials will _____ at your request. Please
6. (A) be provided
   (B) provide
   (C) providing
   (D) provided

send the training results and comments to us as soon as they are available.

Thank you very much.

Clara Wang

Human Resource Manager

Fitness Gym

clarawang@fitness.com.hk

Address: Flat 5, 10/F, Acacia Building

100 Kennedy Road WAN CHAI

HONG KONG

Key to TOEIC Exercises
多益題解答

1. C
2. A
3. C
4. B
5. D
6. A

 結論

被動語態的重心是承受某動作的人或物，而不是執行此動作的人或物，因此在使用被動語態的時候要先確定此情形是否適用，如果不適用的話，就保留原來主動語態。除此之外，還要留意中文常常用主動語態，但是卻有被動含意，例如：「米，煮熟了；菜，炒好了。」，翻譯成英文時則需要用被動結構。

不定詞（Infinitives）&
動名詞（Gerunds）

Unit
1

不定詞 (Infinitives)

1. 不定詞的用法

(1) 不定詞作名詞的用法

例 To get up early is impossible to me.
早起對我來說不可能。

(2) 不定詞作形容詞的用法

例 You need a job to make a living.
你需要份工作來維生。

(3) 不定詞作副詞的用法

例 She was trained to be an English teacher.
她受過作為英文老師的訓練。

> 不定詞的否定式：於不定詞前加上not

例 My mother told me not to go out too late.
我母親要我不要太晚出門。

2. 不定詞原形的用法

（省略to的情況）

P
a
r
t
20

(1) 於感官動詞（see, watch, hear）後面出現的不定詞。

（例） I saw her walk out of the room.
　　 我看見她走出房間。

(2) 於使役動詞（make, have, let）後面出現的不定詞

（例） The nurse made her take the medicine.
　　 護理師要她服用藥物。

> 以上感官動詞與使役動詞改用被動時，to 不能省略

（例） She was seen to walk out of the room.
　　 她被人看見走出房間。

（例） She was made to take the medicine.
　　 她被要求要服用藥物。

3. 不定詞的時態

(1) 時間與動詞時態一致

（例） He seemed to be very angry.
　　 他似乎很生氣。

(2) 時間較動詞時態早

（例） He seemed to have been angry.
　　 他似乎很生氣過。

(3) 不定詞放於 hope, want 後，表示未來

（例） He wants to see her again.
　　 他希望能再見她一面。

(4) 不定詞的常用片語

★ too... to... 太⋯⋯而不能⋯⋯

例 She is too old to work.
她年紀太大而不能工作。

★ so... that... = so... as to... = so... enough to...

如此⋯⋯以至於⋯⋯

例 He is so poor that he has to sell his house.
= He is so poor as to sell his house.
他如此窮以至於要賣房子。

例 He is so smart that he can understand it.
= He is smart enough to understand it.
他是如此聰明以至於他能理解這件事。

★ had better 最好

例 You had better save some money.
你最好存點錢。

例 You had better not to waste money.
你最好不要浪費錢。

Unit
2

動名詞 (Gerunds)

---

1. 動名詞的用法

(1) 當主詞

例 Speaking in public is not easy.
公眾演講不容易。

(2) 當受詞

例 I do not like speaking in public.
我不喜歡在公眾場合演講。

例 He is good at speaking in public.
他擅長於公眾場合演講。

(3) 當受詞補語

例 This course is "Public Speaking".
這門課程名叫"公眾演講"。

2. 動名詞的時態

(1) 表示與動詞相同或之後的時間

★ 相同的時間

例 She is interested in singing.
她對歌唱感興趣。

★ 之後的時間

例 She is interested in becoming a singer after graduation.
她想要於畢業後當歌星。

(2) 表示比動詞更早的時間

例 She is proud of having been a singer.
她對於從前當過歌星感到驕傲。

(3) 動名詞的常用片語

★ **It/There is no use ~ ing** ……沒有用

例 There is no use crying over spilt milk.
覆水難收。

例 It is no use regretting it.
後悔沒有用。

★ **feel like ~ ing** 想要……

例 I feel like crying.
我感到想哭。

⑩ They feel like breaking down.
他們感到快崩潰。

★ **cannot help ~ ing** 忍不住……

⑩ They couldn't help crying upon hearing the news.
他們聽到消息後忍不住哭起來。

⑩ When I heard what he said, I couldn't help yelling at him.
我聽到他說的話，忍不住大聲罵他。

★ **be busy ~ ing** 忙著……

⑩ Recently I have been busy learning Japanese.
最近我忙著學日語。

⑩ What are you busy doing in the lab?
你在實驗室裡忙什麼？

Unit
3

動名詞與不定詞的比較

1. 後面接動名詞與不定詞都可以的動詞：
begin, start, like, love...

 例句：

例 When did you begin to work?
= When did you begin working?
你什麼時候開始工作？

例 Laura likes to sing.
= Laura likes singing.
蘿拉喜歡唱歌。

2. 只能由動名詞當受詞的動詞：
enjoy, finish, mind...

 例句：

例 Larry enjoys interviewing people.
賴瑞喜愛訪問人。

例 When will you finish writing the book?
你什麼時候會寫完這本書？

例 Would you mind opening the window for me?
你介意幫我打開窗戶嗎？

3. 只能由不定詞當受詞的動詞：
want, wish, hope, decide...

 例句：

例 Most children want to go to an amusement park.
大部分小孩子想要去遊樂園。

例 I wish you great health in the year to come.
我祝你來年身體健康。

例 Let's hope tomorrow will be better.
但願明天會更好。

例 He decided to leave here at the last minute.
他最後一分鐘決定離開這裡。

★ 由動名詞與由不定詞當受詞意思不同的動詞：

forget, remember, stop, go on, regret, try, mean, need...

forget 忘記

forget 後接不定詞，表示忘記要做某件事。

例 Don't forget to turn off the heater before you leave the room.

= Don't forget you have to turn off the heater before you leave the room.

離開房間前不要忘記關暖器。

forget 後接動名詞，表示已經做了某件事。

例 Jane forgot feeding the dog.

= Jane forgot that she had fed the dog.

珍忘記已經餵過狗。

remember 記得

remember 後接不定詞，表示記得要去做某件事。

例 I still remember to do the laundry.

我記得要去洗衣服。

remember 後接動名詞，表示記得做過某件事。

例 I remember doing the laundry.

我記得已經洗過衣服。

stop 停止

stop 後接不定詞，表示停下來要去做某件事。

例 Jennifer stopped to send the card.

珍妮佛停下來去寄卡片。

stop 後接動名詞，表示停止做某件事。

⑩ Jennifer stopped sending cards after e-mail was invented.
珍妮佛於電子郵件發明後就停止了寄卡片。

go on 繼續

go on 後接不定詞，表示接下來要去做某件事。

⑩ The professor went on to tell us about the assignment.
教授停下來告訴我們有關作業的事。

go on 後接動名詞，表示繼續做某件事。

⑩ The professor went on telling us about the assignment.
教授不停地告訴我們有關作業的事。

regret 後悔

regret 後接不定詞，表示很遺憾接下來要做某件事。

⑩ I regret to tell you that I am not going to work here
anymore.
很遺憾地我必須告訴你，我將不再於這裡工作。

regret 後接動名詞，表示後悔做了某件事。

⑩ He regretted telling her his secret.
他後悔告訴她他的秘密。

try 嘗試

try 後接不定詞，表示嘗試去做某件事。

⑩ Have you tried to tell him this?
你嘗試告訴過他嗎？

try 後接動名詞，表示試試看做某件事，比起 try 後接不定詞來說較不費力。

(例) Why don't you try writing down your thoughts?
為什麼你不試著寫下你的感覺呢？

mean

mean 後接不定詞，表示意圖去做某件事，意同於 intend。

(例) She meant to fire me.
她意圖要開除我。

mean 後接動名詞，表示「意即為、意味著」，意同於 involve。

(例) Moving out of parents' places means having to pay all living costs by oneself.
搬離父母的家意味著要自己負擔所有的生活費用。

need

人 + need + 不定式：表示「需要」。

(例) She needed to take a rest.
她需要休息一下。

物 + need + 動名詞：含有被動含意。

(例) The carpet needs cleaning.
地毯需要清理。

物 + need + 被動不定式：含有被動含意。

P
a
r
t
20

後接不定詞，表示某物需要被處理，意同於 need to be V-ed。

例 The carpet needs to be cleaned.
地毯需要清理。

一、請於下列句子的空格中填入不定詞或動名詞。

1. Would you mind _____ the window to let air in? (open)

2. Right now we cannot afford _____ a new apartment. (purchase)

3. My sister enjoys _____ very much. (bake)

4. Would you like _____ a walk in the park with me? (take)

5. When did you decide _____ a hair dresser? (become)

6. They seem _____ a lot of money. (have)

7. My aunt suggested _____ Japanese as a second foreign language. (learn)

8. Please stop _____ that noise, all right? (make)

9. If you fail _____ the books you borrowed, you will be fined. (return)

10. I had much work to do, but I managed _____ a couple of days off to be with my family. (have)

二、請於下列句子的空格中填入不定詞或動名詞。

1. remember

   a. I remember _____ that to him, but he didn't reply. (say)

   b. Please remember _____ hello to him for me when you see him. (say)

2. regret

   a. Mr. and Mrs. Sun regret _____ their only son to attend high school in the United States. (send)

   b. I regret _____ you that your son is in serious trouble. (tell)

3. go on

   a. Sorry to interrupt you. Please go on _____ about the issue. (talk)

   b. If you keep working hard, we think you can go on _____ the finance manager in this company. (become)

三、請於下列句子的空格中填入不定詞或動名詞。

1. try

   a. The fish is too bland. Why don't you try _____ a little salt to it. (put)

   b. You should try _____ your temper or you'll get

into trouble. (control)

2. need

   a. The floor of the toilet needs _____. (mop)

b. You don't need _____ the balcony. (clean)

   The balcony doesn't need _____. (clean)

3. help

   a. He passed away too suddenly. I couldn't help
   _____. (cry)

   b. Can you help me _____ the flight in the Internet?
   (book)

Key to Exercises 解答

一、

1. opening   2. to purchase   3. baking

4. to take   5. to become   6. to have

7. learning   8. making   9. to return

10. to have

二、

1. a. saying   b. to say

2. a. sending   b. to tell

3. a. talking   b. to become

三、

1. a. putting   b. to control

2. a. mopping   b. to clean, cleaning

3. a. crying   b. book

TOEIC Exercises
多益題演練

1. She remembered _____ thank you to him when she received his gift.

   (A) to say

   (B) saying

   (C) said

   (D) say

2. It hurt so much that I could not help _____.

   (A) cry

   (B) cryed

   (C) to cry

   (D) crying

3. Ted regretted _____ that to his little brother.

   (A) doing

   (B) do

   (C) did

   (D) done

Questions 4 - 6 refer to the following notice.

Dear Members,

We regret _____ you that from April 1, 2019 on, your

4. (A) inform

   (B) to inform

   (C) informing

   (D) informed

monthly Power Gym membership fees are about to increase.
This increase is due to rising labor costs and rents.
Nevertheless, we opened one gym last month downtown.
Don't forget _____ out the brand-

5. (A) checking

   (B) having checked

   (C) check

   (D) to check

new training equipment we just purchased and installed there. For those who enjoy _____, don't miss the

6. (A) swim

   (B) to swim

   (C) swimming

   (D) go swimming

new 50 meter swimming pool and the spa areas in the new gym. As long as you remain your membership, you can visit the new gym with no extra charge. We wish you great health and thank you very much!

Power Gym

Robert Hay, CEO

Key to TOEIC Exercises
多益題解答

1. B

2. D

3. A

4. B

5. D

6. C

結論

有些動詞需要接不定詞，有些動詞則需要接動名詞，但是
最麻煩的還是接了不定詞和動名詞意思會不同的動詞，還
好本章都已經做了非常詳盡的解說，也提供了清楚的例
句，因此沒有藉口說還是弄不清楚喔。

關係詞（Relatives）

Unit
1

關係代名詞
(Relative Pronouns)

關係代名詞兼具代名詞與連接詞兩種角色，一方面代替前面的先行詞（名詞或代名詞），另一方面則引導關係子句來修飾所替代的先行詞。

關係代名詞的種類：who, whom, whose, which, that, as, than, what。

★ **who**

who 為人的關係代名詞。

例句：

⑲ Do you know the tall girl who is standing over there?
你認識站在那邊的高個子女孩嗎？

★ **whom**

關係代名詞 whom 為 who 的受格，口語中可以用 who 代替，也可以省略。

例 I don't know the person whom you are talking about.
我不認識你們在談的人。

例 They haven't met the girl whom you mentioned.
他們不認識你所提及的女孩。

例 You should not trust someone whom you just met.
你不應該信賴剛剛才認識的人。

★ **whose** 為 **who** 的所有格。

例 There came the guest whose name I happen to forget.
迎面走來這位客人，他的名字我剛好忘了。

★ **which**

which為事物的關係代名詞。

★ 限定性用法

如果關係代名詞所引導的形容詞子句具有「限制住」所
修飾的先行詞為哪些的功能，稱為限定性用法，此關係
代名詞之前不要加逗號。

 例句：

(例) The 3 books which you picked become the best sellers of the year.
你所挑的書當中這三本成為今年最佳暢銷書。

(例) The writer who the professor mentioned before just won the 2017 Nobel prize in literature.
教授提及的作家剛獲得2017年的諾貝爾文學獎。

★ 非限定性用法

如果關係代名詞所引導的形容詞子句是用來補充説明先行詞的性質，不具有「限制住」是哪些先行詞的功能，稱為非限定性用法，此關係代名詞引領的子句前後要加逗號。

 例句：

(例) The 3 books, which you picked, become the best sellers of the year.
這三本你所挑的書成為今年最佳暢銷書。

(例) Kazuo Ishiguro, who wrote "The Remains of the Day", was the winner of the 2017 Nobel prize in literature 2017.
著有《長日將盡》的石黑一雄獲得了 2017 年的諾貝爾文學獎。

★ that

> 先行詞為人或事物，前面的修飾語為：形容詞最高級,
> all, every, any, the same, the only, the very 等等。

例句：

例 The tallest boy that you see there is my son.
　　那邊你所看到最高的男孩是我的兒子。

例 All that glitters is not gold.
　　閃閃發亮的並不都是金子。

例 The first thing that I want to do when I arrive in this
　　city is to call up all my friends living here.
　　我到達這個城市想做的第一件事就是打電話給住在這裡
　　的所有朋友。

例 The only thing that you should remember to do for me
　　is to thank her.
　　你唯一該幫我做的事就是向她道謝。

例 Mrs. Brown is the very person that you'd like to interview
　　as a British survivor of the tsunami in Indonesia.
　　布朗太太是你會想要訪問的最佳人選，她是歷經印尼海
　　嘯的英國生還者。

★ as

> 與 such, the same, as... 連用，在形容詞子句中作主詞或
> 受詞。

例句：

例 Kevin has the same anger issues as his father (does).
凱文和他父親一樣有容易生氣的問題。

例 Mandy is the same sweet girl as we knew in school.
曼蒂仍然是我們在學期間所認識的那個甜美的女孩。

例 Sandy is no longer the same optimistic person as I once knew.
珊蒂不再是我們曾經認識的那個樂觀的人了。

例 The responses of the speech were very overwhelming, such as never occurred before.
對這場演講的反應是如此驚人，真的是史無前例。

例 The number of the tourists to this region have dramatically declined, such as was unprecedented.
來這個地區的觀光客人數戲劇化下降，史上前所未見。

例 As is reported in the newspaper, there will be some subsidies for the young couple who just have their first child.
如同報紙上所報導，年輕夫婦生第一胎會有一些補助。

例 As is known to all, a cheerful personality can contribute to a good immune system.
如同眾所周知，開朗的性格有助於良好的免疫系統。

★ **than**

通常用於 "形容詞比較級 + 名詞" 之後，而比較級後

面的名詞則為than 的先行詞。在這個地方，than 當作
關係代名詞，than之前的名詞為先行詞，也就是比較級
所修飾的名詞。

例句：

(例) Don't give your dog more food than is needed.
不要給你的狗過多的食物。

(例) Don't let your children have more money than is needed.
不要讓你的小孩有超過需要的錢。

★ **what**

what = the thing which, that which, all that, anything that
前面不會有先行詞

例句：

(例) Don't believe what the guy told you.
不要相信這個人告訴你的。

(例) What we see is often the reflections of our thoughts.
我們所看見的經常是我們內心想法的反映。

(例) What's good about memory is that we actually do not remember everything in detail.
關於記憶有一點很好，就是我們不會鉅細靡遺地記住所
有的事物。

(例) This meeting is what we can capitalize on.
這場會議是我們可以好好利用的機會。

Unit
2

關係副詞 (Relative Adverb)

關係副詞（where, when, why, how）通常用來取代介系詞和關係代名詞which，由關係副詞所形成的關係子句用來修飾前面的名詞。

1. 關係副詞分為 where, when, why, how。

(1) where 代替地方

the place 和 where 當中可以省略其中之一，但不能同時省略。

例 I have never been to the place where the film was shot.
= I have never been to where the film was shot.
= I have never been to the place the film was shot.
我從來沒去過那部電影拍攝的地點。

例 This is the city where he works now.
= This is the city in which he works now.
這是他現在工作所在的城市。

例 That is the beach where most people like to practice surfing.
= That is the beach on which most people like to practice surfing.
那就是大部分人喜歡練習衝浪的海灘。

(2) when 代替時間

the time 和 when 當中可以省略其中之一，但不能同時省略。

例 Do you remember the time when we met each other?
= Do you remember when we met each other?
= Do you remember the time we met each other?
你記得我們何時第一次相遇嗎？

例 That was the day when I first heard of his name.
= That was the day on which I first heard of his name.
那是我聽到他名字的第一天。

(3) why 代替理由

the reason 和 why 當中可以省略其中之一，但不能同時省略。

例 Nobody knows the reason why she fell ill.
= Nobody knows why she fell ill.
= Nobody knows the reason she fell ill.
沒有人知道她為何生病。

例 The reason why she dropped out was unknown.
= The reason for which she dropped out was unknown.
她輟學的原因沒有人知道。

(4) how 代替方式

例 Do you know how he learned Korean?
你知道他學韓語的原因嗎？

例 Do you know the way he learned Korean?
你知道他學習韓語的方法嗎？

> the way 與 how 不可連在一起用
>
> 現代英文文法家認為 the way 與 how 意思重複，因此
> 只要於二者擇一來使用，不要兩者放在一起用。

2. 用法

(1) 限定性用法

例 My parents run a hotel where many senior citizens spend
their holidays.
我父母經營一家很多銀髮族在那兒渡假的旅館。
關係副詞對於所修飾的先行詞有限定的作用，稱為限定
性用法，例如在這個例子中，特別指的是所有旅館當
中，來客有很多銀髮族的旅館。

(2) 非限定性用法

例 Anthony would like to spend holidays in Japan, where he can learn to ski.

安東尼想要在日本渡假,在那兒他可以學滑雪。

關係副詞對於所修飾的先行詞只有修飾作用,沒有限定的作用,稱為非限定性用法,關係副詞前要加逗號,例如此例中,日本是全世界獨一無二的,自然不用再加以限定。

一、請將下列句子的關係子句下方劃線。

1. Have you been to countries where English is spoken by the majority of the people there?

2. My ideal job is a job which is related to my major in the college.

3. The police have caught the guy who broke into our apartment last night.

4. This morning I ran into one high school classmate of mine whose name I could not remember.

5. It is unacceptable to give your friend who is getting married money as a wedding gift in the United States.

6. Many people have never been to this place which is not easily accessible by public transportation.

7. They seem to stop funding the organization which was started for charity.

8. These days I seem to be only able to enjoy stories whose endings are happy.

9. Whenever I am down, I would go in the nature where I can always feel the healing power.

10. The bookstore has a special sale which only lasts until end of this week, right before the Easter holidays.

■、請將下列兩句以適當的關係詞連接成一句。

1. The teacher is the person I want to introduce to you. He is in the office.

   _____

2. The nurse is specialized in helping senior citizens. She is out visiting patients at home.

   _____

3. I've got a cousin called Joy. She lives in Seattle. She is an engineer.

   _____

4. I have found the book at my parents' place. The book might be useful to you.

   _____

5. The final exams are only one week away. The final exams can decide if you will pass or fail.

   _____

6. I have always wanted to go to Seoul. All K-Pop fans want to go to Seoul.

   _____

7. In my dream I am in a small town. In the town all people know each other. Over there I am the only stranger.

8. Yesterday I went shopping in the department store. The department store has a special Japanese food expo.

9. Melody is going to hold an art exhibition soon. Melody has learned painting with a teacher for more than ten years.

10. I'd like to invite you to a concert. The concert is given by some Taiwanese musicians. The musicians have studied music in Germany.

三、請將下列兩句以 which 連接起來。

1. This morning Sandy was fired.

   This is not a good news to her family.

2. Our teacher does not have a smart phone.

   This makes it hard for us to reach her.

3. She has a bad temper.

   This means she cannot make new friends with others easily.

   _____

4. It starts to rain cats and dogs.

   This means we won't have the baseball game.

   _____

5. Fewer and fewer babies are born.

   More and more schools are closed.

   _____

Key to Exercises
解答

•找解答

一、

1. Have you been to countries where English is spoken by the majority of the people there?

2. My ideal job is a job which is related to my major in the college.

3. The police have caught the guy who broke into our apartment last night.

4. This morning I ran into one high school classmate of mine whose name I could not remember.

5. It is unacceptable to give your friend who is getting married money as a wedding gift in the United States.

6. Many people have never been to this place which is not easily accessible by public transportation.

7. They seem to stop funding the organization which was started for charity.

8. These days I seem to be only able to enjoy stories whose endings are happy.

9. Whenever I am down, I would go in the nature where I can always feel the healing power.

10. The bookstore has a special sale which only lasts until end of this week, right before the Easter holidays.

1. The teacher I want to introduce to you is in the office.

2. The nurse who is specialized in helping senior citizens is out visiting patients at home.

3. My cousin Joy, who lives in Seattle, is an engineer.

4. I have found the book which might be useful to you at my parents' place.

5. The final exams which can decide if you will pass or fail are only one week away.

6. I have always wanted to go to Seoul, where all K-Pop fans want to go to.

7. In my dream I am in a small town where all people know each other and I am the only stranger.

8. Yesterday I went shopping in the department store, which has a special Japanese food expo.

9. Melody, who has learned painting with a teacher for more than ten years, is going to hold an art exhibition soon.

10. I'd like to invite you to a concert, which is given by some Taiwanese musicians, who have studied music in Germany.

三、

1. This morning Sandy was fired, which is not a good news to her family.

2. Our teacher does not have a smart phone, which makes it hard for us to reach her.

3. She has a bad temper, which means she cannot make new friends with others easily.

4. It starts to rain cats and dogs, which means we won't have the baseball game.

5. Fewer and fewer babies are born, which means more and more schools are closed.

TOEIC Exercises
多益題演練

1. Ryan is one of the few people _____ can give a tour of the ancient temple in English.

   (A) whom

   (B) who

   (C) whose

   (D) which

2. This museum showcases _____ handicraft works were made in the aboriginal villages.

   (A) how

   (B) where

   (C) that

   (D) what

3. If you don't like _____ you just bought, you can always return it in the wholesale store.

   (A) that

   (B) which

   (C) them

   (D) what

Questions 4 - 6 refer to the following e-mail.

To: All customers

From: Jens Schwarz, CEO of Whole Life

Date: March 31, 2019

Subject: Biometric Identification System

Dear Patrons,

    I am pleased to announce that from early May on, we are introducing a mobile payment method with a biometric system. It will include face, fingerprint, hand, and voice recognitions. What's more, thanks to AI (Artificial Intelligence), customers do not have to wait in line to check out of the store. _____ they have to do is to walk

4. (A) As

   (B) All

   (C) That

   (D) Why

through the special gate, and all items will be automatically scanned and shown on the monitor. Then, they can pay with their smartphones _____ have the apps of biometric

5. (A) which
   (B) what
   (C) where
   (D) with

authentication downloaded and installed. The reason _____ _____ we are

6. (A) where
   (B) when
   (C) why
   (D) how

doing it is obvious. It is going to be an efficient and a renovative way of saving time and trouble both for the customers and for the staff members in the store.

Jens Schwarz
CEO

Whole Life Store
Tel: (02) 7765 3421
E-mail: js@wholelife.com
http://www.wholelife.com/

Key to TOEIC Exercises
多益題解答

1. B

2. A

3. D

4. B

5. A

6. C

結論

關係詞的基本結構很清楚，只不過有時在較長的句子，關係子句到底於何處結束，而與所修飾的先行詞如果又相隔甚遠，那還真是難以判定整句的句意。讀者可以本章的練習題來做個關係詞檢測，如果都能輕易答對，那麼就算是沒有什麼大問題了。

分詞片語與垂懸結構

（Participle Phrases and Danglers）

Unit 1

分詞 (Participle)

現在分詞（動詞字尾加上 -ing）表示動作為主動，正在進行中。

過去分詞（動詞字尾加上 -ed 或不規則變化）表示動作為被動，已經完成。

分詞放於 be 動詞或 have 之後。

 例句：

例 I am reading a book.（現在分詞）
我正在讀一本書。

例 The book is read by many people.（過去分詞）
這本書為很多人所讀。

例 We all have read the book.（過去分詞）
我們都讀過這本書。

分詞構句
(Participle Phrases)

用分詞構成副詞性片語，不使用連接詞，若子句的主詞與主要子句的主詞相同時，子句的主詞可以省略。分詞構句是一種從屬副詞子句，用來修飾主要字句，形式如下：

（從屬連接詞） + V-ing / V-en, S + V

 例句：

例 Eating dinner, she saw interesting commercials on TV.
她一邊看吃飯一邊看有趣的電視廣告。

例 Taken with lemon juice, the black tea tastes really good.
加上檸檬汁的紅茶真好喝。

形成的步驟如下：

1. 先看主要子句與副詞子句的主詞是否相同。

2. 如果主詞相同的話，可以刪除副詞子句的主詞；如果主詞不同的話，則要保留副詞子句的主詞。主要子句的主詞如果是代名詞，而副詞子句的主詞為名詞時，於刪去副詞子句的主詞時，記得要將主要子句的主詞還原為名詞。

3. 將從屬子句中動詞前的情態助動詞或 do 刪除，然後將從屬子句的動詞改為 V-ing 或 V-en，be 動詞則為改為 being。

4. 從屬連結接詞可視狀況刪除或保留。

5. being V-ing, being Adj 與 being V-en 當中可以省略 being。

6. having V-ing 可視語意改為 upon V-ing, on V-ing 或 after V-ing。

Unit
3

分詞構句的功能

分詞構句的功能如下：

★ 時間

㊀ When he felt hungry, he went to the cafeteria.
-->Feeling hungry, he went to the cafeteria.
他覺得餓了就去自助餐廳。

★ 原因

(例) As he had no money, he could not buy the movie ticket.
-->Having no money, he could not buy the movie ticket.
因為沒有錢所以他無法買電影票。

(例) Because it is read by many generations of students, the story has become classic novel.
-->Read by many generations of students, the story has become a classic novel.
因為世世代代的學生都讀過這本書，所以這本書成了經典小說。

★ 條件

(例) If you go straight, you will see the bank.
-->Going straight, you will see the bank.
如果你一直向前走就會看見銀行。

★ 讓步

(例) Although he is poor and sick, he often helps those in need.
-->Being poor and sick, he often helps those in need.
雖然他又窮又病，他還是經常幫助需要的人。

(例) Even though he was beaten up by the bully, he still would not give in.
-->Beaten up by the bully, he still would not give in.
雖然他被霸凌者痛打，他仍然不退讓。

可於分詞前加上 not, never 形成否定。

⑩ Not knowing what to do, he called his parents for help.
他不知道該如何是好，只好打電話給父母求救。

Unit 4

垂懸結構 (Danglers)

1. 以帶有分詞開頭的句子

錯誤：

⑩ Seeing his mother return home, the television was turned off immediately.
一看見他母親回來，電視馬上就被關了。

正確：

⑩ Seeing his mother return home, he turned off the television immediately.
他一看見母親回來，就馬上關了電視。

2. 其他造成誤解的句子

(1) 以形容詞開頭

錯誤：

例 Young and inexperienced, the necklace costs too much for her.
年輕又缺乏經驗，這條項鍊對她來說太貴。

正確：

例 Since she is young and inexperienced, she cannot afford to buy the necklace.
因為她年輕又缺乏經驗，所以無法買這條項鍊。

(2) 以副詞開頭

錯誤：

例 Slowly and carefully, we watched as the artist created the painting.
緩慢又小心，我們看著這藝術家創作畫作。

正確：

例 Slowly and carefully, the artist created the painting as we watched.
我們看著這藝術家緩慢又小心地創作畫作。

(3) 以介系詞開頭 (at, on, by, with...)

錯誤：

例 At the age of seven, her mother gave her a doll.
七歲的時候，她的母親給她一個玩偶。

正確：

㉠ When she was at the age of seven, her mother gave her a doll.

在她七歲的時候，她的母親給她一個玩偶。

(4) 以 like 開頭

錯誤：

㉠ Like most students, his father takes him to school by car.

像大部分學生一樣，他父親開車送他上學。

正確：

㉠ Like most students, he is taken to school by car by his father.

像大部分學生一樣，他由父親開車送他上學。

3. 慣用片語例外

這些慣用片語長久以來為人用來作為開場白習慣用語，因此不需要與主要子句的主詞一致。

generally speaking 一般來説

strictly speaking 嚴格説來

given the conditions 在既定的條件下

simply put 簡單説來

to be honest (frank) with you 老實説

to tell the truth 告訴你實話

一、請將下列兩句以分詞構句連接成一句。

1. Sarah slipped and fell. She was getting off a bus in the rain.

    _____

2. The student was hurt by his teacher's words. The student decided to study harder than before.

    _____

3. My grandfather was watching television. He fell asleep.

    _____

4. The girl was being taken photos while dancing. She performed especially well.

    _____

5. The boy saw his mother in the audience. He gave his mother a big smile.

    _____

6. Children hold lanterns. Children like to go around at night at the Lantern Festival.

    _____

7. The policeman was running very fast. He was trying to catch the robber.

_____

8. Our manager was heard to shout at the salesperson. He must have lost his temper again.

_____

9. William was feeding the fish in the pond. He did not see some wild dogs coming from behind.

_____

10. Mr. Lin was hit by a car. He was taken to the hospital on the way to his workplace.

_____

■、請用 -ing 或 Not -ing 來連接兩句成一句。

1. Mike felt exhausted. So he did not go to the office this afternoon.

_____

2. I did not know what to do. So I rang the little boy's mother.

_____

3. Mr. Kim does many projects at the same time. He sometimes mixes up his clients.

_____

4. I thought we needed the boxes urgently. I carried all the boxes home.

_____

5. I do not know why. I do not like the way she talks.

_____

6. The waiter is underpaid. The waiter is not polite to customers.

_____

7. The clerk of the post office did not know where the parcel is from. He could not send the parcel back.

_____

8. Jean did not feel hungry. She did not cook dinner at all.

_____

9. Thomas has health problems. He is going to retire earlier than planned.

_____

10. Her parents did not like the man she was going to marry. Her parents did not attend her wedding.

_____

三、請用 Having… 開頭的句子來連接下列兩個句子。

1. He saw the car accident. Then he called the police.

_____

2. Teresa prepared the dinner. Then she called her family to have dinner.

_____

3. Mr. Yang applied for the necessary documents. Then he was ready to attend the car show in Germany.

_____

4. The doctor read all her medical records. Then he decided that she needed an operation immediately.

_____

5. She finished her postgraduate studies earlier than she had thought. Then she went to France for another half year to learn French.

_____

6. Allen did a thorough health check. Then he confirmed that he had no health issues to worry about.

_____

7. I went to the major museums in Europe. Then I decided not to do oil painting any more.

_____

8. Christine spent seven years studying in the medical school. Then this year he graduated and started to work in a famous hospital.

_____

9. Daniel has bought the train tickets. Then he went on holiday with his girlfriend.

_____

10. Most people learned English for a while. Then they applied to go on working holidays.

_____

Key to Exercises 解答

一、

1. Getting off a bus in the rain, Sarah slipped and fell.

2. Hurt by his teacher's words, the student decided to study harder than before.

3. Watching television, my grandfather fell asleep.

4. Being taken photos while dancing, the girl performed especially well.

5. Seeing his mother in the audience, the boy gave her a big smile.

6. Holding lanterns, children like to go around at night at the Lantern Festival.

7. Running very fast, the policeman was trying to catch the robber.

8. Heard to shout at the salesperson, our manager must have lost his temper again.

9. Feeding the fish in the pond, William did not see some wild dogs coming from behind.

10. Hit by a car, Mr. Lin was taken to the hospital on the way to his workplace.

、

1. Feeling exhausted, Mike did not go to the office this afternoon.

2. Not knowing what to do, I rang the little boy's mother.

3. Doing many projects at the same time, Mr. Kim sometimes mixes up his clients.

4. Thinking we needed the boxes urgently, I carried all the boxes home.

5. Not knowing why, I do not like the way she talks.

6. Being underpaid, the waiter is not polite to customers.

7. Not knowing where the parcel is from, the clerk of the post office could not send the parcel back.

8. Not feeling hungry, Jean did not cook dinner at all.

9. Having health problems, Thomas is going to retire earlier than planned.

10. Not liking the man she was going to marry, her parents did not attend her wedding.

三、

1. Having seen the car accident, he called the police.

2. Having prepared the dinner, Teresa called her family to have dinner.

3. Having applied for the necessary documents, Mr. Yang was ready to attend the car show in Germany.

4. Having read all her medical records, the doctor decided that she needed an operation immediately.

5. Having finished her postgraduate studies earlier than she had thought, she went to France for another half year to learn French.

6. Having done a thorough health check, Allen confirmed that he had no health issues to worry about.

7. Having been to the major museums in Europe, I decided not to do oil painting any more.

8. Having spent seven years studying in the medical school, this year Christine graduated and started to work in a famous hospital.

9. Having bought the train tickets, Daniel went on holiday with his girlfriend.

10. Having learned English for a while, most people applied to go on working holidays.

TOEIC Exercises
多益題演練

1. _____ in the constitution, all people are created equal.

   (A) Writing

   (B) Written

   (C) Wrote

   (D) Write

2. _____ straight, you will see the main post office in an antique building.

   (A) Going

   (B) Having gone

   (C) Turning

   (D) Having turned

3. _____ eaten dinner, Jason rode his motorcycle to do his meal delivery job.

   (A) Had

   (B) Having

   (C) Has

   (D) Hasn't

Questions 4 - 6 refer to the following advertisement.

June 12, 2019

Are you interested in learning English with fun and at low costs? Then join "Mandy's English Fun Club" and sub-scribe to the online English learning magazine! _____

4. (A) Be

  (B) To be

  (C) Being

  (D) been

a member, you canhave access to interactive materials suitable to your level and have English teachers answer your questions online. _____ registered for off-line mind-blowing activities, you can

5. (A) Had

  (B) Having

  (C) Have

  (D) Has

choose among a wide range of events, such as English book reading and afternoon tea. Why not take a look at http://www.mandy.com/? _____ all the factors into

6. (A) Take

   (B) To take

   (C) Taken

   (D) Taking

consideration, you will definitely be satisfied with our English learning products and services. Join now for discounted membership fees!

Mandy Chang

CEO, Head Teacher

Mandy's English Fun Club

Key to TOEIC Exercises
多益題解答

1. B

2. A

3. B

4. C

5. B

6. D

結論

分詞片語的構成看來容易，但是一不小心很容易就犯了垂懸結構的毛病，即使是英文很高竿的人也難以避免，不但如此，有的人還會弄混該用現在分詞或是過去分詞，因此這個文法成了英文考試常出現的項目，叫人想要避也避不開，所以還是好好研讀一下吧。

一致性（Agreement）

Unit 1

主詞與動詞的一致

1. A and B A 和 B

例 Mary and Terry are good friends.
瑪莉與泰利是好朋友。

例 Birth and death is part of life.
生與死都是生命的一部分。（生與死為一體，故用單數
動詞）

2. half of 一半, most of 大部分, two third of 三分之二...

這些片語的 of 後面所接的名詞為複數，則接複數動詞；
所接的名詞為單數，則接複數動詞。

例 Half of the money is gone.
有一半的錢不見了。

例 Half of the students went on a trip.
有一半的學生去郊遊了。

---

3. 表示時間、金錢、距離的複數名詞如果視為一個
整體則用單數動詞，否則則用複數動詞。

(例) Two and half years is quite a long time.
兩年半是相當長的一段時間。

(例) Five years have gone by, and Paul still has not finished
his studies.
五年已經過去了，保羅仍然還沒有完成學業。

Unit
2

時態的一致

時態的一致性：主句的動詞時態決定子句的時態。

1. 若主句的動詞為現在式，子句可以用任何時態。

(例) He thinks that she loves him.
他認為她愛他。

(例) He thinks that she loved him.
他認為她曾愛過他。

例 He thinks that she will love him.
他認為她會愛他。

2. 若主句的動詞為過去式

(1) 子句的動詞若為現在式，則改為過去式。

例 He thinks that she loves him.
--> He thought that she loved him.
他認為她曾愛過他。

(2) 子句的動詞若為過去式或現在完成式，則改為過去完成式；子句的動詞若為過去完成式時，則保留過去完成式。

 例句：

例 He thinks that she loved him.
--> He thought she had loved him.
他認為她曾愛過他。

例 He thinks that she has loved him.
--> He thought that she had loved him.
他從前認為她曾愛過他。

例 He thinks that she had loved him.
--> He thought that she had loved him.
他從前認為她曾愛過他。

(3) 現在式子句中的 will, can, may, shall 於過去式子句中改用 would, could, might, should。

例 He thinks that she will love him.

--> He thought that she would love him.

他從前認為她會愛他。

Unit 3

引述

1. 直接引述

轉述動詞：ask 問, say 說, answer 回答, insist 堅持, tell 告訴, reply 轉述...

轉述動詞可以在引號之前、之後、中間。

例 He yelled: "I have got no weapon!"

他大叫：「我沒有帶武器！」

（例） "I have got no weapon!" he yelled.
「我沒有帶武器！」他大叫。

（例） "I have got," he yelled, "no weapon!"
「我沒有……」，他大叫，「帶武器！」

2. 間接引述

直接引述改為間接引述的方式請見下表。
(以 live 為例)

直接引述	間接引述
現在簡單式 live(s)	過去簡單式 lived
現在進行式 am/are/is living	過去進行式 was/were living
現在完成式 have/has lived	過去完成式 had lived
現在完成進行式 have/has been living	過去完成進行式 had been living
過去簡單式 lived	過去完成式 had lived
過去進行式 was/were living	過去(完成)進行式 was/were living had been living
過去完成式 had lived	過去完成式 had lived
過去完成進行式 had been living	過去完成進行式 had been living

例句：

直接引述	間接引述
He said: "I live in Taiwan."	He said that he lived in Taiwan.
He said: "I am living in Taiwan."	He said that he was living in Taiwan.
He said: "I have lived in Taiwan."	He said that he had lived in Taiwan.
He said: "I have been living in Taiwan."	He said that he had been living in Taiwan.
He said: "I lived in Taiwan."	He said that he had lived in Taiwan.
He said: "I was living in Taiwan."	He said that he was living in Taiwan. He said that he had been living in Taiwan.
He said: "I had lived in Taiwan."	He said that he had lived in Taiwan.
He said: "I had been living in Taiwan."	He said that he had been living in Taiwan.

Exercises 練習題

一、下列句子空格中有兩個選項中，請將不正確的選項劃掉。

1. Physics is / are very interesting to me, and I like to design experiments.

2. The clothes is / are out of style.

3. Don't panic! The police is / are coming soon.

4. Don't you think the water is too hot? 42 degrees is / are not suitable for bathing.

5. Your glasses looks / look very stylish on you.

6. The news is / are indeed very hard to believe.

7. These scissors is / are not very sharp.

8. The staff of the company was / were having a strike.

9. Three months is / are not enough to know an employee well.

10. The committee is / are investigating this case.

二、請填入空格中所缺的動詞正確形式。

1. Some friends of mine _____ (go) on a business trip last month.

2. Some of the bread you bought _____ (be) not fresh.

3. Neither he nor his friends _____ (be) going to be punished.

4. Either Jessica or Mary _____ (be) going to be punished.

5. Both his father and his mother _____ (have) been interviewed by the journalists.

6. One of my friends I hang out with _____ (own) a camping area.

7. Nobody knows that he neither has a lawyer's license nor _____ (have gone) to Harvard University.

8. Our teacher asks us either _____ (draw) or to paint this beautiful flowers.

9. I think both your questions and suggestions _____ (be) excellent.

10. Each of her students _____ (be) required to do a presentation in English in the end of the semester.

三、請將下列的直接引述改為間接轉述。

1. My grandmother said to me: "I will stay in the temple for a while."

   _____

2. Our teacher told us: "I am getting married next month."

   _____

3. Jennifer explained to us: "If you do not register your password, you will not be able to use the free Wi-Fi."

   _____

4. Nilson said: "I did not take the money in the drawer."

   _____

5. Winnie said to her mother: "I am pregnant!"

   _____

6. Winnie told her mother: "I was pregnant at that time in high school."

   _____

7. Mr. President answered: "We're going to build a wall, and Mexico is going to pay."

   _____

8. The secretary told her boss: "Mr. Richardson called at 11:10 and asked you to call him back."

9. She told us: "I have been to many countries and have experienced many cultures."

10. The teacher said to us: "This experiment is to test if the people on the street will give a hand to the people they do not know."

••找解答

、

1. is / are

2. is / are

3. is / are

4. is / are

5. looks / look

6. is / are

7. is / are

8. was / were

9. is / are

10. is / are

、

1. went

2. is

3. are

4. is

5. have

6. owns

7. has

8. to draw

9. are

10. is

、

1. My grandmother said to me that she would stay in the temple for a while.

2. Our teacher told us that she was getting married in a month.

3. Jennifer explained to us that if we did do not register your password, we would not be able to use the free Wi-Fi.

4. Nilson said that he had not taken the money in the drawer.

5. Winnie said to her mother that she was pregnant.

6. Winnie told her mother that she had been pregnant at that time in high school.

7. Mr. President answered that they were going to build a wall, and Mexico was going to pay.

8. The secretary told her boss that Mr. Richardson had called at 11:10 and had asked him to call him back.

9. She told us that she had been to many countries and had experienced many cultures.

10. The teacher said to us that that experiment was to test if the people on the street would give a hand to the people they did not know.

TOEIC Exercises
多益題演練

1. Not only your managers but also his supervisor _____
   _____ going for a drink after work.

   (A) enjoys

   (B) enjoy

   (C) enjoying

   (D) are enjoying

2. Tim told his colleagues that he _____ many
   presentations in English.

   (A) will do

   (B) does

   (C) had done

   (D) is doing

3. Jack believes that his business _____ succeed in
   the coming year.

   (A) will

   (B) had

   (C) has

   (D) is

Questions 4 - 6 refer to the following e-mail.

To: Dr. Jiang

From: Linda Lim

Subject: Thank you

Date: June 3, 2019 11:12

Dear Dr. Jiang,

    I'd like to express my sincere gratitude to you for treating me with such great care that my health _____

4. (A) improves

   (B) improved

   (C) had improved

   (D) has improved

tremendously since I started to see you last December. Over the past six months, my confidence in you and Chinese medicine _____

5. (A) have

(B) has

(C) had

(D) have been

increased all the more each time I receive the acupuncture treatment for the wound from a traffic accident. Previously I was told that I would not be able to walk with a straight back, but now I can walk just as if the traffic accident ____ _____ never happened.

6. (A) had

(B) has

(C) having

(D) have

Thank you again for your kindness and outstanding practice.

Yours sincerely

Linda Lim

Key to TOEIC Exercises
多益題解答

1. A
2. C
3. A
4. D
5. B
6. A

結論

主詞與動詞要一致、時態要一致、引述時的時態要一致，這些聽來是如此理所當然，但是為什麼還是有這麼多人會犯這些方面的錯誤呢？以中文為母語者對於英文單複數與時態總比較難以掌握，再加上引述他人話語的規則，剛開始覺得有點複雜再所難免，所幸熟能生巧，不會過多久就能駕輕就熟了。

標點符號
（Punctuation Marks）

1. 句號（The Period .）

句號是用來表示一個句子的結束。

例如：

(1) 如果有刪節號，省略了某些字詞，後面再加上一個句點表示句子已經結束。

例 After all the things that happened, she would really like to put an end to this project....
經過了這一切，她真的想結束這個專案……

(2) 如果要特別強調音量逐漸減弱，就不要於刪節號後再加句點。

例如：

例 "Alright..."
好的……

(3) 被破折號或括號包圍的句子，不要加句號。

 例句一：

例 Till now he could still hear the voice of that woman--"Buy some bread" --and he wished he had stopped at that time.
直到現在他還聽得到那婦人的聲音--「請買麵包」--他但願那時停了下來。

例 Till now he could still hear the voice of that woman
（"Buy some bread"）and he wished he had stopped at
that time.
直到現在他還聽得到那婦人的聲音（「請買麵包」）他
但願那時停了下來。

 例句二：

例 They were once good friends--That was before the inci-
dence—but now they do not talk to each other anymore.
他們曾是好朋友--那是在發生那件事之前--現在他們不
再交談了。

例 They were once good friends (That was before the inci-
dence) but now they do not talk to each other anymore.
他們曾是好朋友（那是在發生那件事之前）現在他們不
再交談了。

★ **如果括號內有問號或驚嘆號則需要保留問號或驚嘆
號。**

例 They were once good friends (What is the definition of
"friend" anyway?) now they do not talk to each other
anymore.
他們曾是好朋友（「朋友」的定義又是什麼？）現在他
們不再交談了。

例 They were once good friends (Quite good friends!) now they do not talk to each other any more.
他們曾是好朋友（相當好的朋友！）現在他們不再交談了。

2. 逗號 （The Comma , ）

逗號的用途如下：

(1) 分開句子（ 例如 , and , but）

例 He did his homework, and his mother checked it to make sure he did it.
他做了功課，而且他母親檢查確定他做了。

例 He did his homework, but his mother did not believe it.
他做了功課，但是他母親不相信他做了。

(2) 引述話語

例 The teacher said, "No cheating."
老師說：「不要作弊。」

例 "No cheating," said the teacher.
「不要作弊。」老師這麼說著。

例 "No cheating," said the teacher, "or I will ask you to leave the classroom. "
「不要作弊」老師這麼說著，「不然我會叫你離開教室。」

(3) 插入話語

⟨例⟩ That young man, the tall one with glasses, is the exchange student from Malaysia.
那個年輕的男子，就是高高的帶眼鏡的那個，是馬來西亞來的交換學生。

3. 分號（The Semicolon ; ）

(1) 取代 , and , but

⟨例⟩ He did his homework; his mother checked it to make sure he did it.
他做了功課，而且他母親檢查確定他做了。

⟨例⟩ He did his homework; his mother did not believe it.
他做了功課，但是他母親不相信他做了。

(2) 列舉之物中已有逗號

⟨例⟩ The things those who will go camping on Sunday should bring are a suitable tent, a standard one for camping; a flashlight, which should be bright enough; proper camping wear, outfits which should be made of quick drying materials; enough food, which can be immediately heated up like instant noodles.
星期天要去露營的人要帶適合露營標準的帳篷、亮度夠的手電筒、快乾材質製成的合宜露營裝備、足夠的食物，能夠於加熱後馬上食用，例如泡麵。

4. 冒號（The Colon：）

(1) 引述話語，特別是引述內容較長時。

(例) The student said to the teacher: "Tell me a country in which you can speak the language of Mathematics. No such a country, right? That's why I am not going to waste my time to learn Math. "
那個學生對老師說：「告訴我任何說數學這個語言的國家，沒有這樣的國家，對不對？那就是為什麼我不想浪費時間學數學的原因。」

(2) 舉之物之前

(例) The subjects the student likes are: Math, Physics, and English.
這學生喜歡的科目有：數學、物理、英文。

(3) 不可以用冒號將動詞與句中的其他部分隔開。

錯誤例子：

✕ The student likes: Math, Physics, and English.
這學生喜歡：數學、物理、英文。

正確：

(例) The student likes Math, Physics, and English.
這學生喜歡：數學、物理、英文。

或是

The subjects student likes are Math, Physics, and English.
這學生喜歡的科目有：數學、物理、英文。

5. 問號 （The Question Mark ？）

問號用於問句的最後，表示此為一個問題，例如：

例 What should I submit in order to apply for this certificate?
我該交什麼文件才能申請這個證件？

也可以用於表示驚訝或懷疑，例如：

例 "What? Do you mean that I have to sit for an exam in order to apply for this certificate?"
「什麼？你是說我必須做測驗才能申請這個證件？」

6. 驚嘆號 （The Exclamation Mark ！）

驚嘆號常用於驚嘆詞或句末來表達訝異的語氣，例如：

例 "Wow! Did you feel the earthquake?"
「哇！你是否感覺到地震？」

例 "What an earthquake!"
「真是強大的地震！」

7. 括號 （The Parentheses（ ））

於句子中想要提供更多的訊息時，則可以使用括號，例如：

🔖 Jack thinks he can get the job he applied for. (He is always over-optimistic.) So far there are 101 applicants for the position.

傑克認為他可以得到他所應徵的工作。（他總是太樂觀。）到目前為止共有101位應徵者。

★ 以上的句子中，外加的句子是完整的句子，則該句末的標點符號要放於括號內，且句首要大寫。

★ 如果外加的訊息很短，適合放於句子內，則括號內該句首要小寫，且不要用標點符號結尾。例如：

🔖 Jack thinks he can get the job he applied for (over optimistic again).

傑克認為他可以得到他所應徵的工作（他又太樂觀）。

★ 以上的情形若有驚嘆號或問號，則需要將驚嘆號或問號放於括號內，句首要小寫。

🔖 Most of you probably have never experienced an earthquake (lucky you!), but now in this country, you should learn some strategies to cope with an earthquake (how hard could it get?).

你們大部分人可能從來沒有體驗過地震（你們真幸運！），但是現在你們在這個國家必須學一些地震的應變措施（又會有多難呢？）

8. 破折號（The Dash -- ）

★ 破折號可用於思想或語氣突然轉折時。

㊜ Right now I have got everything needed for camping--
almost, except a flashlight.
現在我幾乎準備好露營所需的一切--除了手電筒外。

★ 破折號可用於取代冒號。

㊜ The soup misses the most important ingredient--the
chicken.
這道湯少了最重要的食材--雞丁。

★ 破折號可用於取代括號，使用括號較溫和，而使用破折號則較強調其中的訊息。

例如：
使用破折號

㊜ Jason thinks he can get the job he applied for--he is always
such a daydreamer--even though he knows so far there
are 101 applicants for the position.
傑森認為他可以得到他所應徵的工作--他總是愛做白日
夢--即使他知道至今有101個應徵者。

比較
使用括號：

例 Jason thinks he can get the job he applied for (and he is always such a daydreamer) even though he knows so far there are 101 applicants for the position.

傑森認為他可以得到他所應徵的工作（他總是愛做白日夢）即使他知道至今有101個應徵者。

9. 連字號（The Hyphen - ）

連字號所連接的是不同的單字或單子中的某一部分，例如：

- mother-in-law　　　　　　婆婆，岳母
- sister-in-law　　　　　　　嫂嫂，弟妹
- quasi-official　　　　　　　半官方

★ 不一定要加連字號

有些雙字形容詞，如果放於名詞前則需加連字號，如果放於名詞後則不需加連字號，例如：

例 He is a strong-willed father.
他是位個性剛強的父親。

例 His father is strong willed.
他父親個性剛強

an over-optimistic boy
一個過度樂觀的男孩

He is over optimistic.
他太過度樂觀

現在有省略連字號趨勢：overoptimistic

★ 一定要加連字號

有些形容詞，本身就一定要使用連字詞，例如其中含有 self- 或 quasi- 。例如：

- self-effacing 　　　　　　謙虛的
- self-reliant 　　　　　　自給自足的
- quasi-official 　　　　　　半官方的
- quasi-legal 　　　　　　半合法的

ex-

anti-

-like

例如：child-like 　　　　　像小孩的

(shell-like 沒有連字號，會有三個 l)

兩單字連在一起會造成兩個母音相連，則要加連字號。
例如：

- anti-establishment 　　　　反組織的
- pro-activism. 支 　　　　持行動主義的
  - 例外：pre 　　preemptive 　　先發制人的
  - 　　　　re 　　reenter 　　重新進入
  - 　　　　　　reassure 　　再度保證

10. 撇號（The Apostrophe ' ）

撇號的常用於如下的情形：

(1) 所有格

如果所有格單字為單數名詞，且不以 s 結尾，則於後加上 's 表示

所有格，如果以 s 結尾，則加上撇號即可；如果所有格單字為複數

名詞，則視其字尾是否以 s 結尾，如果以 s 結尾，則加上撇號即可，如果不以 s 結尾，則於後加上 's。

單數：

不以 s 結尾

boy 男孩--> boy's 男孩的

以 s 結尾

Andres--> Andres' （Andres 的）

Russ--> Russ' （Russ 的）

字尾發音為 s 也算

Alex--> Alex'（Alex 的）

複數：

不以 s 結尾

children 小孩們--> children's 小孩們的

以s 結尾

boys 男孩們--> boys' 男孩們的

others 其他人--> others' 其他人的

(2) 省略字母

例如：

aren't ＝ are not

isn't ＝ is not

shouldn't ＝ should not

couldn't ＝ could not

wouldn't ＝ would not

(3) 某些特定的複數形式

A's ＝ 都是 A

B's ＝ 都是 B

i's ＝ 都是 i

帶有撇號的所有格單字後如果要加上其它的標點符號，
則其它的標點符號要放於撇號的後面。

 例句：

例 The food was the girls', and the drinks were the boys'.
這些食物是女孩們的；那些飲料是男孩們的。

11. 引號（Quotation Marks " "）

引述他人的話語要用引號，如果引號內又出現引號，請
將裡面的引號改成單引號。

例句：

㊟ The English teacher said, "Use quotation marks when
you quote others' words."
英文老師說：「引述他人的話語要用引號。」

㊟ "Was it the English teacher who said, 'Use quotation
marks when you quote others' words.'?" asked Mr. Lin.
「是英文老師說：『引述他人的話語要用引號。』的
嗎？」林先生問道。

12. 斜體字（italic）

通常斜體字是用來標示某些特定名稱，有時候引號也會
派上用場。傳統的用法是，遇到較大型的作品，例如書
名、電影名稱、劇名、報紙或雜誌名，用斜體字來標
示，其它的則用普通字體加上引號即可。

通常用斜體字

書名：*Fire and Fury* 《火與怒》

電影名稱：*Seven Years in Tibet* 《在西藏的七年》

劇名：*The Twelfth Night* 《第十二夜》

報紙名稱：*The Taipei Times* 《台北時報》

雜誌名稱：*Reader's Digest* 《讀者文摘》

通常用引號

文章："How to deal with high blood pressure?" "如何對付高血壓"

論文："The Critical Age in English Learning" by Jane Fang "英語學習的關鍵年紀"（方珍著）

詩："The Road Not Taken" by Robert Frost "一條沒有去走的路"（羅伯特‧佛羅斯特著）

歌曲名稱："You Raise Me Up" by Josh Groban "你鼓舞著我"（傑許‧葛羅班著）

Exercises 練習題

請改正以下句子中的錯誤，如果句子正確無誤請於句子後打勾。

一、逗號、冒號、分號

1. Last Sunday we had a high school class reunion, and I met Michael the short one with glasses and his family.

2. As far as I could remember, Michael, and I, had many hobbies in common.

3. Back then we two both liked chess, basketball, photography, reading etc.

4. Michael is now married with 3 kids, I am still single.

5. Although Michael has a well-paid job he is not satisfied with his career.

6. He said "Why don't you come over for a dinner sometime?"

7. I have been teaching: English, Japanese, and sport in the high school we went to.

8. We talked about our English teacher who always prayed before and after each session.

9. The nice lady retired long time ago, therefore I have never met her in school.

10. The English teacher always asked us to learn the following items properly; nouns, verbs, and pronunciation.

二、問號、引號、圓括號

1. "With all due respect." He said.

2. "With all due respect" he said "but you don't seem to have a ticket to this concert."

3. Her grandmother complained (actually she was joking) that she was regarded as a babysitter.

4. Tracy said, "Your buddy said," I'll always be by your side."

5. He asked, "Did she say, 'I don't want to see you again?'"

6. If she was fired I would not be surprised at all.

7. I was not convinced by his words even though he looked sincere.

8. Linda asked herself "have I done it or not?"

9. Linda asked herself if she has done it?

10. Have you heard of a saying?" All is well that ends well." ?

三、撇號

1. My attorney-in-laws son hates that people enter his room without knocking first.

2. On the door of the professors office, there is a schedule of his consultation time.

3. "Welcome to Mary and Mike's house. We two are running a cafe together now."

4. Your son's illness has been confirmed by several M.D.

5. Disneyland is practically an immense childrens playground.

6. After my sister passed away, the responsibility of children's education fell on my brother-in-law shoulders.

7. This watch was given to me by my mother. It's value is beyond money.

8. Its been so long since we saw each other.

9. Where is the department of womens dresses?

10. Who invited Sandy? Sandy attending to a birthday party was unusual.

四、連字號

1. They live in a three story mansion.

2. This is ninth grade learning material.

P a r t 24

3. You should slow-down your speed.

4. Your promotion is surely-deserved.

5. Daniel is considered-established in the publishing industry.

6. My professor is always very self-effacing in spite of his great reputation.

7. Most volunteers do not care about monetary-rewards.

8. Watch out for the negative effects of high-pressure work on you.

9. A high-paying job often comes with a high-stress level.

10. Helping people in need is an important-central part of his family upbringing.

五、大小寫、數字寫法

1. During the '80's and '90's, many Asian students went to the United States to study and then stayed there permanently.

2. The meeting will start at 9:00 o'clock tomorrow morning.

3. Shakespeare's birthday is the 23 of April, and they hold a symposium on that date every year.

4. This dress costs me one thousand nine hundred and ninetynine dollars.

5. I bought this book at one hundred ninety-nine dollars and ninety-nine cents.

6. Many teacher do not like the 1 of April because some naughty students like to play tricks on them.

7. Fortythree people won the award for serving the distant communities in the mountains.

8. As a salesperson here, you can earn from $1000 to $10 million.

9. This dress is .85 cm too long.

10. Eight out of 32 students didn't finish this postgraduate program. The graduate rate was 75%.

P
a
r
t
24

Key to Exercises 解答

一、

1. Last Sunday we had a high school class reunion, and I met Michael, the short one with glasses, and his family.

2. As far as I could remember, Michael and I had many hobbies in common.

3. Back then we two both liked chess, basketball, photography, reading, etc.

4. Michael is now married with 3 kids; I am still single.

5. Although Michael has a well-paid job, he is not satisfied with his career.

6. He said, "Why don't you come over for a dinner sometime?"

7. I have been teaching English, Japanese, and sport in the high school we went to.

8. We talked about our English teacher, who always prayed before and after each session.

9. The nice lady retired long time ago; therefore, I have never met her in school.

10. The English teacher always asked us to learn the following items properly: nouns, verbs, and pronunciation.

二、

1. "With all due respect," he said.

2. "With all due respect," he said, "but you don't seem to have a ticket to this concert."

3. 正確

4. Tracy said, "Your buddy said, 'I'll always be by your side.'"

5. He asked, "Did she say, 'I don't want to see you again'?"

6. If she was fired, I would not be surprised at all.

7. 正確

8. Linda asked herself, "have I done it or not?"

9. Linda asked herself if she has done it.

10. Have you heard of a saying: "All is well that ends well." ?

三、

1. My attorney-in-law's son hates that people enter his room without knocking first.

2. On the door of the professor's office, there is a schedule of his consultation time.

3. 正確

4. Your son's illness has been confirmed by several M.D.s.

5. Disneyland is practically an immense children's playground.

6. After my sister passed away, the responsibility of children's education fell on my brother-in-law's shoulders.

7. This watch was given to me by my mother. Its value is beyond money.

8. It's been so long since we saw each other.

9. Where is the department of women's dresses?

10. Who invited Sandy? Sandy's attending to a birthday party was unusual.

四、

1. They live in a three-story mansion.

2. This is ninth-grade learning material.

3. You should slow down your speed.

4. Your promotion is surely deserved.

5. Daniel is considered established in the publishing industry.

6. 正確

7. Most volunteers do not care about monetary rewards.

8. 正確

9. A high-paying job often comes with a high stress level.

10. Helping people in need is an important, central part of his family upbringing.

五、

1. During the '80s and '90s, many Asian students went to the United States to study and then stayed there permanently.

2. The meeting will start at nine o'clock tomorrow morning.

3. Shakespeare's birthday is the 23rd of April, and they hold a symposium on that date every year.

4. This dress costs me one thousand nine hundred and ninety-nine dollars.

5. 正確

6. Many teachers do not like the 1st of April because some naughty students like to play tricks on them.

7. Forty-three people won the award for serving the distant communities in the mountains.

8. As a salesperson here, you can earn from $1 thousand to $10 million.

9. This dress is 0.85 cm too long.

10. 正確

結論

正確運用英文標點符號看來還真的是門大學問，建議平時在讀英文文章時就要多留意標點符號，如果自己在寫作時遇到沒有保握的標點符號用法，則要查詢後再用。語言是活的，平常就要勤於朗讀英文文章，換成讀自己的子句時，如果遇到要換氣的地方，就表示是逗點要派上用場了；而感到一切都交待完畢，則要毫不猶豫地放上個句號。

附錄

附錄
1

英文不規則動詞三態表

Irregular Verb Conjugation In English

為了方便記憶英文不規則動詞，英文動詞可以歸類為：
AAA、AAB、ABA、ABB、ABC 等形式（依照原形、
過去式、過去分詞排列），各種變化請見下表，各種變
化類型動詞依據字母順序排序，以 ABB 及 ABC 類型為
最多。

★ **AAA**

原形	中文解釋	過去式	過去分詞
broadcast	廣播	broadcast	broadcast
burst	爆開;闖入	burst	burst
cost	花費	cost	cost
cut	切割;剪	cut	cut
hit	打;擊	hit	hit
hurt	傷害;使疼痛	hurt	hurt
let	讓	let	let
lose	輸;失去	lost	lost
put	放置	put	put
read	閱讀	read	read
set	安放;沒入	set	set

附
錄

★ AAB

原形	中文解釋	過去式	過去分詞
beat	擊敗;敲擊	beat	beaten

★ ABA

原形	中文解釋	過去式	過去分詞
become	變成	became	become
come	到來	came	come
run	跑	ran	run

★ ABB

原形	中文解釋	過去式	過去分詞
bring	帶來	brought	brought
build	建造;蓋	built	built
buy	買	bought	bought
catch	接(球);捕獲	caught	caught
deal	處理;對付	dealt	dealt
dig	挖掘	dug	dug
feed	吃;餵養	fed	fed
feel	感覺	felt	felt
fight	打架;作戰	fought	fought
find	找到	found	found
get	得到;拿到	got	got
hang	把⋯掛起;吊	hung	hung
have	有	had	had
hear	聽見	heard	heard
hold	拿著	held	held
keep	保留;保持	kept	kept
lay	置放;產卵	laid	laid
lead	引導	led	led
leave	離開;丟下	left	left

附
錄

lend	出借	lent	lent
make	製造;使得	made	made
mean	意指	meant	meant
meet	遇見	met	met
pay	付錢	paid	paid
say	說	said	said
sell	賣	sold	sold
send	寄發;送	sent	sent
sit	坐	sat	sat
sleep	睡覺	slept	slept
slide	滑壘滑動	slid	slid
smell	聞	smelt	smelt
spell	拼字	spelt	spelt
spend	花費	spent	spent
stand	站;堅持;面對	stood	stood
swing	搖擺;揮動	swung	swung
teach	教	taught	taught
tell	告訴	told	told
think	想	thought	thought
understand	了解	understood	understood
win	贏得	won	won

★ ABC

原形	中文解釋	過去式	過去分詞
be/am/are/is	是;要;有;在	was/were/was	been
bear	承受	bore	born
begin	開始	began	begun
bite	咬	bit	bitten
blow	吹	blew	blown
choose	選擇;挑選	chose	chosen
do	做	did	done
draw	畫;繪製;描寫	drew	drawn
drink	喝	drank	drunk
drive	開車	drove	driven
eat	吃	ate	eaten
fall	掉下	fell	fallen
fly	飛	flew	flown
forget	忘記	forgot	forgotten
forgive	原諒	forgave	forgiven
give	給	gave	given

grow	種植;成長	grew	grown
hide	躲;隱藏	hid	hidden
know	知道	knew	known
lie	說謊;躺	lay	lain
ride	騎;乘	rode	ridden
ring	鳴,響	rang	rung
rise	起身;升起	rose	risen
see	看見	saw	seen
shake	搖動;握	shook	shaken
show	表演;顯示	showed	shown
speak	說;講	spoke	spoken
swim	游泳	swam	swum
take	拿;帶;採用	took	taken
throw	投;拋	threw	thrown
wake	叫醒	woke	woken
wear	穿著,磨損	wore	worn
write	寫	wrote	written

附錄
2

英美不同拼法對照表

美 語	拼 音	英 語
color, favor	o → ou	colour, favour
center, theater	er → re	centre, theatre
fulfill, enrollment	ll → l	fulfil, enolment
license, defense	se → ce	licence, defence
catalog	g → gue	catalogue
check	k → que	cheque
program	m → mme	programme
Judgment	dg → dge	judgement
traveling, jewelry	l → ll	travelling, jewellery
organize, realize, analyze	ze → se	organize, realize, analyse
labor	or → our	labour

附

錄

附錄
3

參考書目 (Bibliography)

Murphy, Raymond. English Grammar in Use: A self-study reference and practice book for intermediate students of English. 3rd Ed. Cambridge: Cambridge UP, 2004.

Schrampfer Azar, Betty. Understanding and Using English Grammar. 3rd Ed. New York: Longman Pearson Education, 2002.

蔣炳榮, 簡明當代英文法 A Concise English Grammar: the structure of contemporary English, 台北：書林, 2013.

Straus, Jane. 譯者：廖柏森, 有文法藍皮書你的英文就通了 The Blue Book of Grammar and Punctuation, 台北：所以文化, 2011.

O'Conner, Patricia T. 吳煒聲, I me 傻傻分不清 ：連莎士比亞也需要知道的文法 Woe is I, 台北：所以文化, 2013.

Le Boeuf, Dennis ＆景黎明, 英文文法全書 World Talk: Dancing with English － A Book of Comprehensive Grammar, 2nd ed. 台北：寂天, 2015.

金形桂＆金英勳, 譯者：都勇, 無敵英語文法寶典 Functional English Grammar, 台北：希望星球, 2012.

20個 最常見的 主題

分門別類規劃 各個主題的架構！

最常見的主題

20個商務

張文娟 著

★ ★ ★ ★ ★

▶▶▶

職場上遇到要用**英語洽商**的時候，

您是否常會感到書到用時方恨少？

本書\
整理出各種商務英語常見用法，\
讓您與國際客戶對答如流，\
溝通無礙，順利達成任務。

 務英語 ＋ 常見用法 ＋ 附贈 **MP3**

Seize Sentence Patter

Translatio

and Writing Become Easy!

只要有翻譯和寫作的需要，

不論是想通過學測的高中生

或是想通過英檢寫作的國高中生、大專生，

或是有檢定考試寫作需求的社會人士，

都可以透過本書提高**翻譯**及**寫作**能力。

何維綺 著

蓋房子不能只有磚塊水泥，
寫文章也不能只靠大量的單字。

蓋房子不能只有磚塊水泥，寫文章也不能只靠大量的單字。

**抓住
文法句型**
翻譯寫作
就通了

何維綺 著

Seize Sentence Patterns;

Translation
and Writing Become Easy!

Useful English Grammar

馬上提升
英文文法

學習**英文文法**其實
Super Easy

本書作者收納了

當代所有必學的英文文法，

並剔除所有艱深罕見過時的文法，

且用最基本易懂的單字構成例句，

讓讀者輕鬆上手，

不需在學習文法的同時還要應付單字。

最**直覺**的**英文文法**

English Grammar

學習**英文文法**其實
Super Easy
一目了然的 動詞時態介紹
➕ 助動詞各種變化 ➕ 馬上提升英文文法！

讓你擺脫繁瑣的了無助詞網各種變化
所有必必學只實用文法觀念要收其中

本書共規劃了**14**個單元，
收錄你最想知道的各種實用文法

包括動詞基本觀念、冠詞、名詞、介系詞、
代名詞、形容詞、副詞、動詞進階觀念、不定詞等。

本書共規劃了**14**個單元，
收錄你最想知道的各種實用文法

美國卡內基
美隆大學
資訊管理碩士

潘威廉 著

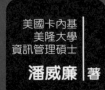

精選
常用生活英語
搭配**使用說明**及**生活情境對**

讓你輕鬆聽懂，並且
說出外國人也天天使用的超好用英文叫

雅典英研所 編著